EFFECTS

A *RIPPLE EFFECTS* NOVEL

L.J. GREENE

Titles by L.J. Greene

Effects Series:
Ripple Effects
Sound Effects
Aftereffects
Side Effects

Standalone:
A Fall of Light

Check out a preview of *Ripple Effects* at the conclusion of this novel. All of the *Effects* novels are standalones, but connected.

This book is lovingly dedicated to struggling artists of every medium. Let's keep at it together, shall we?

It is also dedicated to The Fray, who contributed heavily to the soundtrack in my head while writing the book, and who also unknowingly gave me the best advice for finishing it: *Head down, chin up.*

Chapter 1

Saturday, August 14, 2004
Melody (Mel)

I discovered I was not above enlisting the help of a leek to improve my love life. This realization offered a rather humbling perspective on my present state. Still, I rang the buzzer on the battered front door and, not for the first time, asked myself what in the *hell* I was doing here. My host, Dan Moore, was one of the most beautiful men I'd ever seen in person—that was the obvious answer. But it was an admittedly dubious explanation for meeting him for the first time today in the grocery store and blindly accepting his invitation to a barbecue. A barbecue in the *Tenderloin* District, no less.

Striking good looks aside, the only thing I knew for sure about him was that he was astonishingly well informed on the difference between scallions and leeks, which had actually been quite helpful, if I were being honest. Apparently to my sex-deprived, overworked brain, that was sufficient. Again, some perspective.

Dan answered the door with a look of pleasure and surprise that lit his stunning face like a flame. In that initial moment, I said a silent prayer of thanks to leeks.

In the next, as he leaned in to offer a kiss on the cheek, I debated

1

whether his overpowering cologne could actually *melt* his stunning face. Or mine, for that matter.

"Any trouble finding the place?" he asked.

"Nope, your directions were meticulous."

He smiled widely with those perfect white teeth and intense green eyes, gesturing me inside the small bachelor pad with an elegant flourish of his hand.

The entryway of the apartment was tight and made tighter by the presence of a bicycle leaning just inside the doorway. I pitied the person whose mode of transportation in San Francisco was that bicycle. Cars in the city were no picnic, but you'd take your life in your hands on that thing.

At first glance, the place was tidy, not well appointed, but respectfully cared for. On second glance, a musician lived here—or several of them, judging by the array of equipment I could see.

Dominating the space was a keyboard and three guitars on their stands. A small couch was pressed against the wall alongside a beat-up brown leather recliner. The coffee table, which serviced the two, was stacked high with music composition paper, and off in the corner was a little TV that looked as if it got sparing use.

"Are you in a band?" I didn't think he was. He'd mentioned in the market that he played Division I basketball, which would leave little time for the kind of serious composing that seemed to be going on in this living room.

"No," he said, looking back over his shoulder as we headed down the hallway. "I'm finishing up at University of Virginia—just home from school for a week or so. This place belongs to some friends."

Musician friends. The irony of that just had to be appreciated. I'd spent much of my adult life intentionally avoiding entanglements with musicians, and for a very good reason—three very good reasons, actually: drugs, women, and irresponsibility. The musicians I'd dated could fit neatly into those categories, and one overachiever spanned all three. Finding myself in a musician's apartment felt a little like cosmic payback for the rash decision-making that had landed me here.

As I followed Dan through the kitchen to a small back patio crowded with guests, I cursed myself again for coming.

But I'd spent my high school years focusing on college, my college years focusing on law school, and law school focusing on starting a career. I'm not complaining; I liked the law just fine—it was a good, practical career, and my parents were generous to a fault in footing the bill for my education. But my chosen path had left little time for much of a life, and now that school was finally behind me, I was eager to have something more to my existence than briefs and research. I was only twenty-four, but I felt as though I was on the fast track to cat ownership.

"What can I get you to drink? Beer, soft drink, water?" he asked.

I took in Dan's flawless face with a mixture of awe and wistful regret.

On top of it all—coming to the Tenderloin alone, not knowing anyone here, favoring spontaneity over good sense—this guy was just too good-looking to be anything but trouble. He was uncomfortably handsome. The kind of handsome that is, quite frankly, excessive. He had me with the strawberry-blond hair and the athletic body but throwing in the eyes and that smile; it was just too much.

"Water is fine. I can't stay long."

"What? Why? You just got here." Reading my thoughts correctly, his face changed. "These are all good people. Please stay. I really want you to."

What could I say? He was sweet.

I nodded faintly in uncertain concession, which he seemed to take as a resounding yes. Out came that smile again. Full-on, megawatt.

3

"Don't leave while I'm gone," he said emphatically. "I'll be right back with your water, and I'm going to throw some leeks on the grill like I promised."

I watched him move about the small, crowded yard with confidence and ease. He was especially attentive to the women present, respectful and polite in the manner of someone who genuinely *liked* women—and was probably not going to limit himself to just one.

He disappeared into the kitchen and came out holding two leeks to his head like horns. I couldn't help but laugh. He *was* sweet. But he wasn't for me.

It was a relief, really—gaining my bearings and realizing that, while I did need to get a life, I didn't need a one-night stand, even as tempting as this particular one-night stand might be. I began to feel pleasantly detached from any expectation of what this night could offer and I suppose that's what allowed my attention to casually drift towards the most remarkable voice I'd ever heard.

It was coming from the kitchen, or from somewhere just inside the apartment, but it cut through the space effortlessly. It was a rich, colorful voice—the kind that had warmth and hominess. Genial, with an elusive quality I couldn't quite identify. It took me a minute to realize the voice was Irish.

The lilt was so subtle I might have missed it completely if it weren't for the fact that, against the backdrop of distinctly American English speakers, it had a charming prominence. And it was laughing, a deep buttery sound that oozed vitality and vigor. I loved that voice, before I ever saw the man to which it was attached.

I was watching the door to the yard when he first appeared, emerging as though stepping onto a stage. He was looking down, the dimples on his cheeks still lingering from whatever conversation he'd been having. Just then, he looked up and met my gaze, as though finding me had been his intent all along.

I shifted in my stance and glanced away, feeling an unmistakable blush rise over my cheeks. I'd never been much of a blusher, but I could no more control my reaction than stop my heart from beating. When I looked up again, he was standing in front of me.

"How's the craic?"

Pronounced like 'crack,' I had no idea what he was asking. Dumbly, I just blinked.

"I'm sorry?"

"Are you enjoying yourself?"

He was a physically imposing figure—tall, broad chested, and powerful under his white T-shirt. The intensity in his light hazel eyes sent a hum of electricity right through my body as he stared at me like I could have been his very last meal on earth. I swear to God, every single hair on my arms stood erect.

"Oh . . . yes, but I can't stay long."

One silent beat passed between us and then he was laughing. Not with me, bear in mind—*at* me, dimples deeply cratering both cheeks. His laugh was sexy. Jesus, *he* was sexy.

"Completely fallen to shit already, have we?" In his voice was a hint of flirtation I thought he probably couldn't help.

"No," I said smiling, and no match for his charm. "I just—have a thing."

That sounded *incredibly* lame and we both knew it. He didn't respond immediately. Instead, he just stood there, eyes glistening with humor, drinking me in in a bold, curious way.

It wasn't just one thing about him—his beautiful eyes fringed with thick lashes, the richness of his dark, auburn hair, the curved mouth, or the solid frame—it was how it all came together so devastatingly. This man had a magnetism that was absolutely undeniable, like a secret so big it just oozed out of him, despite any effort he may take to keep it in check. And I knew right then and there, if he ever turned it loose on me for real, I'd be finished.

Because to top it all off, like catnip to a kitten, he was carrying a guitar.

It was beautiful Gibson dreadnought, slung behind his back and positioned in such an organic way that it looked a part of him. The way he cradled it gently with his elbow told me it *was* a part of him. And everything I loved and hated about musicians came rushing back in a surfeit of hormones and horror stories. He was my siren song.

"I'm Jamie Callahan." The siren had a name. *Jamie*, I said in my head. I think I may have sniffed him a little too. Subtly, of course.

Beer, soap, maybe. And something earthy. It was decidedly masculine and tempting.

"Mel Grayson."

He allowed the silence to linger between us, but never dropped that cheeky grin. His smile looked as though it hadn't had the advantage of orthodontics, but it had the good fortune of not requiring it. Any imperfections just added to his charm. God, he was something.

"How can I convince you to stay a bit, lovely Mel?"

I'd just opened my mouth to say something, not actually knowing what sort of something might come out, when Dan returned with a bottle of water and two leeks for the grill. Despite the onslaught of his cologne, it was an enormous relief. How was it that *he* was now the safer of the two options?

"What's with the guitar?" he asked Jamie before loosening the cap on the water and handing me the bottle.

"What's with the leeks?" Jamie fired back, undaunted.

"She likes leeks."

"Goats like leeks." Jamie's smile moved to his eyes, lighting them with humor. "Women want *meat*. Don't they, Mel?"

My heart did a painful *kerchunk* in my chest. How does one even respond to something like that?

His loaded gaze was fixed on mine, and I swallowed hard as something heavy and potent stirred between us. It was a very physical thing.

I wasn't the only one to notice it. When I finally broke away from that look, I realized Dan was glancing between Jamie and me, clearly reevaluating his prospects for the afternoon.

"Can I offer you a burger, instead?" he said with unconcealed mirth.

I cringed.

"You're grand for asking," Jamie answered with a smirk. "I'll take two with sides, as well."

Dan gave no direct response, but the silent conversation that followed was loud enough. It reminded me of every National Geographic documentary I'd ever watched—two alpha males facing off over a female. There really was very little difference between lions, walruses, and men.

Dan tilted his head in gracious concession and left Jamie and I standing together under an entirely new set of circumstances.

"So then," Jamie said.

"So then," I echoed.

The full-dimpled grin that burst across his face lit his hazel eyes with the promise of mischief. I suddenly felt a little off-balance.

I blamed the leek.

§

"Is he going to be upset with you?" I asked Jamie after Dan returned with the burgers but stayed only long enough to deliver them.

"Danny? Nah." His eyes narrowed as he watched his friend navigate back through the crowd. "He'll be all right. He's a gem, that one."

There was an access of pure love in his voice, and I strongly suspected from his tone that the friendship between them ran deep. It left me with a warm feeling in my belly, and maybe a twinge of guilt too.

Jamie ushered me to sit in an elderly lawn chair, and then set his plate down on an adjacent one as he removed his guitar to lean it against a wall.

"Were you going to play?"

"Oh. No, I just had something in my head I was working out. I just . . . well, sometimes it's inconvenient." He waved his hand like it could wait.

But it was a curious thing for me. Not being a particularly creative person myself, I often wondered how it worked for artists. Did ideas come like sunlight bursting through the clouds? Or was it more like wrestling a cat into a bathtub?

"Does that happen a lot? Like when you're in the middle of doing something else?"

He laughed dryly. "All the time. It's a bit of a problem, actually."

I nodded in agreement, taking a small bite of my burger, but in truth, that seemed like a problem of riches to me. The musicians I'd known welcomed any and all inspiration—whenever it came. Good ideas were hard to come by.

"Well, don't let me keep you. I'd hate for the next 'Stairway to Heaven' to be thwarted on my account."

He laughed again, but warmly this time—his dimples underscoring the heartiness of the sound.

"I'd more think you'd be the one to inspire it."

What would come off sounding like a cheesy pick-up line from anyone else seemed completely authentic coming from Jamie. I marveled at this as I watched him proceed to dispose of his burgers in a very businesslike manner. This guy could eat. Though no wonder, he was a wall of a man. A few inches shorter than Danny—

I'd put him at about six feet—but with slightly more mass. Where Danny was elegantly built, Jamie was dense. Not bulky, per se, but he had an air of impenetrability, like Superman, and it likely took a lot of fuel to keep him going. He hunched over his plate to catch any escaping juice and made quick work of anything there that was edible.

I did a decent job with mine too. Danny had talent on the grill.

"So, the instruments I noticed coming in are yours?"

He leaned down and picked up his beer from the ground, taking a deep pull and swallowing.

"Two of the guitars are. The bass and keyboard belong to my roommate, Greg." He gestured with his bottle to a nice-looking guy of slight build and blue eyes. "That bloke over there."

Greg had a chain hanging from the belt loop of his black jeans and with his dark goatee, I could almost imagine him a pirate. He seemed to feel the weight of our attention and turned, nodding his chin by way of acknowledgement.

"D'you play an instrument?"

"No." I shook my head in firm negation. "I took lessons once but . . . let's just leave it that I'm a great appreciator of music and musicians."

That didn't exactly come out the way I'd intended. Jamie's eyes sparkled, but he had the grace to let it pass.

The fact was, I had taken up guitar a few years back, full of determination to get myself to the point where I could just pick up the instrument and play something. How hard could it be, right? I took lessons and practiced religiously every single day. As was my nature, I felt hard work could triumph over any deficiency in natural ability. I was wrong. Hard work is essential for sure, but music is a gift—sadly, it wasn't mine.

"Come," he said, standing up with purpose. "Let's play."

For the record, I had no intention of doing so myself, but I was curious to know what he could do. I followed him back through the crowded kitchen to the living room, where he restored the Gibson to its stand. To my surprise, rather than picking up one of the remaining electric guitars, he sat down on a small bench in front of the keyboard and waved me over to join him.

"See if you recognize this."

With no music in front of him, sitting shoulder to shoulder with me, he began to play "Just Like Heaven" by The Cure. That made me laugh—I was wearing a vintage Cure T-shirt.

"Here, follow along with me. I'll show you how to play it."

He placed the fingers of my left hand on the keys, covering them gently with his own. They were much larger than mine and rough to the touch, but they were warm and sure.

I was suddenly hyper-aware of every point of contact between us—his hand, his strong thigh sheathed in denim, his corded, muscular arm. I could feel my fingers tremble slightly beneath his and fought hard to mask my body's reaction to our closeness.

"A . . . G-sharp . . . E . . . D . . . C-sharp . . . D . . . E. Now, again."

We repeated the unmistakable chord progression together many times—his hand over mine—until I could remember the pattern on my own. Then he drew back and I was playing The Cure. *All by myself!* It sounds ridiculous, but I'd always wanted to be able to play an instrument and this small exercise was thrilling.

I burst out in a face-splitting grin, which, of course, threw me off my game completely, and he had to return his hand to mine for further repetition. A . . . G-sharp . . . E . . . D . . . C-sharp . . . D . . . E.

"There you have it, then," he said proudly. "Well done."

That soft lilt did unfair things to my libido. I was mortified by the thought that he might be able to see it. But even as I told myself that, I felt an inexplicable urge to kiss him.

I didn't follow it.

"Show me another," I said instead.

"How about this one?"

He positioned his hands and launched into a flawless rendition of "Friday I'm in Love." The song was far too complex for me to have much of a roll, but I loved watching him play it, feeling his shoulders flex and give beside me as he effortlessly delivered the piece from memory. He was talented.

"I can't do that, Jamie."

"We'll do it together."

We both knew this was just another excuse to touch, but I did not complain. He laid the fingers of my right hand on a specific set of keys and essentially played over them. With his left hand, he shouldered the bulk of the melody. I was no more than a passive participant but, still, it was amazing to watch. I craved the feel of his hand on the back of mine. I noticed that he often left it there longer than was strictly required. The closeness gave me a rush of excitement every single time.

When we finished, he removed his hands from the keys and rested them on his thighs.

"I think you're a natural."

"I think I'll hold onto my day job."

"What is that, your day job?" He had the most adorable crooked tooth that gave a hint of boyishness to his ruggedly masculine face.

"I'll be a lawyer soon."

I debated with myself as to whether that was an accurate description. The truth was, I had recently taken the bar exam, but wouldn't get the results back for another three months. If I passed— and god, I could not even *think* about the alternative—I'd take my oath and be admitted to the Bar. I was, however, now working full time on a provisional basis for a boutique firm in the city. It was true enough, then, I decided.

"A lawyer?" Jamie seemed surprised. "That's brilliant."

I did my best to wave off the compliment. More than anything, I was growing increasingly aware that even in the small space, we'd somehow managed to draw closer. He was watching me intently, taking in every detail of my face, and at close range, there was no escape from the pull of his magnetism.

"Well, if I get into badness, I'll know just who to call," he said, and out came the dimples in a flash of charm.

I laughed. "Unless your *badness* involves an intellectual property dispute, I'm afraid you'll be shit out of luck, my friend."

Sitting shoulder to shoulder, I could smell the faint scent of his aftershave and feel his warm breath on my cheek. Slowly, his gaze drifted downward to my mouth and my heart stuttered in my chest. He wasn't shy—he intended no discretion in his appraisal of me— and I realized in that moment *how much* I wanted to kiss him. I was breathless with it. Just an inch, maybe two, and I could taste him. I felt a little dizzy—that's the effect he had on me.

He licked his lower lip, but he made no move to kiss me. He just continued to tease me with a look that pulsed like fire through my body.

I stared at his soft lips, his tongue just barely visible.

There was no sound between us. Just the heat of proximity, leaning in too close to be accidental. Longing turned to outright hunger and my composure broke under the weight of his gaze.

I looked away, shifting in my seat. My throat felt parched, and I swallowed sharply. "But if you get into badness by writing something that sounds too similar to this—" and I played A ... G-sharp ... E ... D ... C-sharp ... D ... E— "then I'm definitely your girl."

I glanced back at him, unable not to; he was so *there*.

"Hmm." He pursed his lips, emitting a sexy growl, low and deep in his throat. "I very much like the sound of that."

§

In the same manner, we made our way through a couple songs by The Squeeze and few by U2, and I was beginning to get a feel for his musical influences. It was electrifying sitting with him, watching his powerful hands move over the instrument with supreme delicacy and precision.

"Do you know this?" he asked, and launched into a beautiful descending arpeggio for a song I'd never heard. Unlike the others we'd played, it was slow and soulful, more R&B than rock.

"That doesn't sound like your genre."

"All music is my genre, really." He continued to play the intervals. "I suppose I found my voice in alternative rock, but I listen to everything. This is a song for you. Donny Hathaway's version."

"For me?" I didn't know what he was saying. He glanced at me briefly before turning back to the keys.

"No," he smiled faintly, not wanting to insult my ignorance. "It's called, 'A Song for You.'"

To my surprise, he began to sing softly as he played.

He had a beautiful singing voice that did absolutely nothing to bolster my self-control. It was rich and low, and perfectly pitched. The kind of voice with character. He didn't need any false affectations; his voice had resonance and emotion.

As I watched him play, it hit me like a ton of bricks. He was a lead singer—a frontman. Of course he was.

How could I not have seen it? He had that air of confidence, arrogance almost. Almost. But not . . . quite.

Suddenly, I was seeing him through a different lens, though. I don't know why it changed something for me that he was a frontman. But I'd had enough experience around musicians to know the general type. I'm not saying it was necessarily fair to draw those conclusions, but I didn't think my own experience was an anomaly. Jamie would be like fly paper to a swarm of women who were likewise captivated by his soulful vulnerability on stage. I'd seen it enough times to know better. I did know better. I'd been through it already and knew how this would likely play out. I could see all the images in my head as he sang—the furtive glances, the unexplained absences, the looks of pity from those who knew something I didn't.

It was time for me to go.

I rose from the bench without warning. "Thank you. This was . . ."

Jamie shot up beside me and suddenly, we were standing so close together. There was a moment I could have pulled away. I could have, and I didn't. And then his mouth was on mine.

He kissed me with no preamble. There was nothing tentative about that kiss. His lips and tongue were soft, but commanding. His firm hand caressed the back of my neck in a way that made me feel tingly and weak—as if I'd gone to putty. Without consideration, both of my hands went to his chest, where I could anchor myself against the dizzying effects of that kiss.

Whatever resolve I had was lost. I folded into his body in willing submission. I wanted him—wanted beyond any sense of logic or self-preservation. I *wanted*.

It was so solid, his chest, so formidable, and I let my fingers spread wide over the expanse of muscle and vital flesh, thinly covered by his shirt.

The pad of my ring finger brushed over his nipple and he let out a faint groan as his tongue skillfully worked its way around mine. His kiss was like a drug, warm and disorienting. I moved my hands back and forth over the defined ridges of his torso. And loving the feel of him, I carelessly drifted down his stomach, where I found no give in the slab of muscle that led to his waist.

He seemed to shudder under my touch, gripping my hip tightly with his free hand. He was wearing jeans, and I caressed the soft fabric of the belt loops and felt the sharp edge of a rivet. His mouth was intoxicating, as were the sounds of pleasure sliding from his lips into mine. I ran my fingertips over every ridge and seam I found, drinking in the taste of him—mindless of anything else. The kissing stopped, but with my eyes closed, I continued to touch his body, sliding my hands across the hard, shapely surfaces. Shapely was not the right word. He was beautifully formed—flawless even—every denim-covered rigid curve fitting perfectly in my palm. I pressed and stroked, ran the heel of my hand over his . . . his . . . wait . . .?

OH. MY. GOD!

My eyes flew open in a panic.

It was his . . . I was stroking his . . !

Chapter 2

Mel

COCK!

In a moment of profound humiliation, I glanced up at his face to find him staring at me, wide-eyed and full of wonder. Not lascivious, though he was *undeniably* turned on, maybe even a little painfully so. But more like he was looking at pieces of a puzzle that didn't quite fit together. I swallowed hard, unable to tear either my eyes from his face or my hand from his pants. I suddenly felt flushed and a little sweaty. A tiny droplet ran down the back of my T-shirt.

"You stopped kissing me," I pressed out. Seriously, *that's* what comes to mind when you find your hand accidentally on someone's crotch?

He cleared his throat and swallowed hard. "I liked watching you do that."

"Why?" I whispered through my mortification.

"Because you seemed to like it. And I liked it too."

I was *morbidly* embarrassed. I did not know what had come over me or how to recover from the humiliation of losing myself so fully in a moment. I did absolutely nothing for the space of an eternity while a dizzying array of emotions swirled around my brain, banging into each other like bumper cars. Finally, one managed to escape my mouth.

"Well, I guess now you'll have a good story to tell all your friends." The edge in my voice really wasn't fair to him. None of this was his fault, after all.

I glanced up again, just in time to see the remaining glow drain from his expression.

"Why would I do that?" he asked me, with genuine dismay.

I just shrugged, now feeling as if I might cry. He lifted my chin to meet his gaze, which was indescribably intense.

"Why would I *do* that?" he asked again.

I affected a tiny smile through my sudden shame.

"Your friend invites some strange girl to your house, and she ends up rubbing you in a dark corner. That makes for a pretty good story."

He reached for my miscreant hand, unfolded it, and brought the palm gently to his lips.

"My friend invited over the loveliest woman I've ever seen in my life, and quite inexplicably she thought I was lovely too."

"Jamie . . ."

"What?" He made everything seem like it was so simple and straightforward—so *no big deal that we just met and yet here you are rubbing my junk*. But it wasn't simple and straightforward.

"I don't even know you."

"Is that what you're worried about?"

I was worried about a lot of things, honestly, but yes, my capacity to touch a man intimately without knowing anything about him was a troubling development in my personality. Along with the leeks, of course.

I shrugged.

"Let's remedy that. Ask me anything."

I could not look him in the eye and would not have characterized

17

myself as steady of mind, so I just grasped the first thing that popped into my head.

"You're a band? You and your roommates?"

He nodded. "Us and one other. Cadence is what we're called."

"Is music your full-time profession?"

He laughed and I had to look up. "From your lips to God's ears, angel." He touched me gently on the cheek. "No, not today. But someday. To keep from starving, I work for a commercial landscaper."

"You're a landscaper?" I thought of his rough hands on mine.

"No. I'm a manure spreader, a hole digger, and rock hauler," he said with a dose of humor. "It's steady work, though. And the hours do well for our gigs."

As it turned out, each member of the band had a side job—and none too glamorous. Jamie was the band's lead singer and guitarist, and he and Greg Van de Meer, bassist (and keyboard and guitar, as needed) had founded the band two and a half years ago. Greg made extra money by designing websites and doing some photography for a realty office on the Embarcadero. Nash Aldridge on drums was a graduate of the University of Colorado College of Music and worked for an auto body shop in South San Francisco. And Killian Walsh, lead guitar, was a barista in the financial district.

"Now, may I ask about you?"

We were still standing close, my wayward hands tucked neatly beneath my crossed arms for safekeeping. But he seemed to understand that I needed as much distance as I could have within the confines of our proximity. He didn't touch me, but he didn't back away either.

"There's not much to tell."

"What is 'Mel' short for?"

I hesitated. I hated my name. It was the only blemish on my mom and dad's otherwise flawless parenting record.

"Well, if you must know, Melody."

The story goes that my parents met through friends when they were in their early twenties. My dad was a trial lawyer, dashing with his dark coloring and movie star good looks. My mother was a court reporter, and physically his polar opposite—petite and fair, with delicate features. My dad always said that she was the melody that made his heart sing. It was a romantic sentiment but, as I'd argued all my life, it was not the basis by which to name a child, especially one who was fated to have no musical or vocal talent, whatsoever. In my rebellious teens I shortened the name to Mel. I'd inherited most of my dad's coloring and my mom's stature, and the general consensus among my family was that 'Mel' was far too masculine a name for me. But that, of course, made me want to use it all the more. I'd even gone through a phase when I'd told people the name was short for Melinda. And if I was being honest, I already regretted not doing that again today.

"*Melody?*" His eyes went wide as saucers, and he blinked several times. It was almost comical. His mouth opened a little in a sexy way that made me want to invade it again with my own. I didn't, though.

"Melody Jane, full disclosure."

"Oh, sweet Mary mother of God; I think I'm in love."

I glared at him.

"No, I *truly* am," he said with conviction. "So bloody in love."

I tried hard to work up a stern expression, but he was looking at me like I was a giant ice cream sundae on a hot summer day. A reluctant smile appeared on my face instead.

He continued to shake his head in awe. "Your name is *Melody*. And you're wearing a Cure T-shirt, which means you must have very good taste in music—or at least in T-shirts—both of which I'm a massive fan of."

I laughed. He was a charmer.

"This is it, Melody Jane." The moratorium on touching was over. He reached up and brushed a hair off my face, running his thumb gently over my jawline. That now-familiar jolt hit me squarely. And let's face facts; I knew firsthand what he had to offer.

"It's forever, the two of us," he rasped. "Best you get used to me now."

I gave him a long, level look, to which he responded by making a very undignified face. I giggled, actually giggled. He was fun to be around.

Reaching over to the coffee table, I picked up a black ballpoint pen. I flattened his large, rough hand on the palm of mine, and in neat, careful script, I wrote my phone number. To my own amazement, I also drew a little heart around it. I'd never thought of myself as the girl who drew hearts on a guy's hand.

Apparently, I was.

He looked carefully at the numbers, closed his hand protectively over them, and with the joy of a small boy holding a wild lizard, he raised the large, gentle fist to his heart.

Chapter 3

Jamie

I never could sleep well.

As a boy I suffered night terrors and would keep myself awake by making up new words for things that seemed more appropriate than the real ones.

Dingleollocks, for example.

I won't say what that one was for, but mind you, I was eight.

Once I discovered music though, I found a way to benefit from my sleeplessness. Left alone with my thoughts in the dark, I would focus on a troublesome chord progression or lyric, and actually found that much of my best work was done in those solitary, uninterrupted hours. So much so that I routinely kept a journal and pencil by my bedside to make notes on things I didn't want to forget by morning. Even now, I carried a small pad with me at all times for that very purpose.

But this particular morning, I had more than just a few notes in my head and was propelled out of bed by that familiar urgency to write. I set a pot of coffee on and settled down in the living room with my Gibson to put down a melody that could only be composed for her. Melody. The coincidence was just too brilliant.

I had no idea how much of the morning had passed—that often

happened when I was writing—when I was brought back to awareness by the sound of my mobile vibrating on the table.

"Hey, pickle."

"Jamie, I'm nineteen. Why do you still insist on calling me that?"

I smiled at the sound of my sister's voice. "Because it bugs you, naturally."

"I hate you," she responded casually, and I laughed.

"What's up?"

Cara let out a deep breath into the receiver. "I was just wondering if you've talked to Mum lately? I think Da may be drinking again."

An immediate constraint fell over our conversation. Cara and I were the two youngest of seven kids, and as long as we could both remember, Da's drinking and Mum's excuses for it had been a primary source of dysfunction in our family. Da himself was another.

"How do you know? Did she say that?"

"Not directly. But I called her last night and I could just tell by the way she sounded."

I wedged the phone between my ear and shoulder and pinched the bridge of my nose. It was not the news I wanted. We'd been down this path too many times to count with Mum, always with the same result. You can't help someone who doesn't want it.

"Last time, I practically begged her to leave him and I gave her every penny I had."

"I know you did," she said quietly. "But will you call her again? I worry."

I nodded into the phone. "Yeah, I will."

We fell silent, both knowing exactly how that call would go. People, of course, lived with all kinds of realities; ours was that we'd been born to a brutal man and a damaged woman, and we had to accept the fact that tragedy and chaos would be in our lives as long as our parents were.

With two free hands, I fingered a few of the strings on my guitar and was rewarded by the lovely notes of the song I was composing. It calmed my agitation almost immediately. Writing always had that effect on me.

"Hey, by the way, did you get the email I sent you?"

"Don't know. Which one?"

"I invited you to join a website called MySpace. It's kind of like Friendster, but new. Everyone I know is getting on it."

"Never heard of it," I said absentmindedly, as I continued to work out the bridge.

"You're not listening to me."

"I am. I'm just wondering why I'd want to join a website with a bunch of teenage girls."

"I'm telling you—this is a great way to get some exposure for the band. You can't believe what it's done for the Arctic Monkeys."

Whoever that was.

"You can post music and concert dates, and you can even answer questions from fans. This could be great a thing for Cadence. Maybe you could expand your following in other areas."

"That's called touring, pickle."

She groaned loudly. "You can't tour everywhere, Jamie. Just think about MySpace, okay?"

I heard a soft knock on my front door and hauled my arse up from the couch to answer it. Danny stood on the doorstep looking like shite warmed over. I stepped aside to let him pass.

"I gotta go. How's summer school, by the way?"

"Good. Fine."

"You keeping your grades up?"

Danny's attention turned to me, and he lifted a brow in stern interest. With two overbearing fools looking over her shoulder, you had to feel a bit sorry for her.

"Yes," she answered, and I could picture a well-orchestrated eye roll to go along with the exasperation I heard in her voice. I passed her annoyed reassurance along to Danny with a nod.

"Good. You need money?"

"No, I'm fine. Thanks, anyway."

"I'll phone you up if there's anything to say on Mum."

I hung up and tossed my Nokia on the couch beside me. Danny was sprawled over the brown leather recliner with his eyes closed, arms crossed over his chest.

"Enjoyable evening?" I asked.

"No complaints."

I noticed the shirt he was wearing was misbuttoned near the top, resulting in one tail hanging dramatically longer than the other.

"There's coffee."

He grunted a vague form of acknowledgement, but didn't stir, and I went back to tinkering with the bridge. It needed to be something like . . .

"Fuck you, by the way," Danny said lazily and without much heat, his eyes still shut.

"What?" I knew what.

"You know *exactly* what."

I set the Gibson aside and ran my hands through my hair. Danny and I had been best mates since my family moved to America when I was nine, and he was far more of a brother to me than any of the five I'd been born to. We'd been through a lot together, and it was a dick move on my part to steal his date. He deserved an explanation.

Here's the real truth of it: I knew Danny had invited a girl he'd met, and by the way he was acting about it, I could tell he liked her. But I'd known the bloke nearly my entire life and he had a particular type: blatantly sexy, fun-loving, and casual. He wasn't looking for anything serious, and he rarely involved himself with anyone you'd consider serious. There were a dozen girls in my yard that day who easily fit that description. Never in a million years would I have expected his date to be the reserved, angelic beauty I saw through my window.

I happened to be standing in the kitchen with a bunch of my mates, who were slagging me for my obsession with a song I was writing. In honesty, I was barely listening; I couldn't take my eyes off that incredibly lovely girl.

Compared with everyone else, she was a classic. Perfectly symmetrical features, separated by the blade of a nose, and natural in a way that would likely drive other women mad with jealousy. Gray-green eyes, maybe—hard to tell at a distance—with dark, shoulder-length hair and strawberry lips. I could easily imagine this girl in a prim dress with a cardigan, and yet here she was in black jeans and a . . . Jesus, it was a Cure T-shirt.

But it wasn't even the T-shirt that made me want to know her. She was standing beside a small side table, and on it was a potted succulent that someone had knocked over, spilling out the dirt and pebbles.

I watched her set the pot upright and the plant inside it. Still, she didn't seem satisfied. As though she couldn't resist the impulse, she began scooping up the dirt with her hands, and pressing it back into the pot. She glanced around a time or two, but no one seemed to notice her.

On she went, carefully straightening each branch and gently propping up the broken ones.

It's a revealing thing, actually—what we do when we think no one is watching. It made me wonder about her. I realized I was smiling when I saw her arrange the remaining pebbles into a little happy face on the table. Then she wiped her dirty hands on the legs of her jeans.

That was quite simply it. The moment I knew I could wait no longer to speak to her. I didn't know who she'd come with, or why she was there, but none of that mattered. From here forward, I was determined she would be staying only for me.

"Do ye remember when we were eleven and we climbed the fence where the old water tower used to be?" I finally asked Danny by way of an explanation for my behavior.

He smiled dimly. "I remember we found those banana slugs by the reservoir, and you put one down the back of my shirt. Fuck you for that, too, by the way."

I laughed. "And you retaliated by putting one down the front of my shorts."

He opened one eye in my direction and leaned forward a bit in his chair. "I did you a favor. There wasn't much else to fill the space."

I grinned at him. "The Irish curse, do ye mean?" I asked, holding up my small finger. "Well, I'll have to say no to that. As I recall, the poor little fella was nearly crushed to death by my massive tumescence."

"And as I recall, the banana slug was the only massive thing in your shorts."

He rested his head back in exhaustion, scrubbing a hand over his stubbled face. He'd left the party with two women and looked to be paying the price for it.

Still, I wanted to say what was on my mind. In all the years we'd been friends, I couldn't remember ever competing for a girl. This was a new thing between us, and it left me with an unpleasant feeling in my chest.

"Are you going somewhere with this story, Callahan, or can I sleep through it?"

I ignored his petulance.

"I was just thinking about when we climbed up that gigantic oak tree. Remember?"

"I remember you jumping up and down on your branch like a fucking monkey. And all the sudden I heard a crack. And then you fell."

"And then I fell," I agreed. "Like a shit ton of bricks. Do you know I still wake up in the night reliving that fall?"

Danny snorted with sardonic amusement.

"Everything just gave way under my feet. I remember having no control over what was happening. Putting my hands out to try to grab on to something—anything, really. But there was nothin' I could do. It just happened so fast, and it knocked the wind clear out of me."

The recollection came vividly behind my eyes as I sat staring at my closest friend, who was motionless on the recliner.

"When I finally realized I was on the ground, I was breathless and stunned."

"And alive, despite being an idiot."

"Yes. Very much alive despite being an idiot."

There must have been something in my voice because Danny opened his eyes and I could see the understanding slowly begin to wash over his expression. He studied me for several beats.

"So, it's like that, is it?"

I let out a heavy breath I didn't realize I was holding, and a vision of Melody smiling in front of the keyboard graced my memory again.

"Genuinely, my brother. It's just like that."

Chapter 4

Mel

Jamie arrived at my apartment with a beautiful bouquet of hydrangeas, and a stubborn resolve not to divulge anything more of our plans than *dinner outdoors*.

We made one brief stop to pick up Chinese, and then we headed west towards the water. When we pulled into the parking lot at Fort Point, I have to say, the surprise was worth it.

"Have you been here?" he asked.

"No, actually, I haven't."

Jamie smiled broadly. "I'm very pleased to hear it. This is my favorite place in the city. I come here often for inspiration."

I could imagine why. Fort Point was the site of a nineteenth century military base that protected the city from roughly the time of the Gold Rush through World War II. The three-story brick building sat directly beneath the Golden Gate Bridge. In fact, in the early 1930s, the bridge was constructed literally over the top of Fort Point. As such, it boasted one of the most stunningly beautiful views of the Golden Gate Bridge available anywhere in the city.

"Look at the towers on the bridge," he pointed out as we stood watching the light fade from the evening sky. "The architects understood the importance of scale as a design element. D'ye see how the lights on the towers are dim at the top? The idea was that they appear to the human eye to soar beyond the range of illumination. I've always been fascinated by the effect."

"I never noticed that."

I turned to study his face as he highlighted various architectural details of the bridge and outlined its long and storied past. He was particularly captivated by the tales of the men who built it—what they had achieved, and what they sacrificed.

I'm not sure what I was expecting from Jamie, but he was anything but one-dimensional. I loved that he could be truly awed by things most of us would barely notice—things like composition, and design, and symmetry. His view of the world was an artist's view, and he seemed to be a student of everything he saw.

"I bet you know more about this place than a lot of the people who work here," I observed, and then I watched as innate modesty transformed his expression.

"I've read a few things, is all. Come," he said, gesturing to a set of blankets he'd laid out in the grass. "We've got the best seats in the house. And I have something for you."

Jamie was dressed appropriately for the cooler weather in nice black jeans and a black sweater that showcased his ridiculously fit frame. The all-black outfit was insanely sexy on him, and perfectly complemented his gorgeous auburn hair.

I, on the other hand, was not dressed appropriately. Having had no idea what to plan for, I'd misguidedly selected a cocktail dress for our date. So I was particularly grateful when he pulled from his backpack a thick brown zip-up hoodie, lined in a gray waffle fabric, that he helped me into. The sweatshirt was enormous, reaching half way down my thighs and covering nearly my entire dress. It smelled earthy and masculine.

"*Dinner outdoors* didn't give me much to go on," I said, as he brought the ends of the zipper together. He was focused on his hands, but I watched his sexy lips curl up slightly at the corners.

"Ah, that." He paused, and hazel eyes lifted to mine. He was standing directly in front of me, and our proximity immediately brought back vivid images of his mouth on mine. My heart skipped a beat. "I can't say why, but I expected you'd wear jeans. And then when I saw you in this dress—" he shook his head, drinking in the merits of its plunging neckline and formfitting shape. His was the kind of appreciation I felt deep in my core and the want it created was nearly unbearable. "You just looked so bloody lovely. I didn't have it in me to ask you to change. Forgive me?" he added, with a glint of roguish charm.

But it was those hazel eyes that did it to me, and the thoughts behind them that seemed to instinctively understand that I spent the majority of most days trying to make a male-dominated profession forget that I was a woman. I could hardly resist being prized as a woman by this very handsome and vital man.

"Forgiven."

What else could I say? He was my siren.

§

From where we sat under warm blankets in the grassy area to the right of the fort, the bridge loomed 776 feet above us, a towering edifice painted in its trademark burnt orange. It was lit from below, rising out of the black waters of the San Francisco Bay and stretching majestically across to the Marin Headlands. To the east, I could see Alcatraz and Treasure Island, and beyond that, the Oakland skyline.

"Tell me," he said, as we dug into the boxes of food. "How did you come to study law?"

"Well . . . I guess it was my father's influence. He's an attorney, as well, and he always said a career in law was a sure bet because, come hell or high water, there would always be contracts."

Jamie smiled and reached for a dumpling. "That seems like sound advice. You're close to your family, then?"

"Yes, very. My parents and my brother, both."

"That's lovely." I adored the way he said that word. *Lovely*. With his soft Irish accent, it sounded like LOvely. Similarly, he said COuntry.

"Do you enjoy what you do?" he asked.

I scooped a helping of beef onto my plate as I thought about how to answer. I hated to admit that I was a law school graduate, just launching a career and still asking myself the same question. I had a talent for the law—I knew that—but it wasn't really the same thing as enjoying it. Still, I wondered how many people actually have the luxury of drawing that distinction.

"I think so," I told him with more certainty than I felt. "I mean . . . I'm just starting out so—" I tilted my head back and forth— "so far so good. I think it's the right path for me. My boss, Adam, told me he hired me because he thinks I have a strong protective instinct, which he said is more lethal in a lawyer than a killer instinct. Like a mama bear, he says."

Jamie laughed. "I think, perhaps, he's right. I think you'll make a smashing lawyer." *Smashing*. I added that to my list of favorite words Jamie says.

"Okay, lay it on me. Your best lawyer joke."

"What? I don't have one," he said, working his way through the kung pao chicken on his plate.

I raised a brow. "*Everybody* has at least one."

He grinned at me, deciding. "Right. Well, how about this? What happens when you give a lawyer Viagra?"

I shook my head.

"He gets taller." Jamie raised his eyebrows and made a goofy face, as if trying to draw out a laugh.

"That's not even funny," I teased. "In fact, it's a pretty pathetic showing from someone who calls himself an entertainer."

"Really?"

"Mm-hmm. I think you can do better. In fact, I *challenge* you to do better than that."

"How much time do I have?"

"Unlimited," I said, around a mouthful of dumpling. Then swallowing: "But you have to beat this one: Two attorneys walk out of a bar as a beautiful woman walks by. One attorney turns to his associate and says, 'Man, would I like to fuck her.' The other attorney thinks for a second and says, 'Out of what?'"

Jamie blinked once and then started to laugh. Hysterically. It may have been the very best sound in the entire world. I was happy just hearing it. In fact, I was a little disappointed when his body finally relaxed again. In the waning sun, I realized I couldn't see his features quite as clearly.

Plus, the fog was beginning to roll in. That in itself was quite a thing to see from Fort Point. Long fingers of mist reached under the bridge, rising up and closing like a fist around the steel and cable.

"What about you? Did you ever want to be something other than a musician?"

"I can't think of a single day since I was eight years old that I ever wanted to do anything else," he said, and I wished again I could better see his face. There was a story there; I was sure of it. I envied him that conviction of his life's true north.

"One of my brother's mates gave me and old guitar and an instruction book and told me to learn my scales. I used to sit on a bucket in the alley behind our flat and practice for hours. Probably drove the neighbors bats, but I loved it. I loved the way the notes fit together. You see, there's a pattern to scales. It's very orderly," he said. And then he surprised me by adding almost as an afterthought, "My life was not."

I wanted to ask what he meant—of course I did, but I felt nosy. If he wanted to tell me, I thought he would. He was like that. Instead, I just reached out and squeezed his hand.

He stroked mine with his thumb and smiled to ease any awkwardness.

"Irish mothers everywhere say, 'What's the point of being Irish if you don't know at an early age that life can break your heart?'"

Then he laughed again.

"So, music was an escape?"

He thought about that for a moment. "Yes, I think so. Partially, at least. Music gave me a voice when I didn't have one. It was my emancipation. When I was younger, I was very angry."

"Angry about what?"

He seemed to consider this. "About the world, I guess. About the hand I'd been dealt. I didn't have an easy upbringing. I had a lot of rage when I was younger—still do I suppose, but I channel it into music. I think many musicians are like that. They do what they do because it's cathartic. And being in a band allows people who are slightly broken to feel fixed for a period of time."

"But it's a cruel mistress," he continued, thoughtfully. "I won't say it isn't. It's demanding and relentless—sometimes I don't know who's a slave to whom. I only know it's who I am."

"Do you mean it's cruel because it's hard?"

"Songwriting, in particular, is hard, yes. You write a lot of bad songs before you write a good one, believe me. But I like it, or maybe need it, more than I find it hard. Does that make sense?"

"It does."

"But the part that can be cruel is the compelling nature of it. You get an idea—usually at the most inconvenient time—and it won't let go. You can't be at peace until you put it down and get it out of your head. But even then, it calls to be better. As they say, very good is the enemy of great. It's a frustration to feel like you've fallen short of great. In that way, songwriting is a gift that can sometimes feel like a curse. That seems like a very Irish thing to say, doesn't it?" He grinned.

"That's passion, I think."

He made a small noise of agreement. "Tell me your passion."

My passion? Now, there was a question. One I did not have an answer for. In truth, nothing made me feel more vulnerable than that question.

He waited expectantly, not realizing that in the course of one conversation, he had unknowingly *twice* touched a tender spot. Of course, to someone like him, it would be unfathomable to live your life without a passion. He probably had many of them. But the fact was, I didn't think I did.

I liked lots of things. As a child, I did all kinds of activities— gymnastics, piano, soccer, debate, track and field, and on and on. I was sort of a jack-of-all-trades and a master of none; reasonably good at lots of things, but missing that one thing I lived for. It had always made me wonder if I'd failed to apply myself on some level. Or maybe I was just truly average as a human being. Unlike Jamie, I couldn't think of anything I was really driven by. Not like he was. Not like having something in my life I lived for. Maybe save one thing . . .

"My family, I guess."

I wondered how utterly ludicrous that must sound to him. He had unwittingly just met the most astoundingly vanilla person on the planet.

It didn't help me any that he was quiet for an unnervingly long stretch of time. He seemed to be studying something in me. I couldn't put my finger on it. And then he surprised me by reaching up to touch my face, almost reverently. His fingertips were cold against my skin, and his touch was soft.

"Family is a noble passion," he said. "Beautiful and noble."

I didn't know what to say. How could I? Jamie made me feel as if those deficiencies I saw in myself were, to him, things to be prized. I loved the person I was in his eyes. I loved the world I saw through him. I loved . . .

Well, I couldn't really name it, so I did the one thing that felt absolutely right. I leaned forward and brushed my lips over his, a slow and deliberate kiss of thanks, and affection, and promise. It'd been forever since I'd been close to a man like this. Well, of course the last time was Jamie, himself, but I hadn't really given myself permission to fully enjoy the feel of his body against mine.

"I'm so glad you brought me here."

"Yeah?" He studied me carefully at close range and I could see something that looked like relief or maybe surprise cross his face. If I wasn't mistaken, his smile seemed a little strained. "I was actually afraid you might find this all a bit—" he shrugged— "simple."

Simple?

It took me a minute to realize what he meant.

Cheap. That's what he meant.

Suddenly I was struck by both his candor and the vulnerability it revealed.

I thought about the bouquet of flowers he'd brought me, carefully cut and wrapped in tinfoil to protect the stems. They weren't purchased in a store, more likely procured from a job site.

And since we'd picked up Chinese from the back door of the restaurant—no money exchanged—I was pretty sure it had been some sort of barter arrangement. I had the feeling Jamie knew every side door, every back alley, and every shortcut in the city. He probably had an entire network of bouncers, bus boys, and security guards. He was that sort of guy. Yes, I was beginning to see he didn't have much money, but he was resourceful. That was his gift, and I was far more impressed that he'd put effort into planning an evening, no matter how unconventional, than I would have been with someone whose total investment of thought was in making a dinner reservation.

"I don't feel that way at all. For the record, Jamie, I think you planned an excellent date."

He smiled more easily this time. "I'm happy to hear it. I don't get much practice."

"You don't date?"

He looked at me for a moment. "No. Not normally."

He stirred the remains of kung pao chicken in its box, and something passed over his eyes, but was gone too fast to interpret.

Courtesy dictated that I should have let his comment pass. I would have, honestly, except a prick of curiosity was suddenly outrunning my sense of propriety. In the gray evening light, the definition of his features had washed away and his eyes were hooded.

"Why don't you date?"

He just shrugged, giving away very little. "I have a lot going on right now. Just priorities, I suppose."

"But you made an exception for me?"

"I find you exceptional."

His eyes met mine in a way that made me incapable of a response. Jamie could do that—flatten you with off-the-cuff honesty.

I set down my plate and settled in close to his large, warm frame. He wrapped a strong arm around me and pulled me closer as the fog began to creep over the ground all around us. Through a small break in the mist, we could see the moon over Alcatraz. It was nearly a perfect half circle, and the edges were fuzzy in the fog like a cotton ball.

Jamie pressed a kiss to my temple, and when I turned my head, he placed another on my lips.

"Tell me if you're cold," he said softly.

Honestly, cold was the last thing I felt. I sank gratefully into the sturdy lines of his torso and let go of any reservations that may have lingered about dating a musician. Maybe it was crazy to be going out with him, but, god, I *craved* a little crazy.

Jamie threaded his hands into my hair and separated my lips with his. He angled my head in such a way that our mouths fit perfectly together, deeply and thoroughly.

All around us, the fog was becoming so thick, we couldn't see more than a few feet in any direction. The smell of the mist and the salt water, the sound of distant foghorns and footsteps, I could take it all in on some level, but those thoughts closest to me were focused solely on him. Wrapped in a heavy, protective blanket of mist, the yearning between us running even thicker, we were effectively alone.

Jamie's hunger for me felt ravenous, like he would devour me if he could, flooding every sense until he was satiated, if that was even possible. We kissed wildly, our chests heaving simultaneously with desire, or something else too dangerous to name.

He dragged his teeth along my jawline while he guided my hands to his chest. He wanted to be touched, wanted his body to be explored like before. And he leaned into it, nearly covering me with his blazing hot torso.

Every part of him was perfect. I sunk my fingers into the warmth of his skin, up and under his T-shirt and sweater, and felt the firm muscles of his back that were strong and defined. I began losing myself in his body, and in the feel of his hand sliding inside my dress to cup my breast.

"Ah, God, you're so soft," he rasped, pressing his forehead to mine as the wind whipped around us in its own rough caress. Then he pushed the fabric of my dress aside so he could see my bare skin, could watch with heavy eyes as his hand kneaded my breast and toyed with the nipple.

Suddenly his mouth fastened on it, like he just couldn't help himself—sucking, licking, squeezing it in his rough hand. He groaned at the way it stiffened against his tongue.

Yes, like that, I told him silently.

Just like that.

A tight noise of want escaped my mouth, and in a moment, he was back over me. His body was so close I could feel his heat forcing out the cold. I wanted him desperately and, sensing my desire, his movements took on their own feeling of urgency. His kiss became voracious. I wanted to trap every breath and sound he made and tuck it away in memory.

"All right?" he panted by my ear.

"Yes," I might have said. Or thought. But it didn't matter; my body was telling him everything he needed to know.

I felt his hand move down, between my breasts, across my hips, and over my stomach. On my outer thigh, where his fingertips met with bare skin, he began stroking me with small circles of his thumb.

His body was hard against my hip, and he pressed with it, like he had to.

I was lost to everything else. I forgot where we were; I forgot any sense of propriety and caution; I forgot that I was the most pragmatic person I knew. In that moment, I was the woman Jamie saw. Reckless, just enough.

I let my legs fall open and spread them loosely on the blanket. I felt his breath catch against my mouth, and I kissed him harder with assurance.

Yes, I want this.

Yes, please touch me.

There was a soft Irish growl in my ear and his hands obeyed.

He inhaled deeply, then slid one under the elastic waistband of my lingerie. His thumb found me, swollen and sensitive, and he stroked and pressed with a firm touch, over and over, working me expertly, whispering praises and encouragement, never letting up, never softening until—

I broke with a jolt of electricity, fierce and sharp. Without warning I came apart in his hands, like a million feather-lite pieces that shot into the night before floating haphazardly back to Earth.

And not until it was over did I realize I'd been calling out his name.

He was breathing heavily against me; I could feel puffs of warm air on my face. When I opened my eyes, he was staring at me in absolute awe. His hazel eyes were wide, and his face was mindlessly slack. I didn't know how to take that look; no man had looked at me quite that way before.

The dense San Francisco fog provided a deceptive feeling of seclusion. Still, an awareness of our surroundings began to seep back into my consciousness. I started to say something—I'm not sure what—but he stopped my words with his kiss.

When he pulled back slightly, his soft eyes were intent on mine. "Don't. You're so lovely just like this."

"Jamie . . . I mean—"

"*Holy God*, you're a wonder. I only wish we could stay long enough so I could see you do that again."

He withdrew his hand from my dress and ran his index finger over his lower lip. He was the sexiest man I had ever seen and I wanted more of him like I'd never wanted anything else in my life. Which is why it was several more seconds before my brain caught up with what he'd just said.

"Wait . . . *what?*"

"We need to be somewhere. That is, if you'd like to go."

"It's nine thirty." For the first time I was becoming cognizant of the full extent of my dishevelment.

"We go on in an hour."

"You have a *gig*?" I sat up quickly and tugged my dress and bra back into place with the mist clinging to my hair and skin. "Jamie, why didn't you say something? Don't you have to be there to warm up?"

I knew how important every performance was to an up-and-coming band. I couldn't believe he'd taken me out beforehand.

"It's fine. We loaded in the equipment this afternoon. But I just . . . I can't be late. Would you like to come?" There was hint of hopefulness in his voice. "Or I'm happy to drop you off at home first, if you prefer. There's time."

"No, I'd love to go."

"Yeah?" There was no mistaking his pleasure. He wanted me there. And I was suddenly very excited at the prospect of seeing him on stage.

Chapter 5

Mel

We pulled up and parked on Columbus near a place called Bimbos 365, a big tan building with black awnings and a seventy-year history. Greg, Nash, Killian and Danny were already there, piling out of a white van when we arrived. Bimbos was a very well-known music venue in San Francisco, and it seemed like a big deal that Cadence would play there on a Saturday night. Not that I was, by any means, an expert on the local music scene, but I guess I'd assumed that they were still relatively unknown.

I was wrong about that.

Danny lifted a small duffel bag from the open double doors and turned to glance speculatively at Jamie and me as we walked up. I cringed at the thought of what may be showing on my face.

"I'll take that, brother," Jamie said. "Can you . . .?" He nodded at me.

"'Course."

Jamie reached for my hip with his free hand and pulled me in close.

"I've got to change and get ready. I'll see you in there."

He gave me a quick kiss, and then was gone through the

building's metal door, which was safeguarded by two impressively sized bouncers, with equally impressive tattoos.

Inside, the back of the house was dark, and smelled like a cavern of stale beer and male exertion. The walls around us were literally pulsating with the thump of a bass guitar, and the sound from the stage was nearly deafening. Not a place conducive to conversation, and in a way, I was glad for it. I was still undecided what was the appropriate thing to say to Danny.

As soon as the music cut, there was a furious pace of activity that was almost unsettling to watch; everybody had a purpose. Band members from the previous act emerged from the stage, comparing notes on the performance. A dozen club staff and house technicians organized power cords, called out questions, checked various instruments, and moved this here and that there. The stage manager was barking out requests, which were being executed with military precision.

Where I was expecting chaos, there was a surprising amount of order.

Cadence appeared, fresh from the dressing room in the basement and rechecked all the connections. They seemed remarkably relaxed as they walked around the stage one last time and taped their set lists to the floor.

Jamie seemed very much in his head. He didn't make a move to speak to me, nor I to him.

Finally, I turned to Danny and noticed for the first time that he was wearing a black T-shirt with the band's faces printed on the front and the word *Cadence* emblazoned across the top in some modern font.

"Did you get a mug and a mouse pad to go with that shirt?"

Danny doubled over laughing and turned around so that I could see the word *crew* printed boldly across the back in neon yellow lettering.

"I can't imagine what he must have on you that you would agree to wear that."

"You don't want to know," he said wryly.

It was as good an opportunity as any.

"Danny, about last weekend . . ."

He waved off the coming apology. "You made the right choice." His green eyes were soft and sincere. "Now we can be friends, right?"

"Definitely."

He put his arm around me and kissed the top of my head affectionately, but platonically. I couldn't imagine another scenario in which receiving a decidedly platonic kiss by a man *that* attractive would have made me so happy, but Danny seemed like a very good friend to have.

§

Four clicks of the drumsticks signaled the start. All at once, the stage lights came up and the room burst to life with the sound of the instruments—Nash's drums, followed by the boom of Greg's bass. And then Killian bled in with a cry of electric guitar.

The crowd went wild, which I have to admit was startling. I happened to glance at Danny, who was beaming with pride.

From where we stood near the front left side of the stage, I couldn't see Jamie, but I knew he was somewhere in the shadows. And then, the music ratcheted down to a sustained beat, and Jamie stepped out to the mic.

He was lit from behind, silhouetting his frame with streams of light and particles that seemed almost living and breathing around him. He was an irrepressible presence that appeared to grow in stature before my eyes.

With his left hand arched over the stand, he tapped his heel in time to the beat. I watched him take a deep breath, and then he began to sing.

His voice was low and resonant, and I couldn't liken it to anyone I could think of. It wasn't the kind of voice that reached to sound like someone else. It was distinctly his own, with just a very faint Irish burr underneath. It had beautiful clarity. But as he pushed it, adding power behind the words, that clear voice took on a soft raspy sound that had a definite rock-n-roll edge. He had religion in it, for sure, and an incredible range that moved easily between a deep baritone and a strong falsetto.

But it wasn't just his voice that made him every bit the frontman I knew he'd be; it was his contagious energy and confidence. Jamie was mesmerizing to watch—he was a very physical singer, the way he consumed the floor, interacting with the band and the crowd. He seemed to just lay himself out there, leaving everything he had on stage.

I can't think of a single day since I was eight years old that I ever wanted to do anything else.

No, he was right. He was made for this. And as I watched this incredibly charismatic man, fully in his element, I knew it with one hundred percent certainty—he was going places.

§

Backstage, after the show, was another sort of madhouse.

Anyone with any loose relation to the band seemed to find their way back there, and the band members were pulled in all different directions—pausing for pictures, signing merchandise, and shaking hands.

I was so distracted by the pandemonium I didn't take much notice when a cute brunette with blue eyes approached Danny and me. She didn't look like your typical groupie; in fact, she looked pretty wholesome, dressed in a navy skirt and a white denim jacket.

"Have you guys seen Jamie?"

For a minute, I thought she might have been his sister, but no, Cara was away at school and this girl lacked a family resemblance.

I looked her over more carefully as she glanced determinedly around the crowded room.

"I haven't," I said, "but he should be here soon."

Danny didn't seem to be giving her any thought.

"I can't wait to surprise him. I'm Carly," she said, now turning to me again. "His . . . well . . . I guess, his girlfriend."

That got my attention.

"His girlfriend?"

Carly nodded vaguely as she eagerly searched the area for Jamie. Beside me, I could feel Danny stiffen and glance quickly in my direction, but I was careful not to let any expression show on my face. Certainly not the shock and embarrassment of having been with a guy who already had a girlfriend.

It was loud where we were standing behind the stage. Most of the audience had left the venue, but the dull roar of their conversation had been replaced by the sounds of equipment being disassembled and packed away in cases. House music began playing through the overhead speakers—some techno band whose beat gave me a headache.

Still, I could not take my eyes off Carly. I found myself staring, trying to decide if, maybe in the confusion of the moment, I had misheard her.

Girlfriend?

If that was true, I'd just gone out on a date with this woman's boyfriend. Oh, my god, worse than that, I'd . . . *Oh, my god.*

Danny transferred the beer he was holding to his left hand and reached out with his right. "I'm Dan," he said carefully. All the while, he watched me like I was a pin-less grenade. Carly was oblivious.

"Oh, you're the one he went to elementary school with?"

This revealed some level of intimacy. Danny seemed to realize it too. And as a slew of alarm bells began sounding in my head, Danny placed a hand on my lower back, preparing for the seemingly likely scenario that I would run.

I didn't, but only because I hadn't quite reached that level of clarity. Instead, I began rapidly flipping through my recollection of the conversations I'd had with Jamie, trying to remember if there was anything he'd mentioned that would have suggested he had a girlfriend. I couldn't think of anything overtly but, god, was I that blind?

You don't date?

No. Not normally.

Meanwhile, Carly was looking expectantly at me, waiting for me to introduce myself. It felt like such a ridiculous situation—my brain was spinning, and not by any means operating at full capacity.

"Mel," I said finally, and swallowed hard.

"So nice to meet you." She was very polite.

Why don't you date?

I have a lot going on right now. Just priorities, I suppose.

All men exaggerated, in my experience, and some men lied. I had a feeling Jamie was capable of lying when necessary, but I doubted he was very competent at it. He had such an open, expressive face. Involuntarily, I pictured it: the kind hazel eyes, the boyish, dimpled grin.

Family is a noble passion. Beautiful and noble.

Every muscle in my body was tense, fighting a flood of emotions that threatened just below the surface. I knew I had begun to fall for him. And even worse, my natural instincts had provided no forewarning of anything of this nature.

As Carly went on about having been out of town for the last week and coming straight here from the airport to see Jamie, I could do nothing but nod like a bobble head. I was far too busy battling a full onslaught of guilt and anger. Well, those were the emotions I admitted to; if there were others, I preferred not to acknowledge them.

Instead, the words *women*, *drugs*, and *irresponsibility* circled relentlessly in my head, a swirling mass of censure for every stupid decision that had led me to this very point. Suddenly, I was so disappointed in myself.

Without conscious thought, I leaned into Danny for support and, perhaps on some similar impulse, he tightened his grip on my waist, taking a hasty sip of his beer.

Carly misread the situation completely.

"You guys make such a cute couple!"

Danny sputtered, choking on the beer he'd just swallowed, and coughed forcefully into his fist. Meanwhile, Carly continued, looking directly at me: "You know what would be fun?" *Oh god, please don't say it.* "The four of us should go out after this. Maybe go to O'Malley's."

Danny had turned his back to clear his throat but rejoined the conversation just in time to catch Carly raising her eyebrows in his direction as she said to me in a sing-songy voice, "The booths at O'Malley's get *cra-zy!*"

His eyes sprang open as he struggled for a response. Despite my own discomposure, I honestly felt sorry for him. He had no idea what he'd agreed to when he offered to look after me. Clearly, this was well beyond his expectation.

I was ready to walk out myself, right then and there, and would have, except I was stunned into inaction as another girl approached us and asked about Jamie's whereabouts.

Goddamn that crew T-shirt, which was attracting women like moths to a flame.

Unlike Carly, this girl *looked* like a band groupie—long, blonde hair brought up in a tight, high ponytail, with a short skirt and boobs practically coming out everywhere.

"What do you want with Jamie?" Carly asked suspiciously.

"I want to talk to him. Why?"

She glared shrewdly at Carly, and the tone in her voice suggested strongly that this one was not to be messed with. Carly, to her credit, did not back down.

"I'm Carly, his *girlfriend.*" Carly seemed much more confident about that now.

Danny and I, meanwhile, stood dumbstruck; in fact, I think he was beginning to lean on *me* for support. It felt like we were watching a tennis match between two women who were likely to want to kill each other at the end of it. Anything less resembling the beginnings of a world-class fight club would be hard to imagine.

I think I'd gone numb.

Nottobemessedwith, on the other hand, was undaunted.

"I doubt you're his girlfriend."

"Why would you say that?" Carly demanded.

"Because I *know* Jamie," Nottobemessedwith scoffed. "Plus, I've been sleeping with him for more than a year and he's never even mentioned you." She looked at Carly in the most condescending way. "No offense," she added with a laugh.

I don't know about *my* face, but Carly's face fell instantly. Doubt flickered over her expression, and her eyes darkened with a wounded look. I felt bad for her, given the sheer absurdity of the situation. Under any other circumstance, I'd have probably liked her.

Recovering soon enough, Carly stood her ground.

"Well, he didn't mention you last Friday night, either. Or Saturday morning, for that matter."

Maybe I liked her a little less. Last Saturday afternoon was the day I met Jamie. I was getting dizzy trying to keep track of his love life, and the memories that this nightmare triggered were not good ones for me: women, drugs and irresponsibility. It all came rushing back like one big, giant slap in the face.

Danny spun around quickly, drawing all our attention to a girl standing behind him who had tapped him on the shoulder.

Nottobemessedwith made a very nasty face. "What do you want?"

"Not that it's any of your business, but I'm looking for Jamie."

Oh, for Christ's sake, I thought, and then wondered if I'd accidentally said it out loud.

This new girl looked up at Danny. "Have you seen him?"

Jet-black hair was about all I could register. I crossed my arms over my chest, and let out a soft grunt of disbelief. Carly, who was, herself, coming unglued, turned to me with an *I know, right?*–type glance of solidarity.

"Uh, no," Danny said hesitantly. He looked slightly frightened, and much like a man who was giving the idea of celibacy some very serious consideration. And he was probably as ready as I was to burn that crew T-shirt.

"Well, if you see him, tell him Jessica needs to talk to him ASAP."

"Why?" I shouldn't have asked. I knew that. *Knew. It.* But in that moment, I felt I had very little to lose.

"Yeah, why?" Carly added with a hint of vulnerability that made me feel bad for her, in light of everything that had happened.

"He and I have a problem, that's why. And that's all I'm going to say about it."

An enormous and growing sense of dread began to creep up around me, much like the way the fog had enveloped the Golden Gate Bridge. I felt a chill move through my body, and along with it, the prick of a thousand tiny needles. I was a little lightheaded; I must have looked it.

"Mel," Danny said quietly to me, his face intense with concern.

No one else was looking at me. No one could take their eyes off—

"Are you trying to say you're *pregnant*?" Nottobemessedwith sneered.

That was the final straw; it had all become far too much. I looked around desperately for the door.

"I'm saying I think I'm late," I distantly heard Jessica with the jet-black hair pronounce.

By this time, though, I was so far beyond done with this whole mess.

I pulled a hand through my hair in disbelief, and when I was finally able to hear past the ringing in my ears, suggestions were being made that one or the other may have been a whore, and that one or the other's mother may have also been a whore. Following that were a string of uninspired expletives in which various body parts and diseases were mentioned.

Poor Carly began to cry.

I turned to Danny, who looked terminally freaked. "I'm calling a cab," I said, as calmly as I could manage.

He grasped my arm just above the elbow and tugged me apart from the catfight that was developing.

"Don't leave yet."

"Danny, I will not take a number and stand in line behind *that*."

He looked around, and then over to the women in frustration. "No, you should never stand in line behind anyone."

He was sweet; it made me want to cry. And I was damn close as it was.

"Look, I have no idea what that's about," he said, gesturing to the mayhem. "But please don't leave without talking to Jamie."

No. I couldn't stay another minute. "I'm sorry, but this is humiliating."

It was just then that I looked up and caught sight of Jamie. When his gaze found mine, he immediately broke out into a wide grin. But the toll of that scene was easily readable on my face, I'm sure, and almost immediately, his expression altered. He glanced over at the spectacle to my left.

I didn't hesitate. I turned quickly and pushed the metal rod on the back door to the alley with a loud, abrupt clank. One of the bouncers stood up as I rushed through.

"Can you help me flag down a cab, please?" I hated the shake in my voice.

He didn't waste a moment's time, leaping into action. He'd probably seen plenty of women on the verge of a meltdown and wanted no part of it.

As I watched him signal to a couple of passing cars, I gratefully drank in the night air and tried to regain a little equanimity. Soon, I told myself, I'd be free of this whole nightmare. How had I been so *stupid?*

But just as the door to Bimbos was closing behind me, I heard it swing abruptly open again.

"Mel!" Jamie called out urgently. "Where are you going?" He reached me in three long strides.

"I have to leave." I was struggling to maintain a cool I definitely did not feel.

"Why?"

"*Why?* Really? Why don't you ask one of your *girlfriends?*"

"They're not my girlfriends."

"Not Carly?" I snapped.

"Not Carly or anyone else."

"Oh, right, I forgot. You don't date."

"I don't." His eyes were growing darker again.

"Yes, but you see, when you told me that before, I must have missed the fine print. What you *really* meant is you just fucked around, *a lot!*"

He bristled visibly. "I will not apologize for things I did before I met you."

"I'm not asking you to."

"Yes, you are."

I probably was.

We stood for what felt like an eternity, locked in silent consternation. Finally, I looked away, even so feeling the heavy weight of his stare. Yes, he was right, of course. I *had* wanted him to apologize. For everything I'd seen tonight; for everything I'd been through with other musicians in past years; for a whole bunch of things that weren't remotely his fault. But I had no justification for any of it, and offered none.

"You got a girl pregnant."

"I did not. She damn well knows it."

"How can you say that for sure?" I demanded, though still not my business.

Jamie's face softened, and compassion for me mastered everything else going on between us. "Because I'm always very careful about that," he said softly. "And the timing couldn't—"

He shook his head. He didn't care to get into the details and, frankly, I didn't care to hear them. Tears began to well up in the corners of my eyes.

"Well, you sure have a funny definition of not dating."

He had the grace to look a little embarrassed. He wanted to reach for me; I could feel it. But he didn't. Instead, he scrubbed his face with his hand.

"I'll admit I let your misunderstanding of my meaning stand— partly because I didn't owe you an explanation—" he insisted directly— "but more because I already had enough to contend with when it came to you."

"I don't know what that means."

"It means . . . for Christ's sake, Mel, look at me." He gestured to himself. "I ride a *bicycle* for transportation. The car I drove you in tonight was borrowed. I couldn't even afford to finish junior college. I live in my head too much of the time, and between my job and gigs and rehearsals, my life is fucking *madness*. That's why I've kept my associations with women casual, but I couldn't exactly say all that to you. Not to *you*."

He closed his eyes and ran his hand back and forth over his head in exasperation, leaving his thick auburn hair a perfect mess. I wanted to reach for it—to soothe it back into place along with everything that was awry between us.

"What I had with them," he said, pointing to the door, "I don't want that with you. I want something real." The tightening of the muscles in his throat betrayed his emotion. "But what do I have to offer? You're so *beautiful*. And you're a lawyer. You meet well-to-do men every day who can give you so much more than I can. D'ye think I don't know the odds are already stacked against me?"

His jaw clenched as he kicked his foot at nothing on the ground. When he looked at me again, it was in the most achingly vulnerable way, as if he had just aired every painful truth of himself.

"Jamie . . ."

I was speechless. All my anger deflated, and in its wake I felt a need to protest his comment—to tell him that the way he'd summarized himself was bullshit. Wealth and education weren't the measure of a man. And I wasn't someone who was impressed by those things, anyway.

"No," he said softly, shaking his head. "Please don't."

He wasn't looking for me to stroke his ego or to offer any reassurances. He wasn't saying these things to evoke my sympathy. His intent was brutally straightforward; he didn't think he could give me a lot, but he would give me honesty—even if it came at a cost to his pride.

He just wanted truth between us.

You're a landscaper?

No. I'm a manure spreader, a hole digger, and rock hauler.

He had laid himself bare for me—not an apology, but an olive branch—and I felt I owed him some honesty of my own. I touched his wrist lightly, and hazel eyes found mine.

"You're not the only one who misrepresented."

Jamie cocked his head in question but didn't speak.

"As much as I might want you to believe that I'm the adventurous girl who just accepts invitations to a stranger's house in the Tenderloin, or lets a man make her—" I hesitated, too embarrassed to go on.

"Come," he finished for me, his voice thick.

"Yes. Come in a public park, no less." I took a deep breath.

I had momentarily forgotten about the presence of the bouncers until I realized they were suddenly appraising me much more favorably. Jamie threw them a glare that would honor a headmistress, and they quickly turned their attention anywhere but us.

"I wish I were that girl, Jamie, because you deserve someone fearless like that, but I'm not. It's only when I'm with you . . ."

I faltered, and looked down at my hands, feeling suddenly more naked than ever—far more vulnerable to him with my soul than I'd been with my body.

A taxi pulled up and stopped at the opening of the alley.

"I like it, though," I offered softly. "The way it feels to be with you. I think I may even need it."

The magnitude of that admission was a surprise, even to me. Sometimes you don't know the truth of a thing until you hear yourself say it out loud. And I *had* said it—not just out loud, but to him.

All around us, the air felt heavy and pregnant. I took a long, jagged breath and prepared myself for what I might see in his face. Would it be panic? Awkwardness?

No. What I saw there was truly beautiful. He seemed to understand the trust I'd just bestowed upon him, and his expression enveloped me like a warm blanket. He stepped forward, setting his hands on my hips, and leaned his forehead into mine.

"Don't go," he whispered.

"I need to, Jamie." He squeezed me gently, not happy with the answer. "And you need to deal with . . . *that*," I said, gesturing to the door.

He exhaled and nodded ever so slightly against my head.

Then with great tenderness, he cupped my face with his hands and kissed my forehead, lingering there as though he feared it might be his last. When he finally broke the kiss, I glanced up into his beautiful face. It was a face so full of everything he was: strong and proud, dignified in his way, open to the world. It was a face with so much grace and character, so much determination.

We came from different worlds; that was true. But maybe there was something special in each of ours that we could offer the other.

I'd already admitted to him that I thought I needed that sense of adventure and vitality he brought to my life, but I really didn't know what it was I could give him in return.

All I knew was that a strange new part of me wanted to protect him from the craziness that awaited him back in the club—from everything in the world that could injure him or force him to be more guarded than he was. Another part of me knew I should be protecting myself. I was falling hard, and it was terrifying.

I reached up to stroke his cheek, and he leaned in to press his lips to mine. They were warm and soft, giving instead of demanding. I drank him in gratefully.

"Can I call you?" he asked softly.

I slumped the top of my head into his broad chest, and his arms came around me.

I had arrived at a junction, and no small one. I could easily answer *no* and go back to a life I knew would be prudent. The road more traveled is always the safer one. But tonight I'd glimpsed the other, a gloriously uncertain path that would take me far beyond my comfort zone, embodied by a man whose heartbeat was fast and strong beneath my cheek.

What promise did *that* road hold? And who would I need to be in order to walk it? I didn't yet have the answer, but I closed my eyes and took the first step, anyway.

"Yes," I told him.

I wasn't naive. I knew exactly what I was agreeing to. Not just a phone call, not just another date or another gig to attend. But joy and heartache. Pleasure and pain. Life, if I was brave enough to really live it.

In the cool of the evening, I slid out of his grasp and started for the waiting cab.

"Mel." I turned at the sound of his voice. "What did you think of the show?"

I smiled. "It was . . . exceptional."

Chapter 6

Mel

In my experience, companies are like people. A few are visionary; most are just average. Some act like bullies, others like babies. And most often, the personality of the company reflects that of its CEO. So, the intellectual property infringement action I was currently assigned was like a breath of fresh air. Our client, a public semiconductor company, was facing claims by one of its much larger competitors. This was a common thing. The semiconductor industry is rife with companies that hold large numbers of patents and defend them vigorously.

What made this case somewhat uncommon was the fact that both companies were behaving rationally to resolve the dispute with minimal business disruption. They were both open to discussing a cross license that would allow the parties to avoid a costly litigation. And, ultimately, we felt optimistic that the resolution would be reasonable. No drama.

In fact, all in all, Thursday was a rather orderly day. Which was a good thing because Thursday evening promised to be anything but.

Jamie was coming to dinner.

Jamie's day job entailed strenuous, manual labor and I had seen the man eat—he was like a machine when it came to food consumption. A meal of light fish and a salad would not do. I needed to serve him something hearty and satisfying.

The problem was, I wasn't much of a cook. I thought seriously about buying something already prepared, but then found a recipe online for a beef stew that looked achievable. It was all cooked in a Crockpot.

How hard could that be?

Plus, the great thing was that it needed to simmer for ten to twelve hours, so I could set it up before work and it would be ready when I got home.

No problem.

Well, yes, turns out there were problems.

I dashed home at lunch to check on the meal, but it didn't seem to be cooking fast enough. So, I turned up the slow cooker to speed the process along. I figured as long as I left the office promptly at five o'clock, I would have enough time to get home, quickly change and be ready for Jamie at six.

But my client was late to our four o'clock conference call. By the time we reviewed changes to the licensing agreement, it was 5:20. Traffic in the city sucks at that time, so when I finally burst through the door of my apartment at 5:50, I was sweaty, mad, and plotting to sue everyone for everything.

I should have gone directly to the kitchen, but as it turned out, vanity, as well as a lack of kitchen skills, could be added to my list of personal deficiencies. Instead of noting the smoke that was creeping under the swinging door to the kitchen, I went directly to my bedroom to change into a sexy yellow dress and fix my make-up. My newly adopted stray puppy, Atticus, was right on my heels.

The sound of my fire alarm put an end to said vanity, as well as every aspiration I had of channeling an inner Martha Stewart, who had, to date, never quite materialized.

Everything was unraveling fast.

I had one shoe on and grabbed the other, hobbling down the hall and through the living room.

Unfortunately, the sound of the alarm was followed directly by the sound of my buzzer.

Jamie!

I really wanted to cry. The smell of burning meat was like a slap in the face as I hit the button to let Jamie into my building and left my front door ajar.

I dashed to the kitchen. The whole room was filled with smoke and the alarm was blaring overhead. The Crockpot poured smoke from around the rim of the lid, and the only color I could see through the glass was black.

It was a goddamn mess.

I quickly unplugged the pot and was in the process of waving a dishtowel in front of the fire alarm like a matador to a bull when I felt a cool rush of air behind me.

I turned in time to see Jamie manfully wrestling open a window that I would have sworn was permanently painted shut decades ago. The frame protested with an angry squeak, and then finally gave way to his will.

Suddenly, the alarm stopped and the chaos settled.

And there I stood, in the middle of the kitchen with my yellow dress not yet zipped, wearing one shoe and swinging a dishtowel.

A disgraced Martha Stewart.

Unlike my dinner and me, Jamie looked delicious. He was perched by the window, freshly showered and wearing a navy button down shirt and jeans. His beautiful auburn hair was artfully ruffled, and on his face sat two deep dimples as he watched me with curious amusement.

"How's the craic?" was the first thing out of that sexy mouth.

"The craic is shit," I snapped in total frustration. *Did that even make sense?*

He closed the distance between us in two quick paces and wrapped me up in strong, sympathetic arms. He smelled divine, like soap and the musk of light exertion. I buried my nose into his neck for several seconds and just inhaled. I loved his skin.

Honestly, I could've stayed there all night. But too soon, he released me and grabbed a potholder from the sink. Lifting the lid of my Crockpot, he released a billow of smoke. This was not the dish I had envisioned.

As I stood there feeling hopeless, Jamie launched into action. He opened and closed various drawers until he found a fork, and then he dipped it into the charred remains of the beef stew. I watched in absolute horror as he literally pried a piece of meat from the bottom of the pot.

"Jamie, you can't eat that."

"Why not?" He put the whole piece into his mouth. "Fu—!" He began exhaling mightily around the scorching meat. "Ifs ho—!"

"Of course it's hot, you stubborn oaf! It was on fire a minute ago."

He chewed vigorously, and then swallowed hard, sucking in air to cool his burning mouth.

"Needs a little salt." He reached around me for the saltshaker on top of the stove.

It was a charred mess. It didn't need salt; it needed a Brillo pad and a garbage can.

"Mmm, now it's perfect."

He was pulling off bits of vegetables and meat with his fork, most of it black and nearly unrecognizable from its earlier glory. I drew in a ragged breath and exhaled, bringing the heels of both hands to my eyes. I couldn't bear further witness to this disaster.

"I am so sorry. I'm not much of a cook."

I heard the fork clank upon the counter. Jamie wrapped his hands gently around my wrists and pulled them from my face, pinning them behind my back. In the process, he stepped in very close. I wasn't looking at him, but I could feel his breath. He said nothing, just waited for me to acknowledge him. I didn't for another long moment, and he squeezed my wrists a little. There was no place to hide from my embarrassment. When I finally met his gaze, which was inescapable, his expression was unyielding.

"I'd rather eat a meal from this pot right here than from any other in the world."

"Then you are a fool," I said haughtily.

In truth, this was the stuff that made me melt for him. And melt, I did.

Reluctantly, a little smile began to tug at my lips and was met with a much larger one developing on Jamie's face in response. He glanced again into the pot.

"My mum always says that hunger is the best sauce. And just look at the glaze on this carrot. That's professional grade."

I watched with no small amount of gratitude as he detached one from the carnage with his finger.

Then gratitude became adoration.

And adoration quickly gave way to lust.

I took his hand in both of mine, removing the carrot from his fingertips with my lips. Holding his gaze, I licked away all traces of its existence.

He went still.

It's not just food itself that makes eating so sensual; imagination is an equally powerful aphrodisiac. Jamie's small smile revealed an imagination very much at work, and I couldn't have hidden where my own had gone.

Every inch of his body called to mine. His fingers in my hand were large and rough. I bit down gently on the pad of his index finger as he drew it from my mouth. Then he pressed his thumb to my lower lip and I opened wider to take it in.

His eyes were ablaze. In and out, I sucked the tip of his thumb while he stood, statue-like, staring. Arousal was radiating off him in the short, shallow bursts of his breath and in the rapid rise and fall of his chest.

"Please don't tease me," he whispered, his voice hoarse with desire.

"I wouldn't."

I couldn't. I wanted him that fiercely. I was sure my body was already primed for it.

Suddenly, he spun me to face the sink and I felt the cool edge of the countertop across my abdomen. There was a window directly in my view, but my mind's eye was focused entirely on the press of his body behind me.

His hands brushed my hair forward to one side. As he traced my neck and shoulders, I could feel the calluses on each fingertip from his instruments, and on his palms as a consequence of his work. My own hands clenched into fists and felt soft and untested by comparison.

He crested my shoulder, and my dress slid off into a pool of chiffon at my feet. My bra followed seconds later. With a brief, inelegant struggle, Jamie was out of his shirt and shoes. Heat seemed to pour off him in waves as he stepped close enough to graze my shoulder blades with his torso.

The smell of smoke and burning meat still hung in the air, but the cool evening breeze carried in the scent of the marina as well. It raised goose bumps on my skin that were indistinguishable from those inspired by his proximity.

"Do you want me?" he murmured into my ear.

"You know I do. Let me show you."

His hands came around to cup my breasts and pull me deeper

into his embrace. I felt him lean forward and press his lips to the line of tendon between my neck and shoulder. I closed my eyes and exhaled.

"Turn around."

§

Jamie

Years later, I would write a song about that yellow dress—the way it fell from her shoulders; the way it looked like spun sugar on the floor. That's how deeply the image was branded into memory. A picture worth a thousand words.

There were other images too. A kaleidoscope of them.

A velvet tongue on my nipple.

Soft strands of hair in my fists.

Red lips encircling my cock.

Warm breath.

Relief and urgency. Ah . . . yes . . . sweet Jesus . . .

Relief.

Chapter 7

Mel

Jamie's fly was still open as he held me to his chest and carried me down the hall. He kicked open my bedroom door and set me on my feet beside the bed.

The side table light was on, casting a warm, soft glow to offset the gray cast of the late evening sky. For the first time tonight I felt exposed, standing in front of this man in only my underwear, the taste of him on my lips. He could read it in my downcast face, I'm sure, and lifted his hand to cup my cheek.

"How long has it been?" he asked me.

"Um." I laughed a little nervously. "About, maybe, eleven and a half months. About. Give or take a few days. I think."

His eyes shone—probably because of my embarrassingly precise accounting—but to his credit, his face was soft and serious. He could see how vulnerable I felt. I was shaking. God, I was *shaking*. I wasn't even sure why. Nervousness. Exhilaration, maybe.

But I wanted this; I wanted to tear into him and have him tear into me. I wanted to completely lose myself in pleasure until my brain unraveled into a gooey, messy mess.

Still, Jamie was waiting, letting me catch my breath. He moved his hand to stroke my hair, over and over. He was soothing me, gentling my nerves with soft touches and whispers of how beautiful he found me, how much he wanted me. He leaned in to kiss my neck, teeth grazing my skin, telling me he would take his time and give me anything I needed. The brush of his lips left a trail of heat, and I shivered with anticipation.

I folded my arms around his shoulders and pulled him in closer, until there was only space enough for heat between us. His hands found the sides of my breasts and skimmed down my body to my hips. As he sealed his mouth over mine, the buttons of his open fly pressed into my stomach, and his length, wet at the tip and warmer than any other part of his body, rubbed insistently at my navel.

I grabbed handfuls of his hair and pulled his mouth deeper into mine, our tongues sliding seductively against one another. His hands squeezed my hips, and then glided slowly over the round of my ass, kneading it gently in his palms. His mouth was hungry against mine.

I was getting lost in the intoxication of his kiss when he pulled back, and I dropped my arms from his neck. I missed his warmth against my body immediately.

"Sit," he said softly, and entangled one of his hands in mine. The familiar roughness of his palm was a comfort. I was so nervous. Gently, he urged me to sit down on the edge of the bed.

My heart was beating wildly in my chest, almost painfully, as he stepped in closer between my bent knees.

He touched a fingertip to the column of my neck and traced a line down and across my collarbone. I could not tear my eyes from his face, nor the working of his throat muscles as he swallowed.

"When I was a boy, I made up words for things," he said quietly, watching the drag of his finger over the swell of my breast.

"What kinds of words?"

His expression turned to fascination at the sight of my nipples tightening under his touch.

"Mostly relating to food and girls and comic books. And some other things," he added, smiling faintly, but he didn't name them. His eyes stayed trained on my body, focused on the way he could stretch his hand wide enough to envelop my entire breast. He seemed to like the way my nipple felt between his fingers, and he rolled it gently between his knuckles, and then moved his hand down lower to broadly stroke my ribs from side to side.

I could not fathom what made him recall the memory at that particular moment. It seemed like such a disconnected thought, though he wasn't distracted. His eyes were alive and ardent as he memorized every curve.

When he reached my belly with his hand, he kneeled on the floor in front of me, sat back on his heels and continued his journey over the rise of my hip and the inside of my thigh. I gripped the bedspread tightly on both sides, my body now burning with need.

"Jamie," I gasped. He hooked my lacy waistband with his index finger and tugged it downward and off. I was naked, and would have felt totally exposed, except the sight of his body interrupted any such thoughts. He was an absolute masterpiece. I'd never seen anything like it—every firm ridge of muscle looked as if it'd been shaped from clay, sleek and elegant with strength. And he was so deliciously masculine smelling, with the mingled scent of perspiration and arousal. I could not catch my breath.

"I think if I could have ever imagined this . . ." he whispered, brows creasing slightly as he ran his hands up my calves, between my knees, and then to my trembling inner thighs. "Or could have known at a young age that a woman's body could be as breathtakingly lovely as yours," he tilted his head and spread me a little wider, "I might have dedicated my entire life to coming up with a word that was fit to describe it."

Hazel eyes lifted to mine and he smiled softly.

Words escaped me.

Thought escaped me.

Only the feel of his fingertips drifting higher occupied my consciousness. In the dim light of my bedroom, the moment was almost unreal.

"I cannot be around you and not want you, Mel."

Then he bent and planted a soft kiss on my hip, letting his tongue linger on my skin.

Everything that followed was a blur. A crazy, scattered, mind-blowing blur.

I closed my eyes and let my head fall back, opening myself to his insistent mouth. My chest heaved with huge lungfuls of air, audibly and tellingly. I pulled at the covers and fought against my own colossal craving.

"Look at me when I do this," he commanded.

I tried. I really did. I opened my eyes, but they were unseeing. Too many sensations. Even more fragmented thoughts. How much I wanted this man. Desperately. How much at a disadvantage he had me with just the flat of his tongue. How everything in my world had come to a crashing halt. How, in that moment, he owned me.

A thin sheen of perspiration formed on the back of my neck. I was fighting to control a fire that was quickly becoming an inferno. I realized I was holding my breath, bearing down against a feeling that was likely to wreck me. He knew it too, and he pressed me harder, pushing inside me with rough fingers.

So desperate, I grabbed his hair with two fists and let out a cry of need, loud enough to surprise myself. It was strangled and garbled and utterly incomprehensible.

And then I broke. The orgasm that followed was powerful enough to pull my hips from the bed, ripping through me with vicious intensity and leaving me completely empty yet so very full. A thunderclap, followed by unearthly quiet. I didn't think the pieces of me would ever go back together in quite the same way again.

I felt soft kisses on my thighs, the drag of his teeth over sensitive skin. His fingers left me, and there was both relief and emptiness. My body craved the feeling of some part of him inside of some part of me.

"Please kiss me." I sounded hoarse to my own ears.

Jamie quickly shed his remaining clothing and blanketed me with his gloriously naked body. His mouth slanted over mine, tasting distinctly of my own arousal. I kissed him back with a ferocity that took us both unaware.

I could feel my kiss excite him, and he reached for my hand, pulling it down between our bodies. He wrapped it around himself, and with a groan of sheer relief, he began guiding me to stroke him just exactly how he needed.

He was heavy and thick, powerfully built—silken, and pulsing with heat. Soft hair brushed against my knuckles, and his balls were tight in my palm. I moved to stroke him, over and over, and as I did, watched him begin to come undone.

"Ah God, Mel," he said in a tight voice, "keep touching me like that."

In my hands, I held his manhood, a vigorous, forceful presence. He closed his eyes, causing a crease to form between them, and pressed himself into my firm hold. I could smell the musk of sweat on his body, his face pained in pleasure and restraint.

His lips were at my ear, expelling tight breaths, and his eyes were squeezed shut as he rocked back and forth in my hand, struggling to stop himself from rutting, but not quite able to hold back this primal instinct. It was heady and overwhelmingly arousing to witness, and it made me ache to have him inside me.

"Jamie, please." I could not wait any longer. I was desperate for him.

"Since I first saw you standing there in my yard, I haven't been able to think of anything but feeling your hands on me. I've nearly lost my mind with it."

His head slumped down to my shoulder. As he regained command of himself, he pulled away from me like it pained him to do so.

"Do you want this?" he asked softly.

"Yes." In my voice I heard a hunger as big as his.

With startling efficiency, he rolled on the condom he'd left by the nightstand, and quickly settled back over me. I could not tear my eyes from his ardent face, or from the thoughts that he made no attempt to hide—those focused on one singular goal.

Evening was falling quickly into night. In the last of the light, I ran my hands greedily over the vast expanse of smooth muscle of his chest and arms, and admired the shadows cast across his body by the deep cuts of his torso. His back felt strong and unbreakable.

"All right?" he whispered, as though his throat were as tight as mine. I nodded, unable to say more.

That's when he reached down, lifted my bent knee high between us, leaned his shoulder into it, and opened me in a shockingly vulnerable way.

Suddenly, I was struck with a feeling both terrifying and exhilarating. It was as if I'd somehow managed to harness a stallion, only to realize quite abruptly that when it came to handling him, I was in way over my head.

This man could fuck me into oblivion.

I *knew* it. Could feel it. Whatever reins he bore were flimsy at best.

I closed my eyes, sunk my fingertips deeply into the flesh of his shoulders, and braced myself for whatever may come.

With one hard thrust, he plunged half way inside, causing me to cry out at the shock of it. He was big and I was small, and if there was ever any question about that fact, it ended right there.

"Relax for me," he gasped, but gave almost no time to adjust. He opened me further with his shoulder and pushed inside with a guttural grunt.

I felt winded. The lower half of my body did not feel like my own. He was not only inside me; it felt like he had possessed me. And I wondered if I would ever feel whole again without his body in mine.

I reached down his thigh to the indentation where his quadriceps was flexed, and pulled him still deeper inside.

His answering groan was that of sheer bliss. And in that moment, I knew with unmistakable clarity, I had possessed him too.

His breath was now coming in soft puffs on my skin as he began to move. He felt so tight at first, but soon my body gave way, taking him; demanding him.

He pounded into me, relentlessly, and moisture began springing up on his skin wherever my fingertips trailed—up his strong neck, and into the damp roots of his hair.

I pulled his mouth to mine, holding him, consuming him. Our breath was urgent and tangled.

Finally, I couldn't hold on any longer. I threw my head back against the pillow and shattered. Magnificently—in what felt like a dazzling spectacular of heat and light.

Warm tingles flooded my spine as my body closed around his like a vise. I was too far-gone to see him clearly, but I heard him groan in pleasured agony as my body adamantly urged him to join me.

He thrust deeply, over and over. I lost count, in fact, merely gripping his body for support, until at last, he buried his head in my neck and came hard with a strangled sound and a rush of heat inside me.

§

We were both still breathing heavily when I finally opened my eyes into the stunningly handsome face that hovered directly over mine. He was absolutely breathtaking.

"How's the craic?" he whispered with a cheeky smile, so close to my lips I could almost taste him. I was buried in his arms, in the protection and warmth of muscle and flesh.

"Is that double entendre all part of your Irish charm?"

He laughed and bent to kiss me sweetly. His lips felt soft and inviting, as did the velvety texture of his tongue.

Eventually the kiss was broken and he shifted his body, glancing down between us. I watched him very carefully remove the condom and dispose of it in the can by my bed.

"I'm on birth control, just so you know."

Truthfully, I had no idea why I told him that. It just seemed like a valuable point to make, though there was no way in hell we were having sex without a condom.

His surprise was obvious too, and he seemed to quickly size up the implications.

"I'm not seeing anyone else," he said carefully. "I . . . made my intentions clear."

Jamie told me he would never apologize for things he did before he knew me, but he looked a little contrite as he came back and settled himself between my thighs. "And I get tested regularly. Just so you know. Though I couldn't fault you for wanting proof."

I studied him for a long moment—his open face and painfully honest eyes. I'd been right about women being drawn to him by his soulful vulnerability. How could they not be? He was devastatingly gorgeous. I reached up to stroke his face and he leaned into my touch with a small sigh of contentment. Then, pulling his mouth close to mine so I could feel just the hint of his beautifully sculpted lips, I whispered, "I will *definitely* . . . need proof."

In the space of a breath, the intimacy of the moment transformed. Jamie burst out laughing in exactly the reaction I'd hoped for. I loved his laugh, and I loved the way his eyes crinkled at the corners in amusement.

"Just like a lawyer," he said, shaking his head affectionately. Then he leaned in low and his mouth grazed mine, brushing softly at first, and then pressing and warm.

His kiss was intoxicating, as always. Deep and seductive, and so full of promise and pleasure to come. I drank him in for many long minutes, in the dying stretch of light coming in through my windows. In my arms, he felt—

"Oh, my *god*. How is that even possible?"

"What?" he responded, pulling back to assess my face.

I pushed the covers away and glanced between us to Jamie's now substantial erection.

He grinned widely. *Proudly*, even.

"I told you; I cannot be around you without wanting you." He looked down his body at the impressive presence straining between us. Then he shook his head ruefully. "But I'm afraid *wanting* is all it's going to be because we used all the protection I brought."

For a laughable moment, I think we were both just watching his lonely, superfluous erection lying heavily against my thigh. Then I remembered—

"I bought condoms," I said hastily. "They're in the drawer."

"Yeah?" His relief was unconcealed.

He leaned to one side, and with some effort stretched his long torso to pull the top drawer open. A rush of cool air washed over my skin in the absence of the heat he radiated.

I expected him back over me in a heartbeat, but he stopped, and his eyebrows shot up in surprise.

"Good *Christ*, woman! I don't know whether to be flattered or intimidated. What must you think of me?" He laughed again, still blinking in amazement.

It was true; the drawer was filled to capacity with large boxes of condoms. Well, not just any condoms—*magnums*. I was guessing, of course, when I bought them after the barbecue, but let's be honest here, it was a fairly educated guess. Still, I realized in a flash of embarrassment how that must look. Like either I was planning on screwing him to *death* or I was planning to entertain the entire troupe of an unusually well-hung marching band.

"There was a sale." I winced. Damn my practical nature. But in my defense, it *was* a good sale. And I had no idea how often condoms went on sale. Maybe this was one of those *can't miss* deals. At the time, it had seemed like a prudent decision. Now . . . not so much.

Jamie's whole body began to shake, but his head was down on the bed so I couldn't see his face. Finally, he sucked in an audible breath and threw his head back, practically crying with laughter. A deep flush crawled up his neck and face, and those dimples looked as though they might actually punch holes in his face. He was adorable.

I smacked him, anyway.

"It's not funny!"

He very clearly thought it was. His whole body convulsed over me, causing the bed to shake as if we'd put a quarter in it. Eventually, Jamie wiped his eyes and let out a huge sigh of relief.

"Ah, God, my sides hurt. But I thank you for the compliment. And I'll endeavor not to disappoint."

"Well, you seemed magnum-sized at the barbecue."

"Did I?" Pleased. Jamie's eyes glistened as they moved over my face, and I knew he was looking back in our history together. A look of adoration lingered. Then he grinned suddenly at me, teeth flashing white in the dimness of the room.

"For all you knew, love, it could have been a leek."

Chapter 8

Mel

I don't know long I drifted off before the world came creeping back into my consciousness—people talking on the street below my window, the sound of a car alarm down the street, and the jingling of an animal collar next to my bed.

It felt like a rude disruption when the muscular pillow beneath my cheek twisted out from under me to scoop up an eager and curious Atticus and sit him on the bed between us.

"Well, hello there," Jamie said, scratching Atticus behind both ears with a hand that easily dwarfed little Atticus's head. "Where did you come from?"

Atticus sagged contentedly into the lavish attention, neck drooping, eyes half-mast. Randomly, I wondered if the effect of Jamie's touch was as pronounced in me. Judging by the way I felt at that moment, I suspected it was.

"Hi, sweet boy," I cooed to my little ball of brown and white, furry sunshine. "Were you scared of the fire alarm? I'm sorry." Atticus licked my hand as if I was forgiven for nearly burning down his principal residence, then he leaned heavily into Jamie's chest.

"He's magic." Jamie nuzzled Atticus with his nose and stroked a large palm down his back, over and over. Atticus returned the favor with lavish kisses on Jamie's face and neck until Jamie, laughing, had to physically move him out of range.

"How long have you had him?"

"A few months now, huh, Atticus?" I found his special spot and scratched it until he began thumping his back leg on the mattress. "I saw him running down Van Ness and I was worried he'd get hit. He didn't have a collar or a chip, so I just had to keep him. Plus, he's very cute."

"Naturally," Jamie grinned.

"What?"

"You're very . . ." He hesitated, assessing me critically. And I will fully admit to hanging on each passing second to find out what he thought I was *very*.

"Nurturing," he finally said, pleased with his choice.

"Nurturing, am I?" Could he hear the disappointment?

"You don't like it? What would you have preferred?"

"Oh, I don't know—sexy, devastatingly beautiful, utterly charming. Those are just the first things to come to mind."

"Hmmm." He reached out to cup my breast with his hand. "Well, you're all those things, of course. Perhaps I should have focused my compliment on your tits."

I smacked him and he laughed, prompting Atticus to leap at him with more kisses. I loved to watch Jamie laugh. I loved the crooked front tooth that showed when he wasn't conscious of covering it. I loved the way his dimples would linger on his face for a time after, and how his hazel eyes would shine with humor. Jamie was capable of honest emotion. His laugh always felt genuine.

"Okay, Mr. Charming, tell me, did you have pets growing up?"

"Once. Just for a brief time when I was seven." He paused for a moment, and I couldn't tell if he wanted to continue.

"Foster was his name. He was a mutt. Complete shite of a dog, really," he said with affection. "Barked incessantly, dug in the yard, ran away every chance he got. But, God, I loved him. He was sweet. And if you sang anything, he'd howl along. Every bloody time."

"He sounds awesome. What happened to him?" The moment the words left my mouth, I had an odd sense of dread.

"Don't know," he said simply. By this time, Atticus was in full submission mode. He had rolled over on his back like a pot-bellied frog, his legs splayed out in every direction. Jamie rubbed him from throat to abdomen, absentmindedly, as if looking back in his life. "My da hated that dog. My da is a bit of a brute, you see. A drunk—" he shrugged— "and one day I came home and Foster was gone."

"Where did he go?"

Jamie glanced up at me, as if he could hear the unease in my voice. Then he reached out and brushed a hair off my face with a faint smile.

Shaking his head: "Never asked. None of us did."

"Why not?" I was trying not to sound judgmental of a family I didn't know, but I couldn't understand a dynamic so dysfunctional that you couldn't even ask what happened to the family pet. That was seriously messed up.

"My da was always threatening to put a bullet in him. Or take a fry pan to his head." Jamie paused at the thought. "Anyway, it seemed better not to know. At seven, I just wanted the hope that he'd run away and that one day he'd come home."

"But he didn't." No, of course he didn't.

"No," he said simply.

I could see the pieces of Jamie beginning to come together. I knew he'd had a very different upbringing than mine. But it was no less shocking to imagine what it must have been like to be seven years old and faced with the reality that your dad was as likely to have killed the family dog as he was to have just opened the door and let him run away. What kind of anger would that breed in a child? What kind of survival skills did a seven-year-old need to develop in order to live in that kind of environment? To some extent, I'd always known how lucky I was to have such an incredible family, but I'm not sure I fully appreciated it I until that very moment.

Jamie had said I was nurturing. Maybe to him that was among the highest compliments he could give me.

I leaned in to kiss him over the belly of the dog—not out of pity, but because this man deserved so much more than he'd been dealt in his life. And I'd been given so much more than anyone should keep for herself.

The kiss started as brief, but as was the nature of our chemistry, quickly escalated into something so much more. I got lost in it, in the way his hand wound into my hair, wordlessly declaring his deep affection.

A scrambling of limbs between us broke the kiss and scratched the hell out of Jamie's chest. Atticus wriggled like an earthworm until finally righting himself.

"Jealous little bugger, aren't you?"

Atticus sneezed in response, and then shook himself from nose to tail.

"Does he need to piss?"

"Probably."

"I'll take him out and make us some pasta, yeah?"

It would have been hard to argue. He was up and out of bed remarkably quickly for a man of his size. And I was completely awestruck by his nakedness. He was a masterpiece: tanned skin pulled tightly over the rolling expanse of muscle, the deep indentation of his quadriceps as he bent to retrieve his jeans, his perfectly round ass, and the definition across his back.

Jamie turned, bare chested, and caught the look. The result in his face, one eyebrow half-cocked, was the epitome of male smugness.

"Hungry?"

"Starving."

§

We ate pasta half-dressed over a bottle of wine, and what felt like the whole night stretched out lazily in front of us. We tried a couple of times to clean up the kitchen but found ourselves getting downright dirty instead—against the refrigerator, over the couch, and finally down the hall once more to my bed. Sleep came very easily after that.

I woke to the sound of clothing rustling in the darkness. There was a glow of nighttime coming in through my window, and I could just make out the silhouette of Jamie dressing quietly by the door.

"Are you leaving?" I had no idea what time it was—we'd knocked the clock off the nightstand hours ago.

"I am." He came over to sit next to me on the bed, stroking hair from my face. "Have I upset you?"

I didn't really know how to answer that. I was still a little disoriented and I didn't like that it was too dark to see his face.

"Were you going to tell me you were leaving?"

"Of course I was. You just looked so peaceful. I wanted to let you sleep as long as possible."

I pushed up in bed, and I knew for a fact that *peaceful* was not how I looked. If I had to guess, I'd say Medusa, crossed with a raccoon and exhibiting exceptionally bad breath.

"Why do you have to go?"

"I've got to meet my mates at Nash's place in about half an hour. We have an A&R guy coming to the show next weekend and Greg wants to pull in a new song to our set list. It sounds like shite, though. We're going to rehearse for a couple of hours, is all."

'A&R' was an industry term that stood for artists and repertoire. They were the talent scouts for the record labels. In fact, you could consider them the gatekeepers to the music industry because it was their job to find new artists for the label to sign. But there were precious few of them compared to the number of undiscovered bands vying for their attention. And most A&R guys would not accept unsolicited demo tapes. They were simply too inundated with material from their own trusted sources. So getting in front of one of them was nearly impossible, and there was no other way to break in.

The fact that an A&R guy was coming to the show was a very big deal. Cadence needed to hit it out of the park. They could not afford a misstep. I knew this and decided to be a big girl about it.

"Oh. Okay."

I didn't really feel okay, though. I flipped through the channels on my emotional dial, but none of them felt quite right. I guess I'd assumed that after the night we had, he would stay.

But his leaving reminded me that we weren't officially a couple, and in fact, I didn't really know what we were. I pulled the sheets up tighter around me.

If he could read my thoughts, he was careful not to acknowledge them directly. But he ran a hand down my cheek and into my hair, and leaned forward to kiss me softly.

"Next time, I'd like to stay all night."

I nodded and he rose to head for the door. His broad back cut a swath through the darkness, until he turned abruptly as if he'd just thought of something.

"Ever heard of MySpace?"

I shrugged, shaking my head.

"Some band called Arctic Monkeys?"

"No. Why?" I asked. "Who is that?"

"No one," he said, waving it off. "I don't know why I listen to the opinion of a teenager."

§

True to his word, Jamie came to my place two days later to stay the night. Of course, it was one o'clock in the morning when he arrived. He was amped up from rehearsal, and his enthusiastic lovemaking actually dented my wall. Afterwards, we curled up together, his arm draped around my body with his hand cupping one breast. One of my legs weaving itself between his, and our feet entangled together.

"Love you," he said, yawning widely.

It was nearly pitch black in my room, and quiet except for Atticus's snuffle and a rustle of the covers as Jamie shifted sleepily in my bed.

I wondered at first if I'd heard him correctly. Or maybe he was sleep talking. There was no pomp or circumstance at all.

It wasn't even an *I love you*. It was so off-handed, as if he'd just said it for the millionth time plus one. By the time I'd worked through the shock of those words, so casually spoken, I realized I hadn't responded. But it was of no consequence. His breathing was steady and rhythmic. He was already asleep.

§

When I awoke the next morning, he was gone.

I didn't see him again for close to two weeks. He left me one voicemail in the middle of the night on a Wednesday, asking me to meet him on Sunday night for a gig at the Great American Music Hall on O'Farrell Street in the Tenderloin. All business—that was it. Otherwise, it was radio silence.

I told myself—sometimes even successfully—not to make too much of the fact that following a night of passionate sex and a possible *I love you*, Jamie had dropped off the face of the earth. I spent a good deal more time than I cared to admit, analyzing what this meant and what it foreshadowed for us. I didn't need to see him every day, but if this was actually a thing between us, it might be good to know he was alive, and not crushed under a pile of pavers. And maybe he was thinking of me, too. Just a little.

Chapter 9

Mel

"Why am I just hearing about this now?"

It was a totally fair question and one I had over-prepared for. In fact, my best friend, Hope McClellan, and I had had this entire conversation during my shower this morning—well, in theory we had. She wasn't *actually* present for it, but I thought I'd represented her position quite well. In any case, we were having it again now over lunch.

"Well, it's sort of a funny story, if you want to know the truth," I started. "He's . . . um . . . he's a musician."

For a moment, she just sat like a stone, blinking. In my shower this morning, Hope had found the story *very* funny. Now, in real life, she didn't seem quite as entertained.

"I'm sorry." She leaned over the table in an exaggerated manner. "Did you say *magician?* Because I'm *pretty* sure I was there when you vowed to stop dating musicians."

And this was the part of the conversation that was tricky. Hope was right, of course. She and I had met as first-year law students at Hastings, and she'd had the pleasure of seeing me through my last relationship with a musician that had ended in a classic episode of drunken/high coitus interruptus with some random girl in a backstage dressing room—so ridiculously clichéd that I hated even thinking about it.

Hope had seen me heartbroken, and she wanted something better for me than that. For that reason, I was pretty sure I knew how she would view my starting a relationship with another musician, and that's exactly why I had waited weeks to tell her.

I sighed heavily. "You were, and I did. Are you disappointed in me?"

She leaned back in her chair and studied me for an uncomfortable amount of time. Setting her fork aside, she folded her hands and looked at me straight on.

"I'm disappointed you didn't tell me sooner."

"I'm sorry. I should have—" shrugging— "It just sort of happened fast."

"*Right*," she said, deadpanning. "Because you're such an impulsive person. How could you possibly have had time to tell me?"

She had me there. Honestly, there was nothing I could say to defend my withholding. I'd been a chicken, straight up.

"I'm sorry," I said again sheepishly.

"You are definitely on brand with your choice of men; I'll give you that." She was trying for censure, but ultimately failing. She loved me too much.

I set my fork down and closed my eyes, letting my head loll back in exhaustion.

"Believe me, I was not looking for this. But he . . . he's different."

I could hear her sigh and met her eyes again. That was clearly not the right argument. I tried a different tack.

"Jamie is serious about his career, Hope. He's not into drugs or crazy behavior. And there's something really enriching about spending time with someone who puts his passion at the center of his life. When I'm with him, I feel like I'm actually *living* mine, not just planning for some eventual outcome. Does that make sense?"

Hope took a deep breath and nodded, studying me with what I knew to be a mixture of happiness and concern. She was always after me to be more *in the moment*. She would've just far preferred that my living in the moment didn't involve another musician.

"He has dimples," I added just for fun.

"Dimples are good."

I watched as she generously abandoned her disappointment in me in favor of a renewed interest in scoring some real details. So, I summarized the essential facts about Jamie and did not skimp on the particulars of his ridiculous body and sexy accent. I even copped to the great condom caper, and how he nearly cried tears of hilarity at finding a drugstore quantity in my nightstand.

"He's one of the good ones. I promise. You'll like him."

"Great. When can I meet him?"

"Soon, for sure."

I exhaled heavily as my thoughts drifted for a moment to the disappearing act Jamie was currently performing. And that hesitation was my tell. I knew it, and Hope knew it too. She cocked her head to the side, waiting for me to elaborate.

Sighing, I told her honestly, "The truth is, he may *also* be a magician."

She lifted her brows in a way that compelled me to want to spill every detail. She had a real gift for facial expressions; I thought she might have missed her calling in criminal interrogations.

I proceeded to share with her the one downside I could see to Jamie—how he sometimes just vanished, went off in his head or whatever it was he'd been doing. I didn't really know what to make of it.

"We know this about musicians, Mel."

"You're absolutely right. And yet, I don't think this is just about his being a musician, or being self-absorbed, or anything like that. I think there's more to it."

"Like what?"

"I don't know yet."

The truth was, not knowing why he kept pulling back meant that I also didn't know if this behavior was something that would change. Hope seemed to be making the same calculation.

"Are you happy with him?"

"I am. I truly am, except for that. And part of the reason I think it gets to me is that everything in my life just feels so up in the air right now. What if I don't pass the bar exam? What if I have to give up my provisional employment? And, yes, I worry that this thing with Jamie is more complicated than I can handle. I guess I'm just used to having a little more predictability in my life."

That was a gargantuan understatement and it made me laugh at myself. Hope laughed too, and then her face grew serious.

"You both seem to have a lot going on right now. Promise me you'll be careful. He may very well be a great guy but you have to make sure you're getting what you need."

"I'll be careful. I promise." I didn't know how you could really promise such a thing. And the truth was, *careful* hardly described who I was with Jamie. But I also knew there was no going back on my feelings for him. So I picked up my fork and smiled with more reassurance than I felt. She returned the smile in the very best way.

"So, what's our strategy?" That one question exemplified everything I loved dearly about Hope. If I was in it, she was in it with me. She may or may not have agreed with my decision, but because I'd already made it, she'd have my back. Always.

"I can't say I really have one. But this thing with Jamie aside, I know for my own sanity that I need to broaden my interests beyond just work. I need an outlet for everything that's going on, and I don't feel like I have one right now. I know it's my own damn fault for letting my life get so small."

She shrugged and took a bite of her salad. "Are you saying you think you should take up a hobby?"

"I guess I'm saying if work is my only interest, I'm not even that interesting to myself." Honestly, I was formulating thoughts on the fly, but they felt like the right ones. "I like the idea of doing something that's creative. And something that's just fun."

"*My god*—who are you?"

I laughed and threw a crouton at her, which she caught like a ninja and ate.

"What kind of thing were you thinking of?" she asked, serious again.

I didn't really have anything specific in mind. I began making a mental list of the activities from my youth but none of them seemed right. My future as a gymnast was always dubious at best. Soccer, too, was pretty much out. But there was one thing that had long gnawed at me.

"I kind of want to take a cooking class."

As the words came out, they felt good.

"Cooking? *Really?*" I could see a hundred thoughts crossing her mind as she blinked and nodded absently. None of them were too credible to my achievements in the kitchen thus far. Still, she was the epitome of supportive.

"Cooking . . . yes, you should definitely do that. Definitely," she added one more time with feeling. I thought that last one might have been more of an effort to convince herself, though.

I laughed. "It's a completely practical skill—one I'll use my entire life. I think it's perfect."

"It is perfect," she said with alacrity, and meant it sincerely. Then, her face changed a little as she reached forward and took my hand across the table. "Promise not to leave me out of things from now on?"

"Yes," I said, and also meant it sincerely.

"Then how about we tackle this cooking thing together?"

Chapter 10

Mel

When I arrived at the Great American Music Hall, I followed Jamie's hastily given instructions and asked for someone named Bill. The band was doing a final sound check, and Bill showed me to the wings, where I could hear the disembodied voice of the man who had turned my world upside down in record time.

It was a beautiful voice. I loved the way he said the word *about*. And *part*. I added those to my little list of favorite words Jamie says. *Love you* made the list too, but I wouldn't have admitted it just then.

I hadn't been naive going into this, but I hadn't necessarily expected my predictions of joy and heartache, pleasure and pain to come to pass quite so quickly. Maybe I should have added *hot and cold* to that list.

Jamie walked off the stage and made a beeline for me. In just a few long strides, he closed the distance between us, looking sexier than anyone had a right to. His eyes were on fire, and when he reached me, he swept me up in an ardent kiss that staked my claim on him every bit as much as it staked his claim on me.

"I missed you," he said, sounding vaguely surprised as he pulled back just enough to see my face. "I should have called."

It was a question that masqueraded itself as a declaration. As much as I hated the disappearing act, this wasn't my first rodeo. I'd signed up for this, whether I cared to admit it or not.

"I missed you too. You've been writing?"

"*A lot*. I was feeling very inspired." He smiled so sweetly I couldn't help but forgive him for the radio silence. "It's been a brilliant week."

"I'm excited to hear it. Are you ready for this A&R guy?"

"Ready as we can be. Cross your fingers it doesn't go arseways."

"It won't. You'll be amazing." I smiled at him in reassurance, and he kissed me briefly in return.

"We sold out the venue."

"You sound surprised."

"Well, a little. It's a big place. We typically get a good crowd, but this is more than usual."

"Word's getting out, maybe."

"Yeah. Maybe. Anyway, I've got a good spot set up for you here in the wings."

§

The show was incredible. Whatever condition the new song had been in the week before last, they'd worked out all the kinks. The set was a masterful blend of their distinct sound, delivered with trademark passion and energy. They ended with a song I'd heard them play once before called "False," an angry young man's anthem and clearly a crowd favorite.

Jamie's centripetal presence on stage seemed to make the whole crowd lean in. As I watched him from the wings, I couldn't help but think to myself that maybe this was *it*. Maybe *this* was that pivotal moment in his career when it all came together with a bang—a violent explosion of success that seemed inevitable, if not slightly elusive. Maybe I was witnessing his success story right here.

The band rocked hard through the last chorus of "False." Jamie pointed the neck of his guitar at different sections of the crowd as he played with incredible dexterity. And then he turned back to Killian and slashed downward once more across the strings.

WHAM, he demanded.

WHAM, Killian replied.

Nash's arms were flying around the drums, thrashing the cymbals, as Greg thumped furiously on the bass. The song ended with a crash of instruments, and then the stage went dark. For a moment, nothing happened.

Suddenly, the crowd went *insane*. The roar was deafening. It felt like a physical rush—like something that might actually blow your hair back.

The lights came up, and the band, breathing heavily as if they'd just run a marathon, was smiling like I'd never seen them smile before. They seemed to absorb the nourishing adoration of the audience as though it were a corporal recharge. Nash came out from his drum kit and tossed his sticks into the crowd, while Greg and Killian fielded a handful of items tossed onto the stage.

"Thank you kindly, San Francisco." Jamie grinned at the chanting crowd, waving briefly, and then strode across the stage, pulling an earpiece from his ear to let it dangle across his shoulder.

He was glorious.

When he reached me, he crushed me in a sweaty embrace that made me laugh with its exuberance.

"You were extraordinary."

"I have a joke for you," he beamed. "What's the difference between God and a lawyer?" He raised his brows expectantly as if I might know this one, or maybe in anticipation that the punch line was the greatest in lawyer-joke history. "*God* doesn't think he's a lawyer."

I laughed, less from the joke than from the eagerness of his delivery.

"Nope. Still terrible, frontman. You better get go yourself a record contract—you have no future in comedy."

Jamie's eyes shone brightly as we stood for a beat with chaos whirling around us. Listening to the roaring crowd, I had the distinct realization that this could, indeed, be that moment that changed it all. He took my face in both of his hands and kissed me sweetly. His face was a little rough from his stubble, and he smelled musky and faintly of beer.

"Your lips to God's ears, angel," he whispered. And then he was gone.

§

I could see the five of them talking—Cadence and the A&R rep— off in a quiet corner of the second-floor balcony. I had wondered what someone who changed lives for a living might look like. I thought white robes and sandals might be a little much, but surely, he wouldn't just look like everyone else.

In this case, though, he really kind of did.

He appeared to be in his early to mid-thirties, with a mop of shaggy brown hair and glasses. He was on the heavy-set side, dressed in jeans and a dark T-shirt, and he was wearing a large Rolex on his right wrist. He was definitely not someone who would stand out in a crowd, but maybe that was the idea—that, when he wanted to, he could channel his Clark Kent rather than his Superman. It made sense that he'd want to be inconspicuous in certain circumstances.

From my vantage point near the small bar, the conversation seemed to be going well. There was a lot of smiling and nodding. Jamie looked relaxed. I couldn't have been happier for them. They were hard-working guys with a lot of talent, and if they couldn't make it, who could?

With a little time on my hands, I made my way to the restrooms and resigned myself to the very long line. The wait allowed me to appreciate the ceiling of the Great American Music Hall, a coffered and gilded masterpiece with gorgeous architectural detail.

When I looked around again at my immediate surroundings, there was Clark Kent.

I glanced over my shoulder—unfortunately, too far away to see if the band was still seated in the balcony. But here in the flesh was our guy—our life changer. I realized I must have been staring at him. Finally, he looked up and directly at me.

"How's it going?" he asked casually.

"Oh. Good." A truly brilliant retort. And then I thought of a better one. "What'd you think of the show?"

"It was good. These guys put on a decent act." *A decent act?* He must have been deep in Clark Kent character to be so understated. It was a great act. And, yes, I was biased, but if the reaction of the crowd was any indication, I hadn't been alone in my opinion.

"Do you see a lot of these kinds of shows?" I knew he did, obviously, but he had no idea I knew the band.

He seemed to puff up a little at the question, and crossed his arms so his Rolex was now in plain sight.

Stepping just fractionally more into my personal space than I would have preferred, he eyed me with more interest than he had before.

"Yeah, I'm in A&R." There was an unmistakable element of male bravado in his voice.

"Oh. How exciting. You must love it."

There was a lot of coming and going around us, as well as the constant sounds of a flushing toilet, but he glanced around furtively before speaking.

"If you want to know the truth, I can't stand the music scene.

Can't stand musicians even more." Then he laughed at his own sparkling wit. "It's not personal," he added as an obvious postscript. "But I haven't met one yet who isn't *deep and broody.*"

He made a face and then laughed; he must have thought he was charming; I didn't share the opinion.

"Why do you do it then?"

"Pays good," he said, showing me his wrist. "And it beats a lot of alternatives, right?"

He was no Superman, after all. In fact, it was hard not to take an instant dislike to this man. And even harder not to let those feelings show on my face. I apparently failed at both; his countenance changed in an instant.

"What?"

"Nothing. I guess I just would've expected a little more enthusiasm for the kind of work you do."

Brown eyes assessed me shrewdly. It was obvious our conversation was not progressing as he'd expected.

"Well, what do *you* do?"

"I'm a lawyer." Okay, not yet licensed as a lawyer, but he wasn't interested in the details.

He laughed. "Are you going to tell me you *love* being a lawyer?"

His tone was unquestionably derisive, matching the well-mannered dislike on his face. I didn't get the impression he was looking for an answer, and I didn't offer one. The truth was, I didn't really have one. And unfortunately, while he disappeared into the crowd almost immediately thereafter—good riddance—his question lingered reprovingly in my mind.

Did I love being a lawyer?

I seemed to have been asking myself that question a lot lately. And if I were to be completely honest with myself, I knew didn't. Did that make me no better than Clark Kent, here? Like him, maybe I was just a person going through the motions of a job I didn't really want. Would my clients suffer for my lack of passion?

I didn't *dislike* the law, per se—I certainly didn't despise my industry, as he'd proclaimed to—but I couldn't say I went to work every day excited to be waging and defending intellectual property disputes. And sometimes the thought of doing so for the next thirty years was more than a little stifling. I pushed that reality from my thoughts.

I had to remind myself that the law was a solid career, and like the vast majority of my life choices, it was a practical one. My parents had made a huge investment in me, and my firm had bestowed the ultimate vote of confidence by hiring me before my bar results were even in.

A lot of people had a stake in my success to date, and it was too late for second thoughts. Besides, I expect most people don't honestly love what they do. Maybe they were less obvious about it than my fallen Superman, here. But few have the chance, like Jamie, to make a career out of their passion.

I envied Jamie for that. And that's why it didn't seem right that someone who granted those once-in-a-lifetime opportunities should be so callus about it.

It kind of made me sad. Or mad; I'm not sure which.

But by the time I made it through the line and found Jamie again, he had a Sharpie in hand and was signing T-shirts and CDs for fans. He looked so happy. And I decided then and there I wasn't going to tell him about my conversation.

Business was business, after all. No one needed to tell *that* to a lawyer, unlicensed or not.

Chapter 11

Jamie

The next two phone calls changed my life—both in ways I could never have imagined.

"Hi, pickle."

"Jamie, I swear to God, it's a good thing I can't get a hand on you right now."

I laughed. "To what do I owe the pleasure?"

"I wanted to hear how the show went last night. Was it packed?"

That was a rather odd question. "Yeah, actually, it was *mad*. How did you know?"

"Are you near a computer?"

I'd just arrived home from work when she called, but went to the living room and flicked on Greg's PC at her request.

"Go to www.myspace.com."

"Right." I had literally no idea what to expect.

"Now type in *Cadence* in the search box."

What came up was a fully built-out Cadence page. It was tremendously well done, with photos and recordings of our music, and even a video that Cara had taken a while back from one of our festival appearances. It also had an events page that listed some of our upcoming gigs.

"What do you think?"

I didn't really know what to think. "It's brilliant."

"Want to see the best part? Roll your mouse over the two connecting circles. Those are your connections."

"It says I have two."

"Yes, one of them is me, gobshite."

"And someone named Tom Anderson."

"He's the founder and you automatically get connected to him when you join. That way, you're connected to everyone. But here's the great part: See the other set of circles? Those are people who've connected to *you*."

"There are nearly three *thousand* people here."

"And more and more every day. You can't believe how quickly it's growing. And all these people are listening to the songs I posted and writing comments. Jamie, a bunch of them came to see the show last night."

In shock, I scrolled through some of the comments. I'd never seen anything like this. The whole site seemed to be geared towards connecting musicians directly to their fans. No middle man—no record label, no radio station. Some bands had tens of thousands of connections, and they were posting new material for feedback from their fans. Most of these were bands I'd never heard of. But plainly, MySpace members had. Out of curiosity, I searched Arctic Monkeys. Sure enough, they were a thing. And Christ, did they have a following.

"Hey, still there?"

"Yeah, sorry."

"If you guys add more songs to this and post your shows, I'm telling you, I think it could be big. All my friends are on it."

I wouldn't have believed it if I weren't seeing it for myself. But she was right. These bands were actively using the internet to promote their music. Mostly to teenagers, granted, but in the history of music, especially rock and roll, teenagers almost always got it right.

"Hey, I got another call coming in. Can I call you later?"

"Yeah, fine."

"Do you need any money?"

I always asked her. She had some financial aid, but it wasn't enough. Cara would be the first college-educated member of our family if it killed me. And sometimes it nearly felt like it would.

"No, Jamie. Take your call."

"Cheers."

Switching over, I recognized the voice of Matt Kayes, the A&R rep from Spire Records. My heart went crossways. When we'd seen him at the show, he said he was going to recommend to the A&R team that we be offered a recording contract.

"How's the craic?"

"The fuck does that even mean, Callahan?"

I laughed.

"Anyway, I got news, man. I met with my director and producer, and the label's in. We've decided to offer Cadence a deal."

"Jesus."

I had to sit down. Imagining something and having it actually happen are two vastly different things. I thought my heart was going to pound out of my sternum. My hand was shaking, and I had to switch the phone to the other ear.

"Truly?"

"Yeah, truly. I'll have a deal memo in the mail to you in the next week or so. We can discuss any questions you have after that."

He was so fucking casual about it. I felt quite in shock, myself, like I'd fallen down a rabbit hole. I scratched absently at my chest, waiting for my brain to begin functioning again.

"Brilliant. I'll look for it. Thank you."

"Yep. And Callahan—don't make me look bad."

With that, we hung up, and I just sat there like some nutter. I'm not sure what I thought it would feel like to be offered a recording contract, but the reality of it was quite sterile.

Still, it was a *contract*.

We'd done it.

Years of writing and rehearsing and gigs. Hundreds of demo tapes mailed. Thousands of doors slammed in our faces.

But now we were finally on our way.

There were so many people I wanted to phone at once. Greg, of course, and Killian and Nash. And Danny and Cara; they'd been my bedrocks from the beginning. But even as I picked up my mobile to ring up Greg at work, I knew the person I was aching most to tell was Melody.

Chapter 12

Mel

"You're not going to like it," Jamie insisted stubbornly.

"Why do you say that? Maybe I'll love it."

He plowed his way through the crowd at O'Malley's and somehow managed to wedge himself between two occupied stools at the bar.

"It's an acquired taste," he called back to me.

"So are you."

He laughed like he always did, unembarassable, and received some hearty backslapping from one of the stools' occupants, an older gentleman who looked like he might actually live there on that stool.

"Fine," he said, his dimples betraying his amusement. Then he turned to the bartender and added, "I'll take two pints of Gat, mate."

For a Monday, O'Malley's was a remarkably busy place. And the fact that the five of us, four band members and I, were able to get a table could only be karma-related.

I'd never been to O'Malley's, but I liked it immediately. The bar was located on O'Farrell Street in the Tenderloin—not a great area, but not far from Jamie's apartment, either. The building itself had that old, classic San Francisco feel, with cherry wood in abundance and high, ornate coffered ceilings.

It was absolutely the perfect place for a celebration of this magnitude.

I'd come straight from work in my navy suit and found Jamie, who'd insisted on waiting for me by the bar before ordering. The rest of our group was already seated at the table, but we hung back to have few minutes alone.

"Sláinte!" Jamie raised his pint to me upon his return and took a healthy drink from his glass. I watched the way his throat moved as he swallowed, and tracked his tongue as he licked a smear of the foamy head from his lips. He was so sinfully beautiful, so mercilessly sexy in his dark gray Henley T-shirt and black jeans. I imagined lifting his shirt over his head and applying my mouth to his dangerously inviting chest.

"Sláinte!" I echoed in his Irish Gaelic pronunciation that sounded like *slawn-cha*. "I'm so proud of you, Jamie. You've definitely earned this."

The curve of his mouth lifted faintly, and he reached out to run his fingers gently through the front of my hair. He seemed a little . . . I don't know . . . just less excitable than I would have expected under the circumstances.

"I don't fool myself for a minute that there aren't a thousand blokes just like us who have earned it just as much, but I'll tell you, I'm grateful."

"Even if that's true, it doesn't diminish your achievement. Or the work it took to get you here. My god, Jamie; it's a *recording* contract!"

"It's mad, really, to think about it. I still don't know that I've wrapped my brain around the idea." He took another draft of his beer and glanced over to our table, where the celebration was in full swing. Shot glasses littered the table, and Killian was demonstrating the art of balancing two forks on the edge of a pint glass.

"When you're first starting out you think to yourself, if only I can find a few chaps I want to play with. And then, if you're lucky, you do," he said, gesturing to the group. "And you think, if only we can write that one magic song, you know. But then you do, and for the love of God, there's no one interested in hearing it. And so you tell yourself you're not doing it for the praise or for the recognition— you're doing it because it's in you and it's who y'are.

"The truth is, though, it's been so frustrating at times." He shook his head and brushed a drop of condensation from the side of his glass. "You have to have a following to attract a label, but how do you have a following when every demo tape you mail to record companies and radio stations and magazines and club owners just gets tossed in pile with dozens and dozens of others? Everyone says they love to discover new talent, but they're too busy keeping up with established names. And even more, there's so much risk involved in bringing up a new band; they can't afford a misstep. These days, when you get a chance like this . . . you can't fuck it up."

"Jamie," I said, finally understanding his mood. "Is that what you're worried about? Fucking it up?"

"I don't know."

He stepped aside to let someone pass, and when he came back, I could tell he was distracted by the thought.

"You're not going to. There's a reason you rose to the top of the pile, Jamie—you're *good*. And you're unique. People want to hear you."

He didn't answer, but I could almost see him weighing the veracity of my conviction. I'd always been drawn to Jamie because he embodied for me a sense of adventure and possibility. But, in a similar way, I suspected part of what drew Jamie to me was my analytical nature. I was deliberate and contemplative. I formed opinions slowly and with careful consideration. He respected me for that, and was coming to rely on me for it. And in that moment, I realized that was exactly what he wanted—a reasoned opinion he could trust.

"*Jamie*," I said, forcing him to meet my gaze. "You're someone I would absolutely bet on. I wouldn't think twice."

I watched as his serious expression softened. He seemed to take my words very much to heart. And then without warning, he stepped forward and pulled my mouth to his, kissing me deeply and so abruptly that my Guinness sloshed over the side of its glass and down the leg of his jeans. Neither of us pulled back. Quite the opposite, in fact. I grabbed a handful of his Henley and drew him closer, and he wrapped my head in the crook of his elbow and kissed me until we were both senseless.

Believe in me, his kiss ardently requested. And with a certitude that I could not have concealed if I wanted to, mine answered him. *Always*.

§

Thoroughly serviced, I finally took a sip of the beer I'd stubbornly insisted on ordering and then inadvertently spilled. And sure enough . . .

"Uck." I made a face.

"Let me guess, angel, you *don't* like it?"

Guinness is so dark that it looks chocolatey, with a big, thick, rich creamy head. For the record, it tastes *nothing* like that.

"I had no idea Guinness was so bitter."

"Didn't you, then? You *would* have known if you'd listened to me." With a censorious tilt of one brow, Jamie made a profound showing of male know-it-all-ness.

"I thought you were just being macho."

He closed his eyes and exhaled audibly, growling low in his throat as he did. Annoyance struggled with humor on his face, but humor ultimately won out. Barely.

"Well, look at it this this way, frontman—now you get two pints."

I smiled sweetly at him. He was unmoved.

"No, I'll handle it." I was fortunate enough not to hear the rest of what he grumbled, but I was pretty sure the words *stubborn* and *rock* were mentioned as he cut his way back through the crowd.

At last, he returned and handed me my Guinness, but this time, the head had a slightly purple tint to it. I took an experimental sip.

"Wow! I like that." Gone completely was the bitter taste, replaced by a pleasant sweetness that went well with the richness of the dark ale. "Why is it purple?"

"Black currant syrup. A blush of *embarrassment*," he emphasized, and I thought his Irish accent grew a little broader than usual.

"See, I do like Guinness." I threw an elbow to his iron-like core.

"That's not Guinness," he said levelly. "That's an *abomination*."

Chapter 13

Mel

By the time we left the bar, the band was pleasantly drunk and toasting everything from one's impressive belch to another's sock selection. Fortunately, Killian and Greg could walk home, and convinced Nash to join them. Jamie had other plans.

"You know," he began in careful and precise articulation of his words that only highlighted his drunkenness, "I think this may be the first time I've ever fucked a girl in a suit."

"Is that so?" I glanced at him sideways from the driver's seat. His eyes were closed now, and his head was tilted back against the headrest, but he looked pleased as punch with his sudden revelation. A tiny smile teased his lips. I thought maybe he was being a little optimistic about his chances of following through on that particular promise. He appeared awfully close to passing out in the front seat of my car.

Still, I wanted to capture this moment in my mind—the look on his face was a picture of content. His long, auburn lashes were fanned out across his cheek and a pink blush gave his skin a healthful glow. I reached out and stroked his tousled hair. He was happy, leaning into my touch. Then without a word, he lifted my hand to his lips and licked suggestively at the apex of my index and middle finger. I laughed and pulled away. Drunk or no, he was singularly focused on his goal.

As we headed down Leavenworth Street, I thought more about his comment. I knew what he meant, of course, about fucking me in a suit; I was wearing a suit. But the grammatical ambiguity made me think about *him* in a suit—something I was pretty sure I'd never see.

Did it matter?

I spent all day every day with men in suits—cultured men, highly educated, wealthy. Jamie was none of those things. But he was other things: He was creative, and ambitious, and vibrant. He was the most excitable person I knew. And he was fundamentally resilient. Even in the face of the overwhelming odds of failure in the music industry, Jamie retained that scrappy, headlong self-belief that had launched Cadence from obscurity to recognition. He always moved at a different tempo, always exuded that powerful presence of a frontman, even when he wasn't on stage. He was utterly captivating.

You meet well-to-do men every day. D'ye think I don't know the odds are already stacked against me?

I shook my head in silent remembrance. He had been absolutely wrong about that.

§

Turns out, I had been absolutely wrong about something else.

Parking the car outside my building, I had unwittingly awoken a sleeping stallion. And the stallion in question was presently pressing me against the wall of my stairwell with hungry lips that tasted of whiskey and ale. Six feet of ardent determination were attempting to extricate me from my suit.

It was a very respectable effort.

Jamie had my jacket open and was yanking down one sleeve when

I artfully twisted out of it, laughing, and dashed up the stairs and down the hall to my door.

I could hear him bounding up the stairwell behind me, surprisingly light-footed and agile for such a solid beast, and not the least bit winded. By the time he reached me, I had turned the lock, and was pushing the door open to my apartment.

His body collided with mine with an *oof* that launched me forward into the entryway, him just a breath behind. I felt his warm body at my back, both pressing me forward and holding me captive by my hips. I gave little resistance as he turned me abruptly against the inside of my door, closing it with a bang. He took my mouth like it was the spoils of victory.

His hands went immediately to my skirt, rucking it up over my hips with no thought of removing it. One of his feet nudged at my instep in demand that I spread my legs wider; I shifted my weight to accommodate.

We were both panting wildly. I had my hands in his hair, pulling his mouth harder to mine, which he obliged by returning the kiss thoroughly and skillfully.

Meanwhile, his fingers slipped between us to clear their way past my lingerie. He slid one experimentally inside me, and let out a sharp breath, groaning with words about how warm and soft I was.

He was no longer kissing me—instead, he was watching my face as he pressed slowly and deeply in and out with one hand, stroking me with his thumb.

I braced my fingertips against the door as my hips rocked forward to meet his every thrust. I could hear my own desperate sounds; the sounds of a woman fraying at the edges, feeling as though she might shatter.

He lifted my bare thigh over his hip, while he watched with naked desire the effect his other hand was having on my composure. It was a passionate tangle of his voyeurism and my exhibitionism. Whatever the effect was on me, he was experiencing its twin.

I had begun to open my blouse clumsily, managing to get about three buttons undone when he stopped me.

"No. Don't take anything off. I love the sight of you like this."

Like this. God, I could not begin to imagine what *like this* looked like—glassy-eyed, completely disheveled and totally at his mercy, to say the least.

And yet, I had never felt so sexy.

"Take down the cup." He motioned to my bra and his voice was thick with excitement. "Good. Now touch yourself for me. Tell me how that feels."

My nipple was pebbled hard and cold from a breeze coming in from the kitchen window, but I'm not sure I actually answered—just continued to run a fingertip over the sensitive skin that puckered under my own soft touch.

"Take down the other cup," he rasped, his accent growing more pronounced.

I was beginning to see a side of him that felt deliciously untamed. He growled out sounds of encouragement, mesmerized, as I followed every order without question, spilling out over both cups now, with my skirt around my waist and underwear pulled off to one side. Jamie was still fully dressed, but he seemed every bit as undone as I was. His erection was an urgent presence between us.

"Have you ever let anyone do this to you? In your suit?"

"No."

"Good." There was an unmistakable note of possession in his voice. "Whenever you wear this suit, you'll think only of me."

That tone, and his fevered quest to have me like this, made me wonder in an admittedly scattered way, whether tonight was his way of evening the odds against those cultured men in suits—of proving that while I spent my days around them, not one had ever left me so unhinged. Not one had ever made me *want*. This was Jamie's domain, exclusively. Tonight, he was taking something from those men, and it was obvious he had no intention of giving it back.

I glanced over his shoulder to the window directly opposite. It was fully dark now and the apartment glowed with the soft yellow light from the lampposts outside.

I was beginning to lose control of my one standing leg, which was shaking in my stiletto with anticipation and fatigue.

"Jamie . . ."

I could tell he knew exactly how close I was when he kissed me hard, then dragged his teeth along my jaw.

"Grab my shoulders, love. I'm gonna make this fast."

I felt him rip his fly open as his mouth engulfed my breast. The door was cool behind me. I leaned my head back heavily against it, craving his solid heat inside me, and waiting impatiently for the pounding that would rattle my apartment door in shameless ecstasy.

Suddenly, I was seized by a jolt of awareness.

"Jamie, wait!"

He released my breast from his mouth with a soft pop and met my eyes directly. His hair was standing up in a defiant spray that would have made me giggle had I not been so far past the point of summoning such an emotion.

"Back pocket," he murmured hoarsely, resuming his lips on my skin.

I contorted myself around his body and pushed my hand into his jeans. Expecting a condom, I came up with a folded piece of paper instead.

"Proof." I could hear his smile in the word he spoke, as he licked my hardened nipple.

I closed my eyes. "Oh god, that feels good."

I held that paper against his shoulder—crushed it in my fist, as a matter of fact—as I felt him arrange himself at my entrance. He paused for just a moment and I opened my eyes, aware of the question between us, but feeling it entirely unnecessary.

It is an absolute fact that every civil litigation professor I'd ever had would've failed me on the spot for what I did next: I dropped all evidence of proof to the floor without even a glance. And then we consummated that agreement. Loudly. Again and again and again . . .

§

The stallion in my bed was, for the moment, docile as an old mare—now much more sober, gloriously naked, and blissfully scratching his testicles as he reclined beside me in a tangle of sheets.

"So the question is, will you be able to walk properly tomorrow?" He grinned.

"I think it actually *is* tomorrow." I reached over to the nightstand and turned the clock. Sure enough, it was after midnight. "What time do you have to be at work?"

"Not until seven."

I knew the kind of hours he was keeping and it made me worry that he was overextended. He often rehearsed with the band well into the night, and then got up early the next morning for a full day of physical labor. And on this particular night he didn't have his bicycle or the right clothes, which meant he would have to be up and out even earlier in order to get to work on time.

"I can drive you," I said, laying my head back on the pillow. "I don't have to go in until nine."

"No, you sleep in, love. I'll be fine."

In the glow from the midnight sky, I could just make out the curves of his beautiful body against the white sheets of my bed. Every line looked like an artist's sketch of a man, larger than life. But he wasn't larger than life. He was flesh and blood like the rest of us and I knew he couldn't possibly maintain this pace indefinitely. There was a price for the kind of drive he had. I worried about the debt his body was amassing.

"Jamie," I hesitated. "Do you ever . . . Does it ever . . ."

"What?"

"I mean . . . how long can you keep this up?"

Jamie turned to meet my gaze in the pale light, and affection glowed in the softened curves of his face.

"Come," he said quietly, and gathered me to his chest. He was always so warm, as if he burned with life from the inside out.

"I do what I must, is all," he said reassuringly. "You don't have to be concerned. Besides, it won't always be like this." He was stroking my back broadly from tailbone to midspine. "I'm going to make this happen. Do you believe me?"

Do you believe in me? he was actually asking.

"Of course I do," I said, answering both questions. "You know that." I ran my hand down his arm and curled my fingers into his. He squeezed them tightly and kissed me on the top of my head.

"Truth is, I'd do just about anything to be able to go on stage every week. To have that and you are all I need."

I turned my head and kissed his chest, letting my lips linger there while I breathed in the smell of his skin, where his natural earthiness mingled with the scent of our lovemaking and the distant remnants of O'Malley's.

"Tell me what it's like for you."

"On stage?"

"Yes," I said, kissing him again.

He took a deep breath and blew it out, rearranging his extremities under the covers while he considered my question.

"It's thirty to sixty minutes of bliss, really. It's why we do all the rest of what we must. Onstage you have these surreal moments, like you're standing outside yourself, watching yourself in the most fantastic dream you ever had.

"Y'see, artistry is very lonesome business most of the time. Musicians often work alone. I imagine it's somewhat similar for writers and painters. You have no idea how your work will connect with another person—if it will connect with them at all. But when you're onstage, you get to *see* it. I feel like I can remember every face—the way they call out when they hear a song they like; sometimes they put their arms around a friend or a date. Sometimes they put their hands up in the air or dance or sing the words to a song *I* wrote. They're not thinking about it; they're just reacting to the music, and it's pure magic."

I had seen him perform many times and had witnessed the magic from the side of the crowd. But it was almost unfathomable what it would feel like from the stage.

"And the sounds," he continued. "Those are harder to describe. When the houselights go down, there's this roar of anticipation, and then it gets quiet. Nash will count in the first song of the set and the minute we start to play, the place goes bats. It's like a wave that hits you on stage. There's this electricity that bounces back and forth between the audience and us, each driving the other. I can't tell you how surreal that is."

He went quiet for a moment and then he laughed, detangling his hand from mine, and putting the arm behind his head.

"Unless the crowd is flat, then it's hell," he said succinctly. "There is nothing worse than a flat crowd. You're pulling and pulling and getting nothin' from them. That's when I feel like a dancing monkey on stage because it's my job to get them going. Especially if we're opening for someone—we're the *fluffers*, so to speak."

I smiled against his chest. "Do you mind opening for other acts?"

"No. I mean it's lovely to be the headliner, but now when we open, it's for better bands, at least. That's how it works. And even then, a lot of people come to see us in our own right. Those people deserve the best show we can give them."

"I dated a drummer once who used to get so nervous playing in front of a crowd, he'd throw up in a bucket offstage between songs."

"You dated someone who was in a band?"

"It was high school. Isn't every guy in a band in high school? Wait . . . were you in a band in high school?"

"Yes, or barely out of it, with Greg and two other blokes. But the other two were more interested in getting high, and that wasn't what Greg and I were into. We were young, but sensible enough about that sort of thing."

"I'll bet those two are going to regret their choice."

He laughed. "Possibly. But I think life tends to unfold as it should. Greg brought in Nash; they had gone to school together. And I knew Killian because his mum and my mum are in the same church group. And we all just got on incredibly well."

"Thus, Cadence was born."

"Mostly. But let's get back to your passing fancy with musicians."

"Unfortunately, I wouldn't exactly call it a passing fancy," I admitted reluctantly. "I dated a bassist in college who seemed to have a total aversion to conventional time-telling, and a guitarist-slash-singer who turned out to be a womanizer and a drug addict."

"Three musicians in your past," he said with amusement. "Suddenly, I feel a bit common."

"You shouldn't," I assured him. "I swore musicians off completely after that last one."

He didn't say anything for a long, pregnant pause. Then he slid out from underneath me so I was forced to make eye contact with him. Even in the dim light, I could tell he was intent on something.

"After all that, why would you agree to go out with me?"

It was a harmless and obvious question. But it wasn't asked in jest and I wouldn't answer it that way. Realness. That's what we had. That's what we'd had from the very beginning.

"I honestly don't know," I whispered, knowing I couldn't be more honest than that.

He nodded, though, seeming to understand something that I, myself, did not. But he was generous enough not to pursue it. Whatever it was that was developing between us had come unexpectedly for us both. And I was grateful he wasn't pushing me to name it.

"So you're telling me that if we collect up all your men, past and present, we could form a band?"

I laughed. I'd never thought of it in those terms.

"A really horrible band, but yes."

No answer from the frontman, but roguish thoughts were clearly ping-ponging around his brain.

I went on, dryly. "Slightly off tempo, a little stupid, and sadly lacking in creativity."

"And me," he said, with the humor I'd come to love in him.

"Mmm-hmm. Well, you'd the best of them, of course."

"Of course." He said it slowly and with dramatic flair. "In the kingdom of the blind, the one-eyed man is king."

"Exactly."

Jamie suddenly rolled, covering my body with his own. The weight of his hips was solidly between my thighs and he took both my wrists in hand, holding them tightly over my head on the pillow. My breasts were crushed against his broad chest. His eyes were glistening with humor, and his dimples declared a rather mischievous intent.

"Well, then," he said, shifting slightly so that I could *literally* feel the point he was about to make. "The one-eyed king is ready to take his spoils. And trust me, he'll not lack in creativity."

Chapter 14

Jamie

"It came," Greg shouted into the receiver.

The deal memo arrived at our apartment by courier late on a Wednesday afternoon. I was at a job site when he called with the news.

"Did you open it?"

"Trying." I could hear him tearing impatiently at the envelope. "Fuck, my hands are shaking."

Fuck, my heart was pounding. "You're sure it isn't something else from Spire? Like, I don't know, an invitation or something?"

"No, dude, it's the deal memo," he said, matching my edginess.

He accidentally hit a bunch of buttons on the phone with his chin and the cacophony rang out loudly in my ear.

"Sorry. Okay, got it."

"What does it say?"

"Dear Greg, Jamie, Killian and Nash, Spire Records is pleased to set forth below our proposal regarding the exclusive recording services of, and certain other rights relating to, Cadence—in parenthesis *artist.*"

He stopped reading out loud.

"What?"

"Nothing—there's just a lot here. It's four pages long and there's a lot of . . . legal stuff. Shit, I don't even know what half this stuff means."

His words became an incoherent mumble.

Running a hand through my hair, I tried my hardest to be patient. It was a losing battle. I surveyed the job site, looking for a distraction. Nothing came.

"How many albums do they want?" I finally blurted out.

"Well, I think it's one, plus four 1-LP options. Is it good to have a lot of options or not good?"

"I don't know. What about the advance?"

"It's decent . . . I think."

He breathed quietly into the phone. The adrenaline was beginning to pass, and with it the realization was setting in for us both that we had a legal document in our hands.

"Base royalties, mechanical royalties, accounting . . ." I could hear him turning pages. "Non-record income, ancillary/non-performance income, controlled comps PRO income. Fuck, it's like . . . it's not even English."

"I'm going to phone Mel and have her come over and take a look at it with us. She'll understand it."

"Yeah, good plan."

We both fell quiet. I was standing by a chain-link fence on the outskirts of the site and took a hold of it, pulling absently at the rough metal rungs. There was a hum of activity around me—blokes I'd worked with for a long time were moving pavers into place and trenching irrigation. It was backbreaking work. This was a major project; they'd be here for another year or more.

I wondered where would I be when it was completed. Lord, help me if I was still here.

113

I was lucky to have the job; I knew that. The bit of coin I made paid my necessities and Cara's tuition. But Mel was right; the physical toll of balancing work and music was steep. The idea that I might soon play my guitar without an ache in my hands from cuts and missing fingernails and sprained joints—it was almost too emotional for me to consider.

"We did it, man," Greg said, eerily divining my thoughts. "We got a contract." The last word came out broken and choked.

I felt pinpricks in the corners of my own eyes, and pressed the tips of my thumb and middle finger to them. Turning my back on the work crew behind me, I gripped the phone hard with my other fist.

"We did it." I quickly dashed a drop from my cheek and took in a ragged breath.

Greg sniffled sharply.

"You know what I want to do?" he said, rustling the pages again. "I want to make like a dozen copies of this and send it out to people with a big Post-it note saying, *Fuck You!*"

I laughed gratefully.

"Like that sound technician at Slim's—what was that fella's name?"

"Larry . . . something. Yeah, I'd send one to that douchebag, for sure. And one to that landlady who always called the cops on us when we rehearsed."

"And how about one for the arsehole at SF Weekly who said we were 'destined for great anonymity?'"

In fact, though, one could argue he'd done me a favor; he was the bloke who taught me that an artist must define for himself the value of his own work, or risk that his work be devalued by someone else.

"And I'd send one to Charlotte," Greg added.

"She was genuinely awful, brother."

"She was," he agreed. "But she had that pierced tongue and she used to spread my—"

"Stop! Holy God! Please don't!"

He laughed hard; we both did. Then the sound receded and all I could hear was his breath in the receiver.

"Send one to my father," he said quietly.

I nodded into the phone, though, of course, he couldn't see me.

"And one to mine."

The ensuing quiet spoke unequivocally of the painful understanding we shared.

"Brother . . ." I finally said, though I didn't know the words to continue.

Greg and I had made the pilgrimage into music with the same dream. We'd entered this business together as teenagers—children swimming among sharks. We'd made it thus far with only our determination to break through, and with each other to lean on. Whatever this contract meant for us—whatever legacy would be ours—Greg's life and mine would forever be linked.

Band co-founders.

Songwriting partners.

Friends.

"Brother," he said, mirroring my thoughts. "I know."

Chapter 15

Mel

The men of the indie rock band, Cadence, were gathered in the living room when I arrived. Greg, Killian, and Jamie were sitting on the couch, hunched over the coffee table, working through a complex mathematical exercise of contract compensation. Nash, as was his nature, was circling in the periphery.

Nash was the most mild-mannered of the group, taller than Danny even, with Nordic boy-next-door good looks. He had a tendency to fiddle with things, and therefore always—always—had something in his hands. Today, it was a green apple, which he repeatedly tossed in the air. I had the thought that if he set it down, even for a second, Jamie would eat it.

As was Jamie's nature.

The man at the helm of the exercise was Greg, a notoriously fast talker who shot words from his mouth in rapid succession like bullets. I had a hard time understanding him when we first met, and found myself often gaping at him for multiple seconds while my brain caught up with the spray of sounds he emitted.

Armed with a calculator, Greg was making a series of notes on a yellow pad as Jamie and Killian listed likely scenarios of the costs associated with recording a full-length LP.

To me, Greg was the most unpredictable in the band. He was much harder to get to know than the others: wildly creative and brilliant as a musician, and an introvert to his core.

I was almost certain he was bisexual. He had a girlfriend, Christine, who he seemed loyal to, but she left me with the distinct impression she was game for anything in that area, and she'd sometimes make back-handed comments about his love for Jamie. I asked Jamie about it once; if he had an opinion, he didn't mention it. Men are funny like that—even significant male friendships are often on a need-to-know basis, and Jamie never asked for details of a person's life for his own information. He simply accepted those trusts as they were given to him.

Beneath his hood of dark, unruly hair, Greg had the most stunning turquoise eyes that he often highlighted with charcoal liner. They were kind eyes that hinted at real depth and intelligence, despite his sometimes standoffish demeanor. I think that's why Jamie enjoyed writing with him—Greg had substance, and he absolutely shared Jamie's work ethic and drive to make something of his talent.

The band member most like Jamie in demeanor was Killian. He was Irish as well, but American born, first generation. With dark hair and eyes, he didn't have a great singing voice, but he had real flair on the guitar. Like Jamie, he was a showman. During one of the band's recent gigs, he was in the middle of an intricate solo riff when he opened up a cut on his hand and began to bleed all over his guitar. It wasn't a small thing. We all watched in horror as blood dripped over the body of his Fender and down onto the stage. But Killian just went on playing, and the blood dripping off that guitar only added to the bad-assery of his performance. He was *that* kind of guy, and the girls *loved* him.

Jamie didn't look up from his perch on the couch when I arrived, but reached his arm out for me, then wrapped it around my legs when I stepped in close. The men were deep in a discussion of the need to hire session musicians and how they might be able to minimize the cost of studio time. These were important considerations if they were to stay within the label's recording budget for the first LP.

Of course, I couldn't add anything meaningful to that discussion, and instead gave in to the temptation to run my fingernails through Jamie's beautiful hair. He liked to be touched. He was affectionate by nature and seemed to enjoy the comfort of a physical connection, no matter how small.

The effect of my caress on him was instantaneous. He lolled his head against my hip, making a soft sound of contentment, and squeezed me a little more tightly to his side.

The deal memo was sitting on the coffee table—a four-page document that outlined all the critical components of what would eventually form the center of a lengthier agreement between Spire Records and the band.

I abandoned stroking the fleshy curve of Jamie's ear and leaned forward to pick up the document in front of him.

The idea behind a deal memo was that if key terms could be agreed upon, the rest of the contract would be simpler to structure to the mutual agreement of both parties, thus streamlining the legal process.

"What do you think?" Jamie asked, his long lashes lifting to gage my initial reaction to the document.

He was still in his work clothes and boots, and he smelled of clean sweat and earthiness. Across his forehead was a smudge of dirt.

"Um," I said, reading. "We should talk through this when you're ready."

I flipped to page two.

Handing a contract to a law school graduate is like handing a lollipop to a baby. I immediately became absorbed, so it didn't register right away that all conversation in the room—all movement, in fact—had come to a screeching halt.

"Is there something wrong with it?" Jamie asked.

I glanced up from the page, somewhat surprised to find that I had unknowingly commanded the complete, undivided attention of every man in the room. They were all waiting for an explanation.

§

"Okay. Let's do this."

Every parent has a look that means business. Teachers have the same. Lawyers? We have a tone of voice.

I had taken a position in the center of the room and Nash, with his apple, was now sitting on the arm of the couch next to Jamie.

"First and foremost, this is a legal document," I said, holding up the agreement. "Do. Not. Sign it. Until you are instructed to do so by your attorney."

Entertainment law was a subset of intellectual property law, but it was very much a specialty unto itself. I was familiar with the language of the deal memo, but there was no way for me to keep up with the changing trends of what could and could not be successfully negotiated on behalf of a client. Plus, I didn't have the experience to understand all the possible repercussions of the compensation schedule. That required a specialist.

And in September of 2004, with the winds of change that would forever rock the music industry just gathering, an up-and-coming band needed the very best attorney it could get.

The year prior, Apple had announced a new service—iTunes Music Store.

The significance of this announcement in the decade that followed cannot be overstated. iTunes would revolutionize the distribution of digital music and would usher in the era of downloadable singles.

iTunes wasn't the first commercial attempt to sell music online, but it was the first to get it truly right—offering singles for ninety-nine cents that had far more permissive digital rights management than other subscription services. It offered a convenient and legal alternative to the rampant music piracy that had been unleashed in the wake of the rise and fall of Napster.

Apple dragged the music industry kicking and screaming into the digital age, coupling downloadable music with the user-friendly iPod.

Consumers celebrated.

Album sales plummeted.

And in the face of this change in music, the 360-contract was born.

Recognizing that album sales alone would no longer allow labels to recoup their costs, let alone drive profits, 360-contracts sought to take a piece of every dollar an artist generated—not just record sales, but touring, merchandise, appearances, and more. And contracts were structured so that artists had to repay every penny of the cost of making and promoting an album before they ever saw a dollar of revenue for themselves. For most artists, these *recoupable costs* were insurmountable, keeping them in the debt of the label for years.

Upon a break with the label, many artists lost the rights to their music. Some even lost the rights to their name.

No, even licensed, I couldn't act as Cadence's attorney, but I *could* shed some light on the contract they were holding and, more importantly, I could protect them from making one of the most basic and egregious rookie mistakes in the business.

"If you sign this document as is," I told my captive audience of four, "you will severely limit your ability to negotiate any of these terms when the long-form agreement is drawn up."

They all nodded obediently, if not a little wide-eyed and frightened. That was good. It was healthy to be a little frightened.

"Okay. So let's talk through the clauses and what they mean."

Over the next hour, we walked through each one.

In general, it was best to limit the term of the deal as much as possible. Spire was asking for five LPs—one album, with four additional options. While that sounds like a good thing, the reality was that if the first album didn't generate enough sales to cover all the recoupable costs, what was left would roll over to the next. In this way, the modest advance Spire was offering on the front end of the record deal might be the only artist royalties Cadence would ever see for the life of that deal.

Of course, every artist enters a contract like this assuming that they'll be successful—and in this case, I had every confidence that they would be—but lawyers earned their keep by factoring in worst-case scenarios. An ounce of prevention was always worth more than a pound of cure.

I was quite certain their attorney would press for a shorter term—and likely a bigger advance. I'm not saying that the way this contract was written was usurious per se, but it certainly wasn't generous.

The clause that concerned me the most was the one dealing with creative control. Now, this wasn't the long-form agreement by any stretch, but something about the verbiage surrounding LP song selection and the order of songs released to radio just wasn't . . . right. I kept reading it over and over in my head.

As worded, it didn't seem to grant them any right of approval. That couldn't be . . .

But my train of thought was interrupted by a large crunch followed by a slurp, and I looked up to find Nash searching his immediate vicinity.

Next to him sat Jamie with the apple.

"What's wrong?" he said to me around a mouthful of fruit. "Why did you stop?"

I looked at Nash. As, then, did Jamie.

"What? Did you want this?" Jamie asked him, molested apple in hand.

Nash made a face but shook his head. He was no stranger to Jamie's insatiable appetite.

Jamie turned back to me. "Why are you frowning?"

"It's probably nothing. I just don't like the look of this creative control clause."

Jamie and Greg immediately rose from the couch and came to stand on either side of me, looking over my shoulder at the agreement.

"It looks like the label wants final rights to decide what songs go on the album, including the suggestion of songs not written by you."

"Meaning?" asked Jamie.

"Meaning, I think, that if they don't like the songs you've recorded, they could send you back to the studio to record songs of their choice. Those could be new songs that you would write, or potentially they could be songs that the label chooses for you."

"Fuck that," Jamie said emphatically. "I'm not agreeing to that."

"Well, slow down," Greg inserted. "It could just mean they would want to give us some suggestions, right?" he asked me. "That's normal."

"I'm definitely not the expert here," I said, sensing the growing agitation in the room. "Entertainment law is not my specialty, and things can change pretty fast."

"Okay. But even if they wanted to leave open the possibility of having more creative control, that doesn't mean they would actually exercise it. They wouldn't sign us in the first place if they didn't like our music."

His assertion sounded more like a question.

"Fine," Jamie countered, now teeming with tension. "Then they can take out that clause. No one is going to tell us what songs we can and can't put on an album. Our sound is our sound, and it's based on *our* experiences. I'm not singing someone else's songs."

Jamie's hazel eyes locked directly on Greg's blue ones, and the latter was no less intent in his stare. I was standing between the two men, but for all it mattered, I was invisible.

"And what if they say no, Jamie? You think they'd really give a deal to a brand new band without retaining some creative control?"

"It doesn't sound like we're talking about *some* creative control."

Jamie took the paper out of my hands and reread the clause out loud.

"I know what it says. I don't like the idea that they'd try to tell us what our album should sound like, either. But this is a *record contract*. This is what we've been working for. You knew we were going to have to make some compromises."

"On money, yes."

"So . . . what? You'd flush a deal down the toilet over this one clause? Is that what you're saying?"

The conversation was quickly taking on a tone that made everyone in the room uncomfortable. Killian and Nash weren't saying a word, and as for myself, I sorely regretted voicing my concern. This was an issue for their attorney to pick through.

"Well, let's table this matter for the time being," I put in. "Greg's point is a fair one. Why would they go out on a limb to sign you if they didn't like what they've heard from you? Let's let your attorney work that out."

Jamie nodded in agreement, though his expression was clouded with noticeable concern.

"We don't have an attorney," he said, stating the obvious. "How much do you think a good one would cost?"

I stepped away and took a seat on the edge of the recliner. Killian was looking at the agreement in Jamie's hands as if it were an explosive device on the verge of detonation.

"My boss's best friend is a well-known entertainment lawyer in L.A.," I told them. "Let me see what I can do."

Jamie nodded again. This time he reached out and placed his hand on Greg's shoulder in a rough squeeze of reconciliation. Greg nodded too, and the tension in his lithe frame seemed to drain as he exhaled a deep breath. Then he turned an uncertain half-smile on Jamie.

"Good," he said. "Good plan."

Chapter 16

Mel

Jamie wasn't sleeping. I was growing accustomed to the normal rhythm of his breathing when he slept and could easily recognize when it was off. I had awoken, myself, for no real reason I could put my finger on—just an awareness of him, I think.

Earlier, I'd gone to sleep in his bed, with his solid, naked torso curved around me and his fingertips faintly tapping out a repetitive pattern on the rise of my hip. He did that often, though I'm not sure how consciously aware of it he was.

But now, he lay perfectly still on his back, and perhaps it was his carefulness not to wake me that'd had the opposite effect.

"What are you thinking about?" I asked him quietly.

He turned his head suddenly on the pillow.

"Did I wake you? I'm sorry."

"No, it's fine."

His room was dark, the light from the street dimmed by rough linen curtains that hung from the window next to his bookshelf.

Jamie had a lot of books—fiction, travel, biographies, historical literature. He was well read—better than just about anyone I knew, college educated or not. Most of his books had been purchased at a flea market in the Ferry Building, and as such, many of the spines had a red, blue, or green sticker indicating their modest price.

Stories and words; those were the tools of his trade, of which he was an avid collector. I wondered when he had time to read.

But then again, he didn't sleep well.

"What's on your mind?"

He took a deep breath and exhaled. "The county fair, actually."

Unlike mine, Jamie's brain operated in a very non-linear fashion. He tended to think in a spiral formation. After a month together, I was learning to just go with it. Quite often in our conversations, I couldn't see the eventual destination, but had grown to love the journey as a glimpse into the life experiences that had shaped him.

He turned on his side to face me, and reached out a hand to gently brush a hair off of my face.

"I think I told you my family moved to America when I was nine, yeah?"

I nodded, with my left cheek on the pillow as I watched him in the dim light.

"One day shortly after we'd arrived, Da told us he was going to take us to the Alameda County Fair. We were city kids from Dublin, so we'd never been to anything of that sort. Cotton candy the size of your head, da had said, and funnel cakes and games and rides. It sounded *fantastic*. Really American, you know? And our *da* was taking us. We couldn't believe our good fortune."

Jamie lay back on the bed and tucked his left arm under the pillow behind his head, staring at the memory.

"So, anyway, my brothers and sister and I all drew lots to see who would get to ride in the front rows of our station wagon. Cara and I and my brother, Allen, ended up in the way back. We didn't care, though. We were beyond excited for the fair. I can't even tell you how much we wanted to go. Cara most of all."

"The thing was," he continued after a pause, "my da never intended on going to the fair. He pulled out of the driveway, circled the block, and then came right back to our house. *Came right back*," he implored me to understand. He shook his head in disbelief and his expression darkened. "He just got out of the car, thinking himself *hilarious* for success of his prank. But we were kids; and we were devastated. God, Cara," he said, tiredly rubbing the space between his brows. "She was not yet seven."

His expression was hooded, but that in itself spoke volumes.

"Oh, Jamie." I didn't even know what to say—the cruelty of that one small tale was unimaginable. I knew there must be many others just like it, though they were as foreign to my own experience as could possibly be. My heart broke for him, and I was angry, furious actually, and horrified for the boy he once was.

"No, it's just . . ." He paused, dismissing the sympathy. "I only mention it because . . . d'ye think that . . ."

"No," I said firmly, his destination suddenly dawning. "They mean it. The contract is *real*, Jamie. It just needs some negotiation. Contracts always start from a position that's more advantageous to the party that drafted it."

Jamie was nodding, though I knew he wasn't at all convinced. And truthfully, neither was I. But I wasn't sure if my interpretation of the intent of the contract was clouded by my low opinion of the A&R rep who was driving it.

"Right. Good," he said, anyway.

I moved closer to him, laying my cheek on his formidable chest while his arms came around me once more. He smelled of Jamie—my favorite smell.

"It's all going to work out. I know it will."

I felt him nod and placed a kiss on his chest. He squeezed me tighter to him.

"Sleep now, love."

We settled in to rest, though I knew sleep wouldn't come. Instead, I joined the silent vigil he kept, searching the night for some reasonable and obvious explanation of where all of this was headed.

Chapter 17

Mel

Two days later, I still hadn't found it.

But I set aside the question in order to prepare for one of the most exciting experiences of my life. I was joining Cadence for a four-day tour in the Pacific Northwest.

Adam had done me two solid favors: (1) he convinced his best friend and music entertainment attorney, Gavin Barnett, to take on Cadence for a greatly reduced fee; and (2) he gave me two days paid leave.

The tour itself was arranged by the booking agent of a larger-name band, Echo Transit, that had asked Cadence to be its opening act. As a secondary band, Cadence received a smaller guaranteed minimum fee, but it could leverage the touring crew of the larger band and could make some additional money on the sale of merchandise. Most importantly, the venues booked in Portland, Tacoma, and Seattle held between a thousand and twenty-five-hundred people, so the exposure was priceless. Jamie joked that I would function as Cadence's road manager for the gigs.

So, here's what I learned about touring: other than the fifty minutes per day of stage time, most of your hours are spent driving to the next location and waiting around to perform. As a result, you experienced an odd mixture of extreme togetherness and extreme isolation. The togetherness, obviously, stemmed from the fact that you rarely got a break from each other, except when you could go into your own head. It seemed to me that each member had his own strategy for accomplishing that. The guys did a lot of reading, listening to music with their headphones, sometimes watching TV or tinkering with a song. But it's that very dynamic, in addition to the fact that you're plucked from your life for a time, that can also be very isolating and give you an aching sense of loneliness.

I said as much to Jamie at one point, and he told me that guys who did a lot of touring tended to crave that feeling of isolation after a while. It just became part of their DNA, whether they were at home or on the road. He said it made relationships hard, and I wondered if he was speaking from experience; I wondered if he was talking about ours.

As for my own strategy, I made myself useful during the downtime by seeing to the business side of things that the band tended to put off. I reconfirmed our hotel arrangements, reviewed the contracts to ensure Cadence's modest rider requirements were met by the venue, and saw to it that the band was paid promptly and correctly. Had anyone sliced my head open at any point along the tour, they would have seen dozens of sticky notes on my brain that pertained to a plethora of details, big and small.

I really kind of loved it.

The time together also left us a lot of time to talk and get to know each other. And I really loved that too. To many outsiders, for better or for worse, Cadence was Jamie. That was often true of the frontman. But, in fact, each member was a distinctly strong character—an important leg without which the table would collapse.

Nash was calm and precise, the quiet captain of the beat. His gift to the band was his consummate exercise in restraint in the service of a song.

Greg seemed to be the band's perfectionist and music geek, relentlessly self-effacing about his musical talent, and believing, like Jamie, that music should challenge you, sometimes make you uncomfortable.

And by comparison, Killian was much wryer and unflappable. He was the diplomat, the glue—both musically and interpersonally.

But of them all, Jamie seemed to be the one who most loved the romance of friends in a band. As such, he would likely be eternally broken-hearted over the break-up of the Beatles. And he was also the one who could be most fired up by the prospect of the next experience, the next person to meet, the next record to make, the next . . . anything. He reflected his vitality in his songs, but he was also perfectly willing to air every frailty he had through his music, such that his work would have meaning—not just to him, but also to anyone who cared to listen.

It was the combination of these personalities that transformed four very capable musicians into a cohesive band. And it was likely their mutual love for each other and the dynamic they shared that compelled them over the course of the tour to completely avoid any discussion whatsoever of the pending recording contract.

It was the perpetual elephant in the room. That which shall not be named. The volatile thing that had the power to propel their success or destroy their unity entirely. Nobody wanted to go there. Gavin was in the process of negotiating on the band's behalf, and everybody seemed perfectly happy to leave well enough alone for now.

So the tour took on the feeling of the eye of a storm, a brief reprieve in which they could take a moment just to remember why they wanted to do this in the first place.

And god, what a moment it was. All the shows were phenomenal, but Seattle was especially so, performing to a packed house of nearly two thousand people. And rather than starting in the usual way— half the crowd hanging back by the bar and many coming in late, expecting a mediocre opening act—this show quickly took on the feeling that something very special was happening—one of those *remember when* moments.

From the very first song, the theater came alive with the grinding textures of alternative rock, and the energy in the room was palpable. Killian strummed the opening chords to one of their older songs, "The Shadow One," and the screams rippled back through the crowd. Whether the band was fueling the audience or the reverse was true, in no time the two were feeding ravenously off each other. Jamie was Jamie—he was a force of nature on and off the stage, but tonight he performed with an adolescent glee that was utterly contagious. He was talkative and personable, romping through the vast landscape of his brain for any interesting nugget that seemed worthy to share. Some crowds don't like a lot of talk; this one ate it up and begged for more.

At one point, he took out a small camera and asked a crowd of thousands to lean in for a picture.

"I think I've got you all," he mugged. "Except maybe you in the blue shirt," he added, to which about four hundred people looked down at their shirts and then grinned back at the camera.

Fueled by the party atmosphere, he and Greg shared a mic often, arms around each other and beaming as if they couldn't believe how lucky they were to be doing this. Even Nash, who was not normally prone to dramatic flair, tapped into some secret reserve and pulled out an array of flamboyant fills that drew approving laughter from his band mates.

Watching them in their element brought about a crazy assortment of emotions for me. Pride was the overwhelming one. And joy for their joy. Some trepidation, also, for what we might be returning to.

And envy; I was a little ashamed to admit it. These past four days had been some of the most exciting of my life. But tomorrow, I would return to patents and briefs, while they would continue to have this incredible thing in their lives. I didn't begrudge them anything; they'd earned every bit of their success and more. It just reminded me that I'd never quite found anything like that of my own.

I was so absorbed in the show that I didn't immediately register the presence of Derek White, Echo Transit's lead singer, until he spoke beside me.

"I'm still trying to figure out if I was a genius or an idiot for asking these guys to open for us."

Derek was very tall, like Danny, but wiry rather than athletic, and he had the kind of nerdy quality that looked cool on a musician.

"Better bring my A-game tonight," he added, laughing as he watched Jamie engage the balcony in an exercise of call-and-response.

He shook his head kindly, and I smiled in return, before he disappeared into the wings from where he'd come.

In his departure, I recognized in myself one final emotion.

Fear.

Derek was right—Cadence was becoming a hard act to follow. Their momentum felt more like a freight train barreling down the track. It wasn't just that they were drawing bigger crowds; it was that the crowds were becoming more voracious. These crowds knew the words to the songs, could sing them back to the band with no assistance, pushed their way to the front to swipe set lists off the stage and take hold of Jamie's pant leg if he wandered within arm's length. He was becoming remarkably skilled at fending off their admiration and lust.

As I looked out over the sea of fervent faces, there were dozens of people holding up signs for Jamie—most with some witty variation of "Jamie, let's get lucky!"—but many of the signs indicated that these people had traveled quite a distance to see the band perform: L.A., Denver, Boise, even. I could no longer deny that he and I were trying to build a relationship of substance within a hurricane of intensifying pressures—the next hit, the next pretty face, the next prolonged separation. These felt as inevitable as Cadence's success, and I wasn't sure Jamie and I could withstand them.

I watched as he and Killian dueled with their guitars to the unadulterated glee of the audience, and I felt fear. It trickled down my back like a bead of cold sweat, pulsing inside my body with the monstrous low-end of Greg's bass. Despite the upbeat tempo of their new song, "Two Seconds From Now," my heart was sinking fast.

And rising above it all, Jamie's voice rang out like a swan song:

"From where I'm standing here, we're nothing more than strangers. But two seconds from now, I'm gonna make you mine forever."

These strangers who know you, I couldn't help but think to myself. And who, from here forward, will never want to let you go.

Chapter 18

Jamie

I was starving. And well on my way to getting good and thoroughly plastered if I didn't have something substantial to accompany the Sapporo and sake. I would've gladly settled for anything I recognized as edible or, at a minimum, anything that had been cooked without its tentacles still on. But amongst the colorful assortment in front of me, there appeared to be fish eggs—a meal fit only for a fish just larger than the one that had shat the eggs out in the first place—and what I gathered to be tofu, helplessly tethered to a bed of rice by a piece of seaweed. What man-sized appetite could possibly be satisfied by such crumbs?

With my finger, I pushed a few soybeans onto the end of my chopsticks, but they fell off into my lap before I could get them to my mouth. I was definitely going to starve.

"Try that," Killian whispered beside me, pointing to the backside of a shrimp that looked as though someone had shoved rice up its arse. I squinted suspiciously at it. "Don't eat the tail, though."

No danger there, mate.

For the love of God, I wanted a steak and some potatoes.

"So Jamie, now that we've gotten our appetites out of the way, why don't we talk a little business?"

Richard Stapleton, Vice President of A&R at Spire Records, wiped his mouth with his napkin and leaned forward in his low-back chair. I guessed he was in his fifties and as music executives go, he was far more *executive* than *music*. His suit likely cost more coin than I made in a month.

He was clever, though; I'd give him that. I had no doubt he'd called me out specifically because he sensed I was the one most at odds with Spire's present offer. This dinner—with he and Matt Kayes, our attorney, Gavin Barnett, and the band—was suggested by Spire as a way to iron out the remaining contract issues that largely centered on creative control.

I couldn't fault Gavin for our situation. He had negotiated stronger financial terms across the board. But he'd warned us that concessions in this area sometimes became the label's sticking point on creative control. I sensed from the tone of the negotiations to date that he was right.

What made things complicated was that Greg and I were still very much divided on the question of how much control we were willing to give up in order to make this contract happen. We had cautiously approached the subject a couple of times since our return from Seattle but backed off as soon as things got tense between us. We'd made a lot of decisions together about the band through the years—some quite difficult, in fact—but we had never before encountered anything we couldn't openly discuss. I hated this.

And it was obvious by the way Killian and Nash were avoiding the discussion that they were hoping we could resolve our differences before they had to take sides. I couldn't fault them, either.

There was just no way through this but through. And if Richard wanted to talk business, we'd best get on with it before I passed out from hunger or drunkenness.

I felt Greg's eyes resting heavily on me as I set my chopsticks aside and nodded to Richard in agreement.

"So, I understand you have some reservations with Section 10.3."

Section 10.3. Such a tidy and sterile way to refer to an issue that was highly emotional for the rest of us. It made me wish for the umpteenth time that Mel was here. I liked Gavin; he was an exceptionally capable attorney. But Mel, by her own admission, had a protective instinct that she'd been told was even more lethal in a lawyer than a killer instinct. And suddenly, I completely understood that. Gavin would fight skillfully for our interests; I had no doubt about that. But Mel would have fought for *us*, and I wondered what a difference that might have made if we had had someone like her to represent us.

To Gavin's credit, he snapped to attention at the mention of the contract. He was seated directly across the round table from Richard and me. I sensed he was assessing the distance between us should the need arise to throw himself bodily over the table in order to gag me if I spoke out of turn. I would have quite liked to see it, actually, but I was as eager as anyone to just get on with the discussion.

"That's correct," I said, matching Richard's dispassionate tone. I did not look at Greg. I simply had no idea what I might see in his face and the unspoken strain between us was hard enough.

Richard nodded slightly and at first seemed to accept this without further comment. Then he lifted his sake, pausing half way to his mouth, and gestured at me with the glass, meeting my gaze with narrowed eyes.

"Did you know I started my career as a booking agent when I was just about your age? And then I got my first job in A&R. That was almost thirty years ago." He took a sip and set down his glass. He seemed to be carefully selecting his next words.

"I've seen thousands of bands in my time," he said. "Some made it, most didn't. Do you know what they all had in common?"

I shook my head.

He was quiet, too, for a moment. Then he placed both forearms on the table and laced his hands together in front of him. His eyes locked on mine, so dark blue as to be nearly black, and he smiled without any warmth. "They all thought they were special."

In the span of that one short sentence, the atmosphere around the table changed irrevocably. His words hung between us like an accusation—a cold, wet blanket laid atop of a false air of congeniality. In the pit of my stomach, anger began to rise. I struggled to keep it in check. This wasn't a negotiation; it was a warning shot fired across the bow. Around us, the restaurant was bustling with the clatter of plates and the dull roar of conversation, but at our table, no one said a word. Even Kayes was absurdly focused on his chopsticks.

That's when the sobering assessment of our reality truly set in.

It was much like the discovery of a loose thread on a sweater. One small tug and everything begins to unravel. All of it: the future that seemed right there in our grasp, our hopes of finally breaking through, the end of our shit jobs, the justification that the significant piece of ourselves that we'd given over to our craft had value and purpose. And maybe even something more sacred than that: the brotherhood that had carried the four of us through years of exhaustion and sacrifice.

"Of course, we think Cadence is special," Richard added in a well-calculated afterthought that plainly entertained his own sense of cleverness.

But I'd lived my entire life with a bully, a man who'd mastered the art of intimidation. Sitting before one now, I was reminded of the vital secret they never wish you to know: no one can take your power without your consent.

I was not about to consent.

I arranged my features into an expression that didn't quite sell itself as a smile. "Just not special enough to merit the right of approval, is that it?"

Surprise flashed on Richard's face, and he laughed out loud. "I like you, Callahan. Did you know record companies have only a five percent success rate with the albums they produce? That means only five percent of all records released by major labels go gold or platinum."

"And yet record companies get away with a ninety-five percent failure rate that would be wildly unacceptable in any other business."

He leaned in closer as his growing fascination with me overcame his surprise. "Why do you think that is?"

I drained the last of my Sapporo and set the bottle gently down on the table. Out of the corner of my eye, I saw Greg look down at his hands. His expression was unreadable.

"Because record companies keep almost all the profits," I said, meeting Richard's gaze and not looking away. "Recording artists get paid only a tiny fraction of the money earned by their music. Labels like Spire offer royalty rates that are absurdly low to begin with and then you charge back every conceivable cost to an artist's royalty account. We pay for recording costs, video production costs, tour support, radio promotion, sales and marketing costs, packaging costs and any other cost you can conceive of. We'll probably end up paying for this dinner, am I right? With all due respect, Richard, spare me the Valentine."

Richard didn't respond immediately, yet an extraordinary change went across his face. I happened to glance up at Gavin, whose expression now closely resembled the gaping fish head on the platter in front of him. Nash and Kayes were wearing junior versions of the same thing. Greg wasn't looking at me at all.

The conversation was quickly going to smash and I suddenly had no stomach for the games and the bullshit.

"We want final approval on album content."

Richard pressed his lips together, breathed in through his nose and shook his head. "Can't do that."

"Then why are we here? Why would you want to sign us?"

"I think we can be successful together," he said simply. "You've got talent; you're entertaining. And I like your look."

"Our look?" I could hear my accent growing stronger over the course of our discussion, which was a sure sign I was losing control of my anger.

Richard waved his hand dismissively. "And your voice. And your stage presence. The whole package."

"But not our music?"

"I didn't say that. It's definitely an asset that you write your own material."

"Then why not give us creative control?"

"Because of the five percent. Do you know what your problem is, Callahan? You don't sound like anyone else."

I barked out a humorless laugh, richly embroidered with disbelief. "I hardly consider that a problem."

"In a perfect world, that's probably true. But don't be naive, Jamie; I have to be able to *sell* you. Program directors have to want to play you on their stations. People need to want to buy your CDs. Otherwise, every penny I spend is just a waste of money. *Five* percent."

I opened my mouth to say something, but he stopped me.

"Take "False," for example. What do I do with that song?"

"Our crowds *love* that song."

He made a face, tilting his head back and forth. "Maybe. But it's not quite loud enough for alternative rock stations and it's far too edgy for adult contemporary. We need to make you more commercially acceptable. There'll be a time and a place to work in more of your own stuff. But for the moment, I need your assurance that you'll allow us to guide you. And in return, I'll make you a lot of money. Sound good?"

I felt my lips forming the words *time and place* but no sound actually emerged. It was no wonder; I could not breathe. I was staring at his face, and then at the faces of the rest of our party, and I suddenly felt very, very sick.

"You want to turn us into a fucking *boy band?*"

"That's an overstatement. We want Cadence to be Cadence. We just want to guide you."

I made a noise in my throat, on the verge of rudeness, indicating what I thought of Richard's guidance.

"You'll need to be more specific, Richard," Gavin cut in diplomatically, but I had stopped listening entirely.

All I'd ever wanted to do was to play music. It had been the one constant in my life from the time I was very young. When my life fell to shit as it did often in my youth, I could always find solace with my guitar. Songwriting, in particular, had helped me to make sense of a world that, at times, seemed purely senseless. I hadn't dreamed of fame and fortune then; I had dreamed merely of survival—just making it through that one day, and then, God willing, the next. Music had been my talisman. It was still my talisman.

I had no idea how to be myself if I couldn't play music that was my own. Just the thought of it made me feel entirely hollow.

I looked up at Greg, and for the very first time that evening, he was also looking at me. His eyes were as blue as the sky, outlined with dark liner and weariness. They were pleading, and I understood their need implicitly.

Greg and I had met in a record store when we were seventeen. He worked there, and I was in, browsing the aisles for inspiration. But between my accent and his habit of talking insanely fast, neither of us could understand a damned word the other was saying. It was mad. We were in America, both speaking English and both squawking at each other like two parrots in a pet store. Two odd birds who both liked telling stories and who loved to have a good laugh. We'd been the closest of friends ever since.

As I discovered, his father was a Protestant minister whose intolerance had led to Greg's leaving home at sixteen and living on the street for a time. Like me, music had been his salvation, and it had given him one singular, obsessive point of focus for his life. It was justified; he was among the most brilliant musicians I'd ever met. He was creative and unconventional, taking the beginnings of songs and working out full compositions that became the cornerstone of our unique sound, the same sound that Richard was so ready to dismiss.

A part of me *could not* understand how Greg, of all people, would be willing to accept any interference from the label when it came to our music.

On the other hand, a part of me did understand. For Greg, this contract represented the end of an era of *literal* hunger and fear in his life. This was his ultimate validation—a chance to silence those critical voices in his head that had told him for years he was nothing.

Furthermore, we had worked so hard to make this contract happen. There were thousands of struggling bands, just like ours, who would have given anything, accepted any terms to have this kind of offer. To turn it down under any circumstances seemed absolutely bats—like looking a gift horse in the mouth and telling it to fuck right off. This was a rare opportunity to actually live the life we'd dreamed of. We had no idea if or when we'd ever have a chance like this again.

And yet, for me, the choice was not so simple. Without creative control, I could easily imagine scenarios in which the contract became a noose around our necks. I imagined bubblegum pop songs with no substance or relevance to our lives, and silly videos of us making hijinks with cartoon characters. And even more basic concerns: what if they insisted that we work with a producer we didn't connect with? Or wanted ultimate control over album cover artwork and the selection of our first radio single? If we became puppets for a struggling label in a struggling industry, there was no telling what we may unwillingly become.

Greg wanted to roll the dice and take a chance on our dream, believing that over time, the label would grow increasingly comfortable with our creative choices. His pleading eyes told me so, and begged me to go along. But I had no faith in the men sitting before me, and less in those behind them with their calculators and their business agendas. I *was* my music, for better or worse, and I simply could not live with any agreement that sought to change something so fundamental about me.

So here we were at a crossroads, hope battling with doubt. We stood poised to sign a contract that could ruin what we were. And yet *not* signing the contract could have precisely the same effect. These three mates were my family—the first real one I'd ever known. And sitting here in this moment, my hands clenched in my lap, I could not fairly say what we stood to gain and what we stood to lose.

A wave of anxiety washed over me, enveloping me entirely. The room began to spin, and I put the heels of my hands to my eyes to stem my growing disorientation and fear.

"Hey, man," Killian said with concern, laying a gentle hand on my arm. "Are you okay?"

The room was very warm, and my heart was beating far too fast.

"Here," he whispered. "Take this."

I lowered my palms and he pushed a water glass into one of them. Shaking visibly, I lifted the glass to my lips and forced the cold liquid past the lump in my throat. I realized I was sweating, and wiped my brow carelessly with the back of my other hand.

Killian was alarmed. He traded a quick glance with Nash, sitting three seats away, and leaned in close to my ear.

"We can go outside if you need to."

I truly didn't think I could stand up at that moment. I felt far too out of sorts.

"No," I said hoarsely, and cleared my throat.

Killian grabbed another glass of water and handed it to me.

"You need to look at this practically," Richard was saying to Greg. "You have a long, promising career ahead of you."

It was a classic case of carrot and stick. I got the stick; Greg was getting the carrot. Richard must have sensed that if he could divide us, he could sign the band more easily and have the freedom to mold us into what he wanted. He'd give us just enough to draw us in, but never so much that we would feel we could be something without Spire's backing. And the contract documents were *right there* on the table beside him; I didn't have a clue how or when they'd appeared.

Holy God, I'd always known we were swimming with sharks, but I hadn't truly felt bitten until this very moment.

Without a clear purpose in mind, I pushed my chair back abruptly and rose to my feet. All heads turned in my direction and the conversation ceased.

"Where are you going?" Richard asked sharply.

I hesitated for just a moment, and then, as though by magic, I found a bit of clarity on the one thing I knew for sure.

"I need to eat."

"We have a negotiation to finish."

I shook my head. "This isn't a negotiation. It's an insult."

Striding purposefully from the restaurant into the sanctuary of the cool San Francisco night, I promptly and thoroughly vomited my guts out into a bush on Washington Street.

Chapter 19

Jamie

"*I need to eat?* What the *fuck* was that?" Greg shouted as he charged through the front door of our flat. But there were so many other questions between us that needed to be asked and answered. Sitting on our old brown couch with a heart as heavy as stone, I wasn't going to bother with that one.

"What do you want, Jamie?" he demanded through my silence. "You want to dig holes and shovel shit for the rest of your life? Because it sure sounded like that tonight."

The mere suggestion made me physically bristle.

The bus ride home and a turkey sandwich had gone some distance towards restoring my own equilibrium, but plainly the same could not be said for Greg. As I'd feared, it was all beginning to come apart. We'd stemmed the tide for as long as we could, knowing the deluge was inevitable, and at last it rolled in.

"Is that so?" I fired back. "I didn't realize. Because no one else at that table tonight said one *bloody* word in defense of the band. Not one bloody word!"

"*Defending* us? Is that what you call it? I'd call it jeopardizing everything we've been working for! How can you not get that?"

His voice had been rising since the moment he stepped inside, Nash and Killian behind him, and now he threw his hands up in vast frustration. But he wasn't the only one grappling with volatile emotions.

"You're accusing *me* of standing in the way of your plans while you're not the least bit angry with the label for trying to sell us on a deal they know is *shite*?" I could not fucking believe what I was hearing. I truly thought I might lose my mind. "I've given everything I have to this band—every ounce of energy and every spare penny I've got. You think I'm not interested in makin' somethin' of myself? Of getting out of this godforsaken dump? I ride a *bicycle*, for Christ's sake, and haven't even got the coin to take my girlfriend out for a proper meal!" I could feel an intense flush darken my face and realized that, somewhere in my venting, I had made it to my feet without any recognition of when that had occurred. "I've practically opened up a vein and bled myself dry for *years* with the responsibility for writing our material. And you so arrogantly now accuse me of putting our future in jeopardy?"

Greg flinched, but I went on, my voice growing harder.

"Don't think for a minute I don't know that our music would not be what it is without you, without all of you—" I said, gesturing broadly to the group— "that's why *I* was the one whose idea it was to share the songwriting credits equally among us for whatever financial gain that may mean."

"No one ever asked—"

"No, you didn't! And it's a decision I'd gladly make again. But don't ye *dare* accuse me of bein' selfish!"

"And don't accuse me of being naive! You act like I don't know—or somehow don't care—as much as you do about the risk we'd be taking. I just happen to believe that once we put together a great album, all this bullshit back-and-forth on creative control goes away."

The angry color was beginning to fade from his face, but his blue eyes were still bright with passion. "Aren't you tired of just scraping by and fighting for every inch of progress we make?" he asked in exasperation. "God, I am." His shoulders slumped in such a way I could see just how tired he was. We all were, really. "I just want us to get *on* with our lives. We've been killing ourselves long enough. And Christ, Jamie, we always knew we'd have to bend a little in order to get there."

"Bend on what?" I wiped a hand carelessly across my forehead and into my hair. "Money? Fine. But *never* on authenticity. I don't happen to share your optimism that what we think is great, Spire will find acceptable. I'm sorry, brother, but I'd rather keep shoveling shit as you so eloquently put it, than wake up every day and not be able to recognize the bloke I see in the mirror. He's no great prize to begin with and he's skint for sure, but at least he's true. At least I can say he's honest."

He shrugged his shoulders, uttering a short, bitter laugh. "So that's it, then? Doesn't matter what the rest of us think?"

"Of course it matters," I shot back in dismay. "I want us to be of one mind on this."

"No, you want us to be of *your* mind on this."

"Meaning what, exactly? You think I've dismissed your opinions?"

I turned to Nash, who was leaning his weight against the living room wall, and his face went pale with the realization that the deluge had now reached him precisely. He straightened, and faced it head on. Nash was not loudly spoken, but neither was he meek.

"I'm a drummer, Jamie, not a songwriter. I'm always playing someone else's material. So, I don't know, maybe I am a little less passionate about that. I just know that if you're asking me for my vote, I vote for *us*. Whatever will get us back to the way we've been. Not the way it is now. I want Cadence. *That's* what I want."

I nodded in acknowledgement—I wanted that too, Lord knows. Then I shifted my focus to Killian.

"I happen to like our sound the way it is," Killian said succinctly. "I don't want someone to come in and try to change it. But I agree with Nash that none of this means shit if we're tearing each other apart. You two need to figure out what you can live with and, whatever that is, settle it between you. There's only one side to take on this—and that's the *band's* side. Anything else is just wrong."

Each of us looked at the others for a long moment without speaking. We were in a dead split, none among us feeling like any progress had been made, and none sure where to go from here. Victims of our own success—the irony was pure fucking madness.

I'd never been one to blindly trust the universe to award favor based on merit, but it felt like a cruel joke that we should be given a Trojan horse when we'd merely asked for a pony.

"So?" Greg finally asked me pointedly. And the look on his face told me the distance between us was cavernous. "What's it going to be, *brother?*"

Chapter 20

Mel

When the buzzer rings at 2:27 in the morning, most people would think *apartment fire!* I thought *Jamie*. And was right.

It was a big night for the band and he promised he'd call when he got back from dinner with the Spire team but, of course he didn't, so I went to bed once again feeling the distance of a relationship conducted at arm's length. As much as I felt for him, it was growing tiresome and a little lonely, if I was being honest. I hadn't even had a chance to tell him about my cooking classes because he'd had so much on his mind and our time together was usually so frenetic: late night visits with early morning departures, gigs, quick conversations at work. We were trying, but it was hard.

I thought a lot about what he'd said to me on the road about musicians often craving isolation, and I was beginning to wonder if he'd been trying to tell me something he didn't have the heart to say straight out. Our relationship was a big change for him—maybe it was too much change.

On a positive note for the evening, I'd made short ribs. Edible ones, in fact.

It took three hours, two pans, one shallot (finely minced) and a

Martha Stewart cookbook, but I had done it. And while Martha may have been having her own challenges in the area of securities fraud and obstruction of justice, she was above reproach when it came to short ribs. I couldn't wait to tell Jamie.

As it turned out, this was not the night to tell Jamie.

When I opened my front door, he was leaning heavily against the nearest wall, glassy eyed, blinking slowly, and intoxicated beyond any state I'd previously seen him.

Alarmed, I reached for his arm and pulled him inside. He was wearing his good navy shirt, but it was wrinkled and half untucked, and he smelled strongly of musky sweat and alcohol.

"Hi," he said stupidly with a tiny smile that pressed his dimples into service. His cheeks had a pink, ruddy glow, softening the blow of his rumpled appearance.

"Jamie, how did you get here?"

He turned in the doorway, and pointed sloppily to his bicycle, which had been abandoned in the hallway in front of the stairwell where it obviously couldn't stay.

Though I was hesitant to let go of him, I hurried to retrieve the bike and rolled it into my dining room for the night.

When I returned to the entryway for him, I noticed a sizeable bandage covering his entire right forearm where his sleeves were rolled up. It was gauzy and white, and secured on all sides with medical tape.

"Oh, my god. What did you do?" It was very easy to imagine that he'd veered his bicycle into a parked car or an unsuspecting telephone pole. But then *somebody* had bandaged him up, and I was mad as hell they'd allowed him to ride off in this compromised condition.

He heaved a breath as if my question was going to require some fortification.

"A lot of things," he said, and nodded once to underscore the point. "For one, I told the label to go *ffffuck* themselves." His lashes fluttered with the effort of pushing the drawn-out expletive over the threshold of his lips. Then he belched into his fist.

"Oh . . ." He drew his brows together as if he remembered something else. "And I think I may have banjaxed my band. That's when I went to O'Malley's for a bit of Old Rosie."

He'd had a lot more than *a bit* of Old Rosie. The night had obviously not gone well; I felt awful for him. And while this startling, albeit brief, account of his evening was sufficient to explain his level of intoxication, I held no illusion of getting any more in the way of lucid details tonight.

Jamie was swaying on his feet now, and looking as though he wasn't going to be vertical for long. I took his uninjured arm and led him down the hall to my bedroom, hoping he'd make it before he passed out. Otherwise, he'd be spending the night on the floor, for all I could do to move him. He followed me dutifully with a wanton smile, as if he honestly believed he could be of some particular use to me in the bedroom tonight.

"Here," I said, as we stood together next to my bed in the warm yellow glow of my bedside lamp. "Let me get you undressed." He stood perfectly still, trying to be helpful, and also trying hard to focus properly on my face. He looked so young standing there. Jamie *was* young—younger than I, in fact, by a couple of years, but I didn't imagine he'd ever had the luxury of *being* young.

As soon as I placed my hands on his waist to pull out the tucked-in side of his shirt, he closed his eyes and let out a small sigh of contentment. Jamie liked to be touched—took more comfort in it than anyone I knew. He liked to be cared for.

So I unbuttoned each white button slowly, letting him feel the warmth of my hands as they went about their work down his chest and stomach. A little smile lingered on his lips. When I finally had the shirt open, I stepped in closer so he could feel the press of my body near his. I ran both my hands through his thick, auburn hair, down his strong neck, and across his broad, sturdy shoulders, where I gently eased the shirt from his body to drape it neatly over my desk chair.

The physical contact had him immediately aroused; his penis had clearly not gotten the memo that the rest of his body was in no condition for follow through.

"You smell nice," he murmured sleepily. "Like pie."

I had to laugh, pathetic as he was at that moment. *Like pie*. Well, there were worse things to smell like. *Him*, for example, though his smell was improving with each article of clothing I removed.

Once I had his pants down and around his ankles, I tipped him over onto the bed with an *oof*. He was not light. But from there, the rest of his garments were easy to slip off and I was able to pull the blankets up around him.

He seemed to hover on the verge of consciousness, not yet ready to let himself fully drift off into much needed sleep. I sat on the bed beside him, leaning back against my headboard, and stroked his hair as he rested next to my hip. *What had happened tonight?* I wondered about that as I watched his chest rise and fall with each breath. He shifted beneath the sheets so his body was now curled up against me, seeking closeness in the early morning hours. His hand cupped my thigh, making his bandage pucker slightly around the edges.

Carefully, I peeled it back. I was curious to know the extent of his injury should I need to treat it in some way. But I found it wasn't an injury, at all. Surprisingly, a large tattoo now graced his entire right forearm, a detail of his evening's adventures that he seemed to have forgotten entirely.

He must have felt my astonishment and opened his eyes, turning his wrist in my hand. He stared hard at his arm for a minute, reacquainting himself with the design.

The tattoo was really very beautiful and intricate, though the skin around it was mildly red and angry looking. It was a design of a treble clef that suggested the body of a bird, with eagle wings spreading out on both sides to wrap partially around his arm. At the bottom, near his wrist, the symbol was anchored by a shackle and key.

"My captor and my liberator," he said quietly, hearing my thoughts, and then closed his eyes again.

I studied the design more closely, with its swirling lines and detailed application. There was definite artistry involved here, though I was deeply suspicious of any all-night establishment that granted tattoos to the intoxicated. At least he hadn't come out with Pac Man gobbling up his nipple, or *Never Don't Give Up* across his chest. Alcohol and tattoo parlors notoriously produced far more horrendous offspring than this poignant piece. It was actually very fitting for a man who lived both for, and in service of, his incredible talent.

It's a gift that can sometimes feel like a curse. I truly believed it.

I'd suspected the toll that all this was taking on him, but didn't fully appreciate the extent of it until tonight. He was strong, but he was only human.

I rose from my bed, washed my hands and gently coated the new tattoo with antibiotic ointment.

Jamie had spent the evening nursing wounds I couldn't fix; but this was one I could—and wanted to, even if it was the smallest of all the things he was dealing with.

When I was finished with the aftercare, I slipped out of my own clothes, turned off the light, and climbed under the covers behind him, wrapping my arms around his waist and feeling the reassurance of flesh and rib. In the darkness, his fingertips found my outer thigh and he softly pressed a rhythmic pattern on my skin, as he often did just before he fell asleep. I squeezed him a little tighter in response, just to let him know, in case he could know such a thing from his slumbers, that it was right that he had come here. It would always be right—no matter what time of day or night—to come, lay down his burdens, and just rest for a while.

"Love you, too," I whispered and kissed his warm back, though I was sure he'd long since succumbed to unconsciousness. It was better that way.

§

Morning came painfully for Jamie.

When I entered the bedroom with a large plate of scrambled eggs and sausage, he propped himself up in a seated position to the obvious detriment of his head.

"How are you feeling?"

It was Sunday, thankfully, and neither of us had anywhere we had to be. Jamie gratefully accepted the meal I handed him along with a glass of orange juice—almost as gratefully as he accepted the Tylenol.

"Other than the fact that my arm is sore, and I've got Old Rosie banging through my brains, I feel smashing. You're just grand for this, by the way. Thank you." He dug in with the enthusiasm of someone who hadn't seen food in days, stabbing as many eggs onto the tines of his fork as was physically possible, while I settled in beside him in my white satin robe.

"From the looks of things, you had quite a night."

He swallowed a large bite and paused at his work. His brows pulled together and I could see what appeared to be regret on his face. "I'm sorry to have disturbed you. I shouldn't have."

"Yes, you should have. That's what it means to have someone in your life."

Jamie considered this carefully, like he was examining something in me, and yet at the same time, examining something in himself. He didn't respond directly, and though I couldn't quite pinpoint what I saw in his expression, it felt complicated.

He cleared the hoarseness from his throat. "It was a hell of a night." Setting the plate aside, he emptied the last of the orange juice, and over the next short while, acquainted me with the essential facts of his evening.

"What I can't understand is why Spire would bother with us. Why not just find a band with the exact sound they're looking for?"

I wasn't sure if this was a rhetorical question, but it was one I'd given considerable thought to myself, actually. And what I kept coming back to was this:

"A few years ago, my parents remodeled their house—kitchen, bathrooms, that kind of thing. It was a huge deal for them and my dad, being my dad, got seven bids for the work. All seven for the exact same job using the exact same types of materials." Jamie nodded, following. "The bids came in wildly different. The guys who really wanted the work were competitive, and the ones who were only mildly interested in doing the job seemed to price the work at its highest. And they were the least willing to negotiate."

"They'd do the work if they got their price—otherwise, they were fine letting the job go. I get it. The company I work for does that too. You think that's what's going on here?"

"I think it's a risk calculation. All these contracts are structured so that even an album with mediocre success can recoup a lot of direct costs for the label. But they can vastly improve their chances of making money if they have a greater say in ensuring that what you put out is commercial. I think these guys are just doing the math. They see potential revenue in your music, but they're hedging their bets by asking for more control."

He nodded slightly. A small crease formed between his brows as thoughts moved rapidly though his aching head.

"Could be."

I picked up his right hand, cupping it between both of mine.

"What are you going to do?"

He sighed and flexed his shoulders, resettling his upper body against the headboard. His face was calm and smooth as he watched me stroke the calluses on his palm. He had an inward look that suggested he was searching for an answer in the worrisome void of an uncertain future.

Jamie didn't need to say it, he clearly felt a crushing responsibility for other lives whose fortunes were tied to his own—the band, his sister's education, maybe the needs of other family members, though he rarely mentioned them. In addition, the contract represented a financial gain for him personally—not just the advance, but the publishing and songwriting credits for which he could also negotiate a relatively lucrative deal.

Walking away from it meant putting all of that in question, and it meant continuing a juggling act that was obviously taking its toll on him physically. He had to take time off work in order to tour, but the lost wages made it hard to make ends meet, not to mention taking away from the resources he could contribute towards touring, booking studio time, producing CDs, etc.

I was sure all this was going through his mind, though he'd never, ever talk to me about money, proud as he was. But in the end, I also knew that money would never be his deciding factor. His sense of responsibility *would* weigh heavily in the equation, though, and would haunt him no matter what choice he made.

"I cannot sign it."

The solemn words came out as barely a whisper, but there was no question he was suffering for the decision.

"Honestly, Jamie, I think you're right not to."

I knew the repercussions of his decision were going to be significant. I wanted to offer some insightful words of encouragement, but I didn't know what else to say that could possibly make a difference, so I just squeezed his hand instead.

He shrugged, returning the squeeze, and stroked his thumb idly over the back of my hand.

"Even if that turns out to be true, there's no comfort in it. This whole situation is my fault. I should have seen it coming and put a stop to it before we got this far."

"How could you possibly have known?"

He heaved a sigh. "There were signs. Most A&R guys will go to the mat for the bands they recruit. Kayes never seemed to be all that committed to us. The thing is, Mel, I ignored it because I wanted so badly to believe it, too—that this was our big break. I'm just afraid now that we won't come out of this untouched."

"If it's your fault, then it's mine, too. I didn't like Matt Kayes from the very beginning and I didn't say anything. I didn't want to sound like I doubted you. I'm sorry, Jamie."

Jamie Callahan studied me silently for a long moment, his beautiful light hazel eyes serious, but drenched in tenderness as they noted every detail of my face. Sitting with the sheet low on his waist, he exposed a torso of the most perfect lines and proportions. He reminded me of Atlas, bearing the weight of the heavens on his shoulders—endurance personified. At times, I thought he felt his burden in a very similar fashion. Unlike Atlas, though, Jamie never sought to hand it off.

Lifting one arm, roped with veins and now adorned with ink, he cupped my cheek in his hand.

"You, my Melody, are above all blame for all things. And if you still believe in me despite the mess I've made, then I count myself to be an exceptionally lucky bloke."

"I believe in you now more than ever. You *will* make it because it isn't in you to give up. And because you are so incredibly talented and deserving. But I will say this, I'd like you to point me in the direction of the tattoo parlor that gave you *that* while you were drunk."

"What will you do?" He lowered his hand, but his eyes sparkled with amusement.

"File a complaint, that's what." I wasn't amused at all.

"With who?" His mouth was now twitching at the corners.

"I don't know yet—the city of San Francisco, the Better Business Bureau, *someone!*"

"You don't like the tattoo?"

He was going for nonchalance, but he fell shy of his goal. He didn't have much of a poker face.

"Actually, I like it a lot." I ran my fingertips down the sides of his arm, tracing the veins that curved through the soft springy hair. "The workmanship is beautiful. And it's fitting for you." I lifted my gaze to hazel eyes that were watching me so intently. "I just don't like the possibility that someone might've taken advantage of you when you weren't in a position to be making good decisions."

His lips curved in a shy smile, expressing something much more heartening than amusement. Then he leaned forward and kissed me softly on the lips, a feather-lite kiss that made my heart feel ten times bigger. He was warm, with a faint scent of cider that hung about his body, and with a taste of oranges that lingered on his mouth.

"Well, I'll save you the trouble. I got the tattoo *before* going to O'Malley's."

"Hmph," I said, and reached up to stroke the golden stubble that had sprung from his jawline overnight. "Okay, then. Good to know it was premeditated."

He smiled. "Good to know you care."

"You know I care, Jamie."

"Yes, well. That still confounds me."

The mood had suddenly turned serious. He reached for me and pulled me over to straddle his hips. Then he took my hands in his, and his thumbs caressed each ridge and hollow.

Dark auburn lashes lifted to reveal an artist's eyes that saw me in a way no one ever had before him. I wanted to know what he saw with those eyes. Every time I guessed I was wrong.

His palms drifted over the satin of my robe, his fingers spread wide, exploring, memorizing every line—the short lines that curved around my breasts, to the long ones that ran down my hips, around my backside and up my inner thighs.

He pulled at the tie around my waist and it easily slipped open.

"Take it off," he murmured.

"Jamie," I whispered and obeyed.

He drew his finger down my throat, pausing to feel my racing pulse, and he leaned in and pressed his mouth to the throbbing beat.

"You are so very lovely," he said, each word spoken reverently.

I could feel his arousal burning beneath me, but he was in no hurry. He was memorizing my body as he continued on a path down to my belly and lower, where he found me more than ready for him.

The way his hands moved over my skin, the way he took his time, it felt as if he was composing a song in real time—my song—carefully selecting a note or a chord for every detail he saw, many of which I knew I might never see, lacking the capability to appreciate things in the way he did. My body was his private muse, and he played me with expert hands. I welcomed it—loved it, actually.

Reaching behind, he lifted me to my knees to take my breast in his mouth. I took more pleasure than I could have imagined in watching his tongue drag over the rise of my skin, and then suck my nipple to a fully erect state. A rush of air left my lungs.

I wrapped my arms around his head, his gorgeous hair brushing against my forearms. I could feel his shoulders flex as he pushed back the sheets from his lap and then moved his hands to my hips to work me down until he was deep inside.

There was no preamble; we were both primed and aching for completion. I let my head fall back as he thrust, steely and pulsing, inside me. His skin was so warm and slightly damp across his chest. He was holding himself in check, and the effort was costing him.

But as we moved together, he implored me to find my rhythm, to take what I needed from his body. I did, with an urgency that drove me nearly to the point of exhaustion. We melted hard into each other, until I was beyond words or thought.

"Let go," he commanded. "And let me see you."

I closed my eyes and cried out, tumbling uncontrollably—my absolute pleasure sealed in that one beautiful command.

That's what Jamie did in all things—pushed me just to the edge of my comfort zone, then inched one step further because he knew I craved to feel more, enjoy things more, risk more. Reckless, just enough.

My undoing was Jamie's, as well. He thrust powerfully up inside me, again and again and again, until he tumbled too, spilling himself exhaustively with a hoarse grunt.

His body stilled, but his fingertips continued to clutch my hips, holding me tightly to him. A rough cheek lay vulnerably on my slick breast, and neither of us moved.

"I need you, Mel," he whispered against my skin.

I was still regaining my wits, so I can't say that I fully understood or appreciated the depth of his declaration in the moment, nor how hard it may have been for him to make it.

Jamie always said things easily, big things, without any self-consciousness or regret. But somehow, this felt different. He had come to me last night in a way he'd never come to me before. Perhaps in need of something he thought only I could give him. I wasn't sure what, but I had the strong feeling that we were finally becoming a part of each other, truly connected. Not just through our bodies, but by something much, much older.

And despite everything that had happened the night before, and everything troubling him still, sleep came very easily to the man after that.

Chapter 21

Mel

I heard almost nothing from Jamie over the course of the workweek, though his 2:00 a.m. message on Wednesday led me to suspect he wasn't sleeping well. And Killian didn't offer much when I returned the call, but he did leave me with the distinct impression that things in the apartment were tense. Understandably so, and it was a worry.

Per Jamie's instructions, I arrived at Slim's in the SoMa district of San Francisco at eight o'clock in the evening. Slim's was one of the best music venues in the city, with a cool New Orleans vibe and standing-room-only capacity of about eight hundred. Jamie had left instructions with the stage crew to show me back to the dressing room when I arrived.

Generously named, the dressing room was a small, utilitarian space, but served its purpose well for a vocal warm-up and a quick change of clothes. Unlike many you encountered in the club scene, this one had no leaking water, no peeling paint, and no odd, unpleasant odor.

The band was all there, dressed for the show when I walked in. What was immediately apparent, though, was that no one was talking to each other. Jamie's back was to the door, his guitar on a table in front of him, and he was in the process of changing one of its strings.

The rest of the guys were just reading a book or listening to some music. I gave them a quick wave and headed for Jamie.

"Hey."

"Hi," he said, leaning in to give me a perfunctory kiss before picking up the peg winder from the table and continuing his work.

It was very clear things weren't right, but I could hardly bring it up with all of them sitting right there in the room, and wouldn't anyway. What was there to say? *Sorry this situation sucks; don't be mad at each other.*

Instead, I did the only thing I could think of: I reached up and rubbed Jamie's back over the black Henley T-shirt he was wearing.

He barely acknowledged the contact, and that was, maybe, the most startling indication of what was going on in his head.

I stood dumbly and watched him as he silently tightened the new string. He probably could have done it in his sleep, and if I were a betting woman, I would have guessed he wasn't even thinking about the process as he completed it, far off as he seemed in that moment.

"Well, if it isn't Cadence."

Jamie and I both turned around at the familiar voice to find Matt Kayes standing in the doorway.

"What are you doing here?" Jamie asked dryly.

Out of the corner of my eye, I saw Greg get up slowly from his chair and set his headphones aside. Nash put down his book.

"Scouting another band."

Jamie nodded wordlessly, and began to turn back around to his guitar.

"You guys were fucking idiots, you know that?"

Jamie's eyes flashed at the insult. He set down the tool he was holding and faced Matt directly.

"You should go." His face was even and calm, but there was strain beneath the cool exterior.

Killian instinctively moved in closer, looking as though he was perfectly ready to intervene physically.

"I will," Kayes said, though his shorter, pudgy frame seemed to be bristling with anger, as well. "But you know what really pisses me off? I *told* you. When I called you about the deal memo, I told you— don't make me look bad. You *fuckin'* prick."

Jamie's bulk loomed at my shoulder. He stepped forward to stand directly in front of Kayes, who was now right next to me, though fixated as he was on Jamie, he probably didn't realize it.

Jamie's voice was steady, but his gaze was locked on Kayes' face. "I think you managed that all on your own."

Kayes' mouth twisted sharply and he seemed to be contemplating various forms of replies.

Meanwhile, Nash stood up from his chair, a towering presence that, despite his mild nature, only added to the tension in the room.

Inside the venue, Slim's guests were now filing in in droves. We could hear a low roar of conversation and activity that echoed off the brick walls and metal beams of the high-ceiling concert hall. But in the tiny cement dressing room in the back, adorned with an old couch, a few folding chairs and a small table, nobody moved.

I was standing so close to Kayes that I could see his eyeball twitch. And the more I studied him, the angrier I became. He was still wearing his big Rolex that he seemed so proud of, and exhibiting a look of indignation that I didn't think he had any right to. He was as guilty for all of this as anyone. He wasn't Superman; he was a *bargain* hunter. And shame on him for it. He didn't even like musicians.

It was just then that Kayes' attention cut over to Greg, who had silently joined our little circle. Kayes gave him a long and pointed look.

"Did you agree with this decision, Van de Meer?"

It was the one question no one wanted asked. Though he made no outward move, Jamie seemed to recoil slightly. Greg had *not* agreed with the decision. In fact, he had vehemently disagreed.

All eyes in the room went to Greg, who was done up for the show with heavy black liner and a Kinks T-shirt over black jeans and army boots. He took in Kayes' question with no visible reaction. Unlike Jamie, he *did* have a poker face.

In the weight of that moment, I might have expected Greg to waver. I couldn't have blamed him for it; it was a terrible position to be in. He was still the most unpredictable member of the band for me. But as it turns out, he was beautifully unpredictable.

"Of course I did," he said evenly. "The deal was shitty."

It was as if all four members of the band exhaled at once. There seemed to be something glowing around them specifically, if only for that one fleeting moment. A brotherhood. All in, for better or for worse. Any conflict between them was their business, and theirs alone.

I glanced very quickly at Jamie, whose outward expression was indiscernible, yet his face burned with emotion.

Kayes uttered a short snide laugh, now focusing again on Jamie.

"You're going to regret that. I gave you a chance to *be* something."

"I *am* something."

Kayes smiled a deeply cynical smile. Then he leaned in towards Jamie and pointed at me. "Let's see how much longer she thinks so."

There are moments in your life when you stand outside yourself and think, *Wow, I'll be darned. Look what I just did.*

This was such a moment.

It started with my watching in horror as Kayes' hideous comment about me struck a direct hit with Jamie. He didn't say a word, but his eyes darted to mine with a look so painfully vulnerable it broke my heart, utterly.

I don't think, in my lifetime, I've ever been so angry with anyone as I was with Matt Kayes in that exact second—so angry, in fact, that wild thoughts began racing through my brain—disconnected, random thoughts that bore no correlation to what was happening in that room.

It felt like a fight or flight reaction. For some weird reason, I remembered some self-defense moves I'd been taught years ago. Strike quickly, and aim for the throat, balls or shins. Eyeballs if you can.

No correlation whatsoever to rational thought.

Fist to the throat; knee to the balls, heel to the shins.

I was mad as hell at the thought of being used as a weapon against a man I loved dearly.

So maybe it wasn't a complete surprise that things got jumbled up in my head. Maybe I can't be faulted entirely for the fact that in those first crazy seconds, when everything seems to stop and you're standing outside yourself thinking, *So that happened*, sometimes things actually do happen.

I watched disconnectedly as my fist shot out sharply from my body with astounding force. Where it landed in a pillow of softness was as much of a surprise to me as it was to poor Matt Kayes.

He dropped like a sack of potatoes, howling in pain and clutching his testicles like he was protecting a precious baby chick he kept hidden in his pants.

"Whatthefuck!" he squeaked, rolling around in circles like a pinwheel on the floor. To say it was undignified was an understatement.

I tore my gaze from this spectacle to find all four members of the band gawking, eyes wide as giant saucers at the action unfolding before them and Kayes still yelping, "Whatthefuck! Whatthefuck! Whatthefuck!"

"Oh, shit!" Nash gasped, probably with more amusement than was polite, under the circumstances.

And here's the thing about men: they are very careful with that particular appendage and they are especially wary of any attempt on it. The four standing males in the room seemed to take a collective step back from Kayes, as if his present condition might somehow be contagious. Killian and Greg checked themselves discreetly, just to verify that their own equipment was all accounted for and in good, working condition.

Satisfied that it was, both looked over at me, beaming with enormous boyish grins. It was the first time I'd seen them smile in ages.

Jamie was likewise distracted, if just for now, from the insidious seed that had been planted in his head. He glanced at me as if he was seeing me for the very first time; or maybe like I was a Martian stand-in for the woman he'd been dating for the past couple of months. Having given up every attempt to pinpoint an explanation, he simply shook his head in amusement and put his arm around my shoulder, pulling me in close.

"Come on, champ. Why don't we give Kayes some privacy?"

The five of us left the dressing room, with Kayes still squeaking in a girlish voice, "It hurts!"

That's when the reality of my crime of passion began to sink in.

"Jamie, he could press charges against me!" I said in horror. "For assault! On his *balls*!"

Jamie chuckled deep and easy. "He's not going to press charges, angel. He'd have to admit to getting dropped by a tiny girl. And believe me, that would be more damaging to his manhood than anything you just did."

"Besides," Killian agreed, still smiling. "It would be his word against ours."

§

Unfortunately, the palliative effect of my unintended actions didn't last long. Something had been broken between the members of the band, and it wouldn't be so easily fixed.

In a cruel twist of fate, the show also had its own problems. Cadence took the stage and immediately began having technical issues with the earpieces. These are custom-molded earplugs whose speakers feed a pre-determined mix of sound to the performer by way of a wireless transmitter pack tucked into his waistband. If the mix of sound isn't right for each member of the band, they can't hear what their counterparts are playing. They may not even be able to hear themselves. It can totally throw a performer off his game.

In this particular case, it seemed as though Nash wasn't getting any drums in his earpiece, so he was beating his kit with a much heavier hand. In turn, the rest of the members were struggling to hear themselves over Nash, and were signaling as best they could to both he and the monitor engineer to make adjustments mid-song.

Jamie, as the lead singer, had necessary priority in terms of the engineer's attention, but it seemed as if, even with the corrections they were making, he still couldn't hear Killian properly. He kept glancing questioningly in Killian's direction as if trying to sync his own guitar and vocal level with what Killian was playing.

And Greg was coming totally unglued. In fairness, the bass is the hardest to regulate because the low-end tones don't translate well to the in-ear monitors in the first place. He looked the closest of all of them to just throwing his hands up in frustration and walking off the stage.

But technical issues weren't the only problem. All four seemed to keep to their own corners of the stage, rarely interacting with the others. Jamie, in particular, was disconnected and distracted from his performance, never quite catching his groove. There was no absolutely chemistry between them—nothing to suggest that the band was anything greater than the sum of its parts.

And so, it was no surprise that the crowd was flat and uninspired. The audience stood politely and listened to the music, some clapped or bobbed their heads to the beat, but very few were dancing. The entire show lacked the fervor and frenetic energy I had come to expect from Cadence's performances. And Jamie couldn't pull them out of it, no matter what he did. He just didn't seem to have it in him.

It absolutely broke my heart.

The fifty-minute set felt like an eternity, and when it was over, the band left the stage unceremoniously to a light helping of applause and no calls for an encore.

I was standing just beyond the wings when Jamie walked off, sweaty and spent. The look on his face was one of utter defeat. He met my gaze for a gut-wrenching moment and then closed his eyes and shook his head softly, holding up one hand as if to say he needed space.

I watched him make his way to where he'd stashed a clean shirt and a bottle of water, downing the water in one long swallow. He tossed the bottle in a nearby can and stood with his hands on his hips in faraway thought. The lines of his shoulders hung low in desolation. Where his natural exuberance might normally have carried him past this, tonight he just didn't seem to have the strength; his reserves were depleted.

A part of me ached to offer some consolation, admittedly without a clue of what that might be. But I knew there was nothing to be said, except maybe *I'm here for you*. And I was, wholeheartedly, but I was not enough.

In the end, it didn't matter. Greg got there first, and the conversation that followed appeared far too private for me to join. Jamie was turned slightly so that I could see the men in profile, and I watched as Greg said something to him, the effect of which seemed to hit Jamie squarely. Greg looked troubled too and shook his head as Jamie fired back a response.

By the time they were joined by the remaining members of the band, an unsettling feeling was churning in my gut. It was then I realized what I was witnessing. I stood breathless, refusing to believe in my heart what my eyes already knew to be true.

Cadence was breaking up.

Chapter 22

Mel

In mid-November, I received word that I passed the California Bar Exam. Both Hope and I did, and we had a cursory drink to celebrate.

The first phone calls I placed were to my family, as they always were for news, both good and bad. More than anything, though, I wanted to call Jamie.

But he had disappeared from my life.

His infrequent phone calls became increasingly so, until they were non-existent. I emailed him a few times—even invited him to a party my firm was planning in honor of those of us who had taken our oaths and were admitted the State Bar—but I never got a single response. On one occasion, I spoke with Killian and learned that Greg had moved in with Nash, and Killian and Jamie were picking up some extra shifts in order to pay the rent until their next move became clear. Jamie never seemed to be home, probably by design.

As for me, there were plenty of tears shed, damn him, but I was determined not to lose myself in grief. Instead, I focused considerable effort on my work, and continued to invest my energy into a new hobby I found to be exceptionally and surprisingly cathartic.

Cooking. Who would have thought?

I became *that* person in the office, the one who was always bringing in treats and leftovers and new recipes I was perfecting. 'Rou' and 'deglaze' became part of my active vocabulary, and I actually subscribed to a couple of cooking magazines—something my former self would have found stressful and disheartening.

But in the low moments, those tearful ones I could not fairly blame on an onion, I missed Jamie terribly and wondered how he was.

In some ways, one could argue, Jamie had left me better than he'd found me—more accepting of myself, more sure of what I wanted and needed in a relationship—but he had also left me brokenhearted, and I didn't know how long it would take for that wound to heal, or if it ever would, completely.

It was hard to imagine I'd ever meet another man like him—that I would ever feel for anyone the way I felt for him, the way I felt when I was with him. The thought of future relationships with anyone else seemed utterly colorless by comparison. I feared that in my practicality, I'd settle for someone who would complement my personality, but not necessarily challenge me. Someone who could give me a nice life, but not a partner with whom I could create an extraordinary one.

Very good is the enemy of great. Jamie had said that.

Still, as time went on without a word from him, I couldn't continue to hold out hope for us. He had developed a pattern in his life of isolation and retreat when faced with adversity. It was a survival technique for someone who had probably been in survival mode his entire life. But it wasn't healthy for a relationship, or for the individuals in it. He had a circle of supporters, but he wouldn't let himself be a part of it. And I hurt for him, but I knew I couldn't change him. He had to do that for himself.

I'd always expected that the pressure on our relationship would come from the demands of his work—and mine, frankly—and from a constant presence of female fans and the lengthy separations necessitated by touring. I'd actively prepared myself for those things, had strategies mapped out in my head. But I hadn't expected that the biggest challenge would come from within, and I was at a loss how to fight it—how to fight for us. He was either going to be in this relationship with me, or he wasn't. And for now, he wasn't.

He was off fighting his own battles, and I knew there were many. The break-up of the band must have been a devastating blow. And it wasn't caused by one bad show; it was the culmination of their differences of opinions, hard feelings not communicated, and the aggregate effect all that had on their chemistry. They weren't Cadence without it.

Maybe it was impossible to know for sure who was right and who was wrong when it came to the contract. Maybe it would have gone as Greg had suggested: the label would offer some guidance that Cadence could live with, and they'd put out a great first album that would give the label a reason to back off.

But I was a student of the law, and I thought it was much more likely to go as Jamie had predicted. When companies invest in drafting complex agreements, they usually do so with the intent of exercising their full rights. The music industry was no different from any other. After all, Prince didn't become 'The Artist Formerly Known as Prince' for nothing. His dispute with his label led him to change his given name to an unpronounceable symbol.

These contracts weren't small gambles—they had the power to make or break an artist, even for someone of the magnitude of Prince. And in the end, for Cadence, the gamble wound up in a loss.

It was a loss for me, too.

Chapter 23

Voicemail from Danny

"Hey. I've been trying to reach you, man. Cara told me what happened with the band. Listen . . . This isn't the end of the road. I know it feels like that right now, but you're just at the starting gate. And you're going to be just fine; I know it, Jamie. I've always known it. Anyway . . . I love you, my brother. I think you know that. Wish I were there . . . Okay . . . well . . . call your sister back. She's worried about you. And don't fuck things up with Mel."

Chapter 24

Mel

"Please tell me you're bringing these to the party."

My boss, Adam Silverman, took another enthusiastic bite of my third attempt at lemon pepper chicken wings as we stood together in the firm's small kitchen, napkins at the ready, trying earnestly to keep from smudging our work clothes as we tested my latest recipe.

"I am. Stanley tried the last ones I brought in and kind of insisted." I cringed. "I think I'm the only one bringing food, though. Is that weird? The party is being catered."

"Stanley's wife is vegan."

"Ah." Leftovers.

After a few more silent bites, Adam glanced up at me pleasantly.

"So, I'm looking forward to meeting Jamie on Saturday."

"Oh . . . uh . . ."

I swallowed and set down the bone in my hand. I wasn't prepared for any talk of Jamie at work.

And Adam had absolutely no idea of the emotional landmine he'd just triggered. How could he have known? It was just a casual conversation among coworkers, spoken innocently over a batch of lukewarm chicken wings. Decent wings, by the way.

But with one simple, harmless statement, my face fell and my heart with it. I went silent, and I think I may have accidentally looked like I was going to cry.

I only know this because his eyes went wide, and he immediately developed an expression of *Fuuuuuuuuck! Whatdidido?* His eyes were darting around in little panicked movements as if desperately searching for help in every corner of the room. He sort of looked like a chicken, actually, in a very expensive suit.

Then, coming to grips with the fact that he was, indeed, alone in a confined space with an emotional person, and no help was to be found, Adam seemed to settle to his task, handing me a paper napkin and patting me awkwardly on the shoulder.

"I'm sorry," he finally said in a touching and genuine way. "I didn't realize. That was the wrong thing to say, I'm guessing."

"No." I dabbed my eyes and laughed a little at the cartoonish nature of the situation. "It's fine, really." I waved off his sympathy and he seemed greatly relieved for it. "You know how it goes."

Adam nodded without comment. He was a great boss, after all— very supportive of me and encouraging in my work. And we were friendly, for sure, but I would not say we were *friends*. Not like cry-on-your-shoulder friends. *At all.* I was mortified by the idea of crying in front of him, and he seemed equally mortified that he'd unwittingly been responsible for it.

"Well, the wings are outstanding," he proclaimed with a smile. "They'll be the best things at that party, as far as I'm concerned. Everything else will be catered and *fancy*." He made a goofy, scary face.

I laughed. "I'm glad you think so. I'm good at doubling and tripling recipes; less good at halving them."

Chapter 25

Mel

Turns out, I was right. I was *literally* the only person attending the party at the stately Pacific Heights home of Stanley and Irene Baker who was bringing food. If it weren't for the fact that I had come in a red dress, I could easily have been mistaken for one of the caterers as I walked in. What worried me most was whether Irene Baker had even been told that one of her husband's guests was bringing what amounted to a carnivore's extravaganza. Stanley, a founding partner of my firm, Baker Harris, LLP, had assured me heartily that she would be thrilled.

I truly believed one of them would be.

On the flipside, this was the very first time in my entire life that anyone had singled me out for my cooking—in a good way, I mean. Quite the contrary, I'd come to accept the fact that, when it came to events of a potluck nature, I was always the one asked to bring wine. Or chips. My friends and family had full confidence in my ability to employ my credit card effectively.

I decided to put this odd situation in the win column, and rang the doorbell with the self-assurance that any non-vegan would be glad for my contribution to the spread.

Fortunately, the foil pans were whisked from my hands in the entryway and carted off to find more suitable plating for the festivities.

And true to all expectations, the party in progress was elegant.

Shortly after my arrival, I found myself in conversation of mutual congratulations with the team of attorneys assigned to represent our semiconductor client in its patent infringement case. The beneficial resolution had been that our client was required to pay a small $15 million settlement, but in total, this was peanuts compared to what it could have been. Plus, the cross-license agreement we negotiated would allow it to enter an attractive adjacent market without fear of further legal action from its competitor.

It's often that way for attorneys and their clients; the things that *don't* happen are usually the things that define our success—those things we help our clients swerve to miss. That made me think of the Spire contract. And Jamie. I cursed myself for thinking of him as often as I did.

So it was an eerie twist that I should glance outside the gracious front windows of the Baker residence for the first time that evening and notice a bicycle chained to the low wrought iron fence that outlined this magnificent home. Funny, it looked just like . . . it *really* looked like . . .

Jamie.

I turned my head in the direction of the front door to find him standing in the entry of the grand living room.

I had to blink for a moment, mistrusting my eyes, but it *was* actually him. He was handsomely dressed in a crisp white shirt, rolled up at the sleeves and tucked neatly into gray wool slacks, with a black belt that showcased his trim waist. His hands were in his pockets, and he was staring directly at me with an expression I could not decipher.

Myriad of conflicting emotions crashed through my body at once. I had an urge to run to him and throw my arms around him, burying myself in his strong hold for comfort from the sadness that had become my norm these past weeks. I had an equally strong urge to march right up and slap him hard across the face for every bit of pain he had put me through. And there was another inclination, urging me to send him away, but in truth, I didn't think I could do that.

I didn't have time to execute any of these actions before he strode across the room in my direction. I couldn't break from his gaze, frozen as a deer in headlights and blinded from anyone or anything else in the room. He was my everything—and damn, damn, *damn* him for it.

"Congratulations," he said softly, coming to a halt right in front of me with an expression full of wariness and uncertainty. He was so close that I had a strong impulse to touch him, to run my hands across his chest and breathe in his manly scent.

God, I'd missed him. So vivid was he by comparison to anything else in my life.

But I felt so hurt by him that I refused to acknowledge it.

"What are you doing here?" I demanded, as if my state of mind were as simple as mere anger alone.

"You invited me," he said plainly.

I think I actually laughed in disbelief, completely at a loss to understand how he could possibly just waltz back into my life—*here*, nonetheless, at a work event—after so much time had gone by. Without so much as One. Damned. Word.

"But that was—!"

"Hello. I'm Stanley Baker."

In an *astounding* example of poor timing, the senior partner of my firm—my boss's boss's boss—inserted himself into our terse conversation with an outstretched hand to Jamie and total oblivion of the chaos he'd just stumbled into. Jamie, well accustomed to managing the unexpected, didn't miss a beat.

"Very pleased to meet you, sir. I'm Jamie Callahan, Melody's guest." He was cool as a cucumber, damn him, and he completely ignored my growing outrage. "I was just admiring your lovely home."

"Oh, you're Irish!" Stanley beamed. "You know, I have a relative who's Irish."

God, don't we all? I thought uncharitably.

"Yes, sir, I am." Jamie smiled, full of warmth and sexiness. I resented him for it. "My family moved to America from Ireland when I was nine, in fact."

Ireland. It was so pretty the way he said it. Sort of like *AR-land*.

As I distantly listened to their ensuing conversation, I reached into the wastepaper basket in my head and retrieved the crumpled and wadded up list entitled *My Favorite Words That Jamie Says*, a list I had convincingly discarded weeks ago. Reluctantly, I added *Ireland* to it.

And then I noticed that *Love You* was still on there too. It had no right to be, for all the good it had done me.

But the mere memory of those two little carelessly spoken words made my eyes prick with tears, and I bit the inside of my lip to keep from crying. It was a stupid list, anyway. And I'd be damned if I would get emotional at a party at least partially thrown in my honor. In my head, I angrily crumpled up the list again and threw it back in the can where it belonged.

"Well, I can still get Kerrygold butter and pretty much any biscuits I want—whether it's HobNobs or whatever," Jamie was saying. "There's a shop in Los Angeles imaginatively called The Irish Shop. It sells Taytos and whiskey fudge and Aran jumpers and whatnot. When I'm in L.A. for a gig, sometimes, I'll stop by there and go a little mad with nostalgia." I had no idea what he was talking about, nor did I care. It was impossible to follow over the crisis in my head.

I couldn't make myself rejoin the conversation. Instead, I studied him as he talked to Stanley, and analyzed every single line of his face and neck as if I had to decide whether he was really here, or just an apparition. His lustrous auburn hair had grown a little longer—I liked it. And he was tan; had he been working a lot? The warm coloring made his amazing hazel eyes stand out even more than usual. But he also looked worn down, like he hadn't been sleeping well. And I remembered that I hurt for him, despite the impact that his coping mechanisms had had on me.

As I watched him talk, I wanted to move in closer, to drink in his body heat and the intoxicating scent of his masculinity. At the same time, I wanted to walk away. Far away.

In the end, I did neither, just stood there silently in my candy apple red dress and gave my very best impersonation of someone who was all right.

Jamie seemed to feel the heaviness of my stare, and pulled his gaze from Stanley for just a moment to meet mine directly. There was a polite smile hanging artfully on his face—his little crooked front tooth lending character to his already expressive visage—but his eyes told a different story entirely. They were solemn, seeking mine for an answer to a question he could not bear to ask, but knew he had to, nonetheless.

"Come with me," Stanley said, as part of a conversation I had missed completely. "I have something you'll appreciate."

Stanley was a dear man, quite taken with Jamie, and so eager to show him . . . whatever it was . . . that we had little choice in the matter, awful as the timing might have been.

So follow Stanley, we did. Jamie ushered me in front of him, placing a firm hand on my lower back. Whether it was a gentlemanly gesture, or insurance that I wouldn't run, I didn't know. I just knew that as we mechanically made our way across the great room to a small parlor adjacent to it, I felt each and every point of contact where the heat from his skin touched my body to a riotous effect.

The small parlor was cozy and sumptuously appointed. It had the same big picture windows that looked out onto the quaint San Francisco street, and the same soothing color palette as its larger counterpart. As soon as we walked in, I knew exactly what it was he wanted to show Jamie.

Positioned right in the middle of the room was the most magnificent grand piano I'd ever seen. 'Magnificent' didn't really cover it, though—the piece was . . .

§

Jamie

'Regal' is how I might have described that Fazioli piano. The construction was pure artistry, made of red spruce with ebony wood keys and a high-gloss polyester ebony finish. It was undoubtedly the most beautiful instrument I'd ever seen. I couldn't stop myself from running a hand reverently over its lid.

"Did you know that Fazioli only produces a hundred pianos a year?" Stanley asked. I could believe it, given the flawless craftsmanship of the piece. "And now that my daughters are grown, this one sits quiet most of the time. It's such a shame."

I nodded, quite in agreement. An instrument like this was too special to lay in neglect.

"Why don't you give it a try?" Stanley asked me.

It was obviously important to him, and though my heart wasn't in it, I obliged for Melody's sake. I sat down on the bench, a piece of furniture as sturdy as the piano itself, and arranged my fingers on the keys. It took only a fraction of a second to decide on the song, and in doing so, I reached back in time to when everything in front of me felt like a promise.

A . . . G-sharp . . . E . . . D . . . C-sharp . . . D . . . E, played in a slow and soulful arrangement.

"Just Like Heaven" by The Cure. Melody recognized it instantly and her face transformed from one of careful composure to something far more clouded.

"Will you excuse me?" she asked Stanley suddenly, now unable to look at me directly. "I'd like to use the ladies room."

"Stay for this," I said to her, with an urgency that must have sounded strange to our host, and immediately switched over to George Gershwin's "Someone to Watch Over Me."

I didn't want her to leave—though she did, anyway—and would have done anything to erase the hurt in her eyes that I knew I'd put there.

She was the loveliest woman I had ever seen in my life—tonight all the more so in a beautiful crimson dress. I loved that she wore that dress. It was feminine, like her, but it said unmistakably that she would not live quietly. Nor should she. She was passionate and intelligent, and she should never, ever blend in with a crowd.

But like the piano beneath my hands, valuable so far beyond my reach, she seemed not meant for me. She belonged in this room, with these people who were more her equals. After all, outside the front window was chained a bicycle that represented a substantial portion of my personal net worth. I couldn't so much as give her a ride home, let alone provide her the life she deserved. And it didn't seem fair to hold her to me just because I wanted her so very much.

If only I could have convinced my heart of that.

I had come tonight, knowing it was selfish. Maybe I needed to prove to myself that I was right to let her go; or maybe I'd come in secret hope that somehow I was wrong . . .

§

I excused myself from Stanley's company as soon as I could. I needed to seek out Mel. And I fully understood that my urgency to speak with her was grossly hypocritical since I was the one who had let six weeks go by without calling. But now that I was here, near to where she was, the distance between us felt excruciating. If it was a mistake to have come tonight, I could accept that—but I could not leave without talking to her, if only to say I was sorry beyond words for the pain I'd caused.

I chose to wait for her return in a location that gave me good visibility to the collection of rooms in which most of the guests were mingling—a buffet table by the entrance to the dining room. I felt foolish at this gathering, and very out of place. Genuinely, I could not have been less interested or capable of making small talk with anyone. I avoided it by surveying the buffet instead.

The table had an incredibly odd assortment of items. On one end were a variety of small finger foods, like caviar on toast—not to my liking—and other things like tiny lettuce leaves, sprinkled with . . . something. Cheese, maybe, with nuts? I didn't know, but as I waited, I ate one anyway.

At other the end of the table were literally piles of chicken wings in three different flavors. I could not imagine the schizophrenic caterer who had dreamed up this menu. Still, I put one of each kind of wing on my plate and couldn't decide which one I enjoyed more. So, I tried all three again. And again. And yet again, at which point I thought it wise to wipe my hands and ditch the small graveyard I was amassing.

"Jamie, is it?"

I looked up to find a man standing beside me whom I did not recognize. He was quite possibly the tidiest human being I'd ever seen in my life—pleasant looking, and about my height, with brown hair clipped just a bit too short so that, even with gel, it stuck straight up like needles at his crown.

"Yes," I said, holding out a hand to shake.

"I'm Adam Silverman." He returned the gesture.

Adam Silverman. It clicked in my mind. Mel's boss.

I shook his hand firmly and appraised him a little more carefully. He was a handsome chap, particularly in his bespoke suit, though he could've probably managed that equally well in a tracksuit. And he was much younger than I had envisioned. For some reason, the reality felt like a bit of a shock.

But he was also the person responsible for helping us secure Gavin's representation, which we never could have afforded on our own.

"I owe you a debt of gratitude. I should have reached out to you sooner," I said, still recovering from the disconnect between the man standing in front of me and the one I'd had in my imagination—a *decidedly* less attractive one.

"No, not at all," he insisted sincerely, dropping my hand and shrugging off the apology. "I'm sorry the guys from the label turned out to be such dicks."

I nodded. There was little to say about that. The whole experience had the storyline of a music industry horror film. Except that it wasn't. It was our lives.

"Anyway," he continued, now gesturing to the wings, "These are great, aren't they?"

"Fantastic."

"I know!" he said, smiling. "That's what I told Mel. She felt weird about bringing something she'd made, but everyone loves them."

Something she'd made? I wasn't sure I'd heard him correctly. I continued to stare at him blankly, as the words banged around in my head. Mel was a treasure beyond all others, but I had a hard time imagining that these masterful treats had come out of her kitchen.

Adam regarded me oddly, and then answered my unspoken

question with a note of uncertainty, as if maybe he was speaking out of turn.

"Mel brought these. The recipes came from that cooking class she's taking."

He looked at me like I should know this; from his perspective, I was her boyfriend, after all. Why *wouldn't* I know this about her? But I didn't, of course, because I hadn't spoken with her in more than a month. Because, unlike Adam Silverman, I didn't talk to her every day, or see her every day. Unlike Adam Silverman in his bespoke suit, I wasn't there.

If he'd punched me in the face, he couldn't have landed a better blow. My thoughts staggered, and speaking as much to myself as to him I admitted, "She didn't tell me she was taking a class."

He stared at me for a long moment, and I couldn't decipher what it was I saw in his face. It wasn't aggression or gloat; it was worse than that. It looked very much like sympathy. Or maybe censure. Or disappointment. Maybe all three. It made me feel like absolute shite.

Then he nodded, still eyeing me closely and apparently warring with himself about something. Finally, he answered with quiet assuredness, "Too bad you never asked."

That was the worst blow. Because he was right; I'd been a bastard. And the feelings those simple words dislodged were not to my benefit.

Of course, in hindsight, it was obvious that what I was experiencing was fear and regret, coupled with inadequacy, I suppose. But, as is often the case, anger is a much safer emotion to express, and provides the path of least resistance. The anger was self-directed, but it didn't come out that way.

Chapter 26

Mel

Not offering any explanation whatsoever, Jamie grasped my elbow and all but pulled me through the kitchen to the back door. We were outside before I knew what had happened. The night was cool and clear, not a trace of a cloud in the sky. Just so many stars that it would have been romantic had I not been burning with such confused emotion, and he not been so boorish that he was dragging me off like the house was on fire.

"Let go of me!" I demanded. We marched down a fine gravel path towards a white gazebo, situated on a hill below the main house. "What are you doing?"

"We need to talk."

"Do we?" I said, gathering my sarcasm around my body like armor. "Oh, I don't know . . . why rush it?"

He ignored me, of course, and just continued to tow me along as though I had no say in the matter. Clearly, I did not have a say in the matter.

"Let go!" I hissed when we finally reached our destination.

Jamie whirled me around to face him, but he did not let go of my arm. In the soft glow of the yard's accent lighting, his face looked like it was carved from stone. Shadows highlighted every angle of his strong jawline and broad cheekbones, and every muscle in his face appeared tense and hard. If it hadn't fully registered before, it was easy to see now that he was every bit as upset as I was.

"He seems to know an awful lot about you, this Adam Silverman."

"My *boss*, you mean?" I wrenched my elbow free of his restraint.

"A bit chummy for a boss, don't you think?"

I stared at him in shock, emitting a sound that ran somewhere between outrage and incredulity. "Are you *jealous*?"

Jamie didn't answer. He was very nearly vibrating with fury, though. Cords stood out on his neck and a deep shade of red began to rise across his face and ears. Lines had formed between his brows, and his impressive frame loomed over me in daunting silence. But I wasn't backing down, either.

"Oh, that's just *classic* considering the fact that I haven't heard from you in nearly two months!"

"And it appears you wasted no time moving on."

"For all you cared, you selfish ass."

"At least I never had a desire to even *look* at another woman!"

His bullshit self-righteousness was the final straw—I drew my hand back and slapped him hard across the face. My palm wrung with the force of the contact, but he stood statue-like and unflinching, his eyes boring into mine with the twin of my rage.

"How dare you, Jamie. How dare you barge in here after all this time and make insinuations like that. You have *no* right!"

Out of sheer frustration, I pounded his chest with my fist. It was like hitting a wall, completely useless.

All the while, tears were welling up, just below the surface, and I fought them as hard as I fought him.

Finally, growing tired of my thumping, he took hold of my wrists in one large hand and pulled me tight against his body. With masculine savagery, he kissed me, long and hard. It was an access of pure passion, not of affection or desire. Still, with his warm lips on mine, I disintegrated into that kiss, struggling to stay standing on my own two legs, and struggling to find an anchor point between a crush of raging emotions.

My head was swimming with them, and I could not gather my wits. I pulled back slightly and bit his lip, hard enough to taste the tang of blood in the soft flesh of his mouth. His eyes lit with fire, but he released my wrists from his hold.

"You have no claim on me!" I was so upset that I needed to hear myself say it, knowing full well that his claim on me was self-imposed, and that he could easily argue for the opposing side.

But Jamie was not interested in my argument, and even less in making one of his own. He pressed me to him and took my mouth again, deliberate and ruthless, staking his claim in his own way, and making his case, even as I protested.

It was all so bewildering and infuriating and ardent, and I kissed him back hard, matching his passion breath for breath, and staking my own claim while punishing him at the same time.

I wasn't thinking about where we were. I didn't care about my recklessness or what good sense might tell me. I wasn't listening to anything but the demands of my body and his.

I was finally finding an outlet for all the pain and confusion and anger and resentment, and it felt absolutely intoxicating. I reached my hands up into his hair and pulled hard, then raked my nails down his neck and chest as I kissed him deeply.

We were both breathing heavily, struggling concurrently to tear each other apart, even as we pulled each other as close as was physically possible. And in the midst of this insanity, Jamie lifted me to the ledge of the gazebo railing and stepped between my legs, ignoring the kicks and blows I rained down on him.

He let me hurt him, over and over, until finally, I had exhausted my rage.

Only then did he break the kiss. He stared at me with the wild look of a stallion, hesitating only for a moment. But in that moment, something passed from me to him, and he tore at the front of his pants. He was massive—thick and steely, and made ready by so much more than lust alone.

Was it true that there are only two emotions, love and fear?

Jamie pushed aside my clothes and plunged into me with a tortured groan. Was this love? Or was it just the fear of losing me?

With one powerful thrust, he asserted his claim without speaking a word. Then he took my mouth again in the same manor. My mutinous body welcomed his intrusion with no small amount of pleasure, and half-hearted curses and broken sounds were the only objections I could muster.

All around us hung the faint musk of desire as Jamie rutted against me in quick, merciless motion.

I was lost, driven by a compulsion I didn't understand, but felt compelled to obey. I held on to the folds of his shirt, and opened myself to him even as my mind fought his stake on my body.

"You have no right," I said feebly.

I pulled at the buttons of his shirt, tugging him closer as my nails clawed at the smooth skin of his chest, and dug into his vital flesh.

"You have no right to me," I whispered again, as he pounded my body, making my words come out individually through punctured breath. Sweat beaded on his brow and on his chest.

We were locked in a struggle of possession, garnished with frustration and anguish, love and fear. It was love for me, for sure. I pulled him to me and pushed him away, wanting so badly, I hurt with the need. Gripping him viciously with the desire to own him completely, then crumbling in his arms, and melting as if I was made of nothing substantial.

"I know that," he said bitterly, exposing his own torment. He plunged forward with the full weight of his body, and his taught frame stilled as he came copiously inside me.

His heaving breath was at my ear, warm and humid against the crisp night air. I felt his hands flex on the curve of my waist and then relax again to a soft hold.

And then neither of us moved a muscle for a very long time.

This whole night had been too much, a release of emotion so powerful and so overwhelming that I felt absolutely drained. The body, it seems, has its own language, capable of speaking in a voice more demanding than words.

Love or fear?

"Why did you come here?" I managed to ask him. *Please tell me it was for love.*

He exhaled into my hair as though admitting defeat. "I missed you."

I leaned back from the warmth of his neck and chest so I could see his wary face. "If you missed me then why did you stay away?"

"I . . ." He looked at me, distracted momentarily by the sight of the tears I could not contain. Gently wiping one away, he answered quietly, "I guess maybe it's all I know."

Jamie was never anything but honest. And he had the heart of a lion but, by his own admission, he lived in his head too much of the time and he retreated there when he needed to gather himself. It was a songwriter's sanctuary, I knew, but it was hell on a relationship.

"You can't just *do* that," I insisted, straightening my dress. "You can't just come into someone's life and then leave without a word the moment things in your own life get hard. Because people *care* about you—*I* care about you—and it's not fair."

Love or fear?

Jamie examined my face with considerable absorption and then exhaled deeply. "I *know*. I can see that now . . . how much I've hurt you. I never intended that. I just thought . . ." He did up his slacks and rubbed his palm against his forehead. "Well, I just . . . I thought you'd be better off."

"*What?*"

All around us, the night was still, barely a breeze to move the leaves overhead. And it was too late in the season for insects, so the only noise came from the far-off sounds of the city. I sniffled unattractively and quickly dashed away a rogue tear with the back of my hand.

"I *know* when I'm bein' selfish," he said. There was a note of steel now in his voice that told me he had regained his composure in full. "It's not right for me to have you when I can't provide for you."

He might as well have slapped me, for the way those words felt.

"You cannot be serious." But he *was* serious, dead serious, and he met my eyes unblinking. "You have *no right* to make that kind of a decision for me. And furthermore," I said, my ferocity now restored, "I can provide for myself! I don't need someone else for that."

"I know that, as well."

"Does it bother you? Is that the problem here? Are you threatened by my career? Because I need to know that right now."

There was a very traditional side of Jamie that rankled, but he was no chauvinist.

"No, Melody," he said. "I'm not threatened by your career." Then he fixed a determined gaze to mine. "But I want to give you the world, and I don't know how long it will be before I can give you anything at all. Not like these people can. And that isn't right. At the moment, I don't even have a band."

We both fell quiet again but did not take our eyes from each other. He honestly thought all of that mattered.

"Don't cheapen my feelings for you by saying something like that," I told him.

191

He shrugged, half impatient, and shifted his body restlessly in answer—proud, stubborn fool that he was.

"Do you care about me because of my job?"

"You know I don't," he said.

"Well, the same goes for me. And do you *really* think something is going on between me and my boss?"

He exhaled and shook his head, looking out into the night behind me. I watched his tawny eyes sightlessly take in the landscape from end to end. "I guess I didn't like hearing from him that you've been learning to cook. That was a bit of a surprise. As were the wings. They were delicious, by the way. And not burned at all," he added.

One corner of my mouth curled up irrepressibly.

"I cook a lot of meat," I said wryly. "I think you're my muse."

He smiled sweetly, dimples appearing now on both cheeks.

"You're mine too, you know. 'Two Seconds From Now' was written about you. About falling in love with you the first day we met."

For several long moments, we both just looked at each other, measuring the impact of the words he'd just spoken. If I had any thought that his declaring his love for me was an accident, that thought was erased by the look on his face that challenged me to disagree. And if I'd wanted to somehow conceal my love for him, well, that was impossible.

But the truth was, this was the first time we'd ever spoken openly about the word *love* in the context of *us*. It was long overdue. And I guess I felt like if we were going to finally speak of love, I wanted to be touching him when we did.

I reached out and picked up one of his hands, spreading his fingers wide and pairing it with mine. His was much bigger, warm to the touch, and rough with life and labor. I reacquainted myself with every ridge and callus.

"You can't fall in love with someone just because you like her name," I said practically.

"Ummm," he said, shaking his head and watching the movement of my hand against his. "I fell in love with you even before I knew your name."

"Ah. That little rub down I gave you in your living room?"

"Well, *no*," he said with precision. "Although I will admit, that did sweeten the pot a bit."

I gave him a brief and dirty look, and he laughed before touching my cheek with his fingertips.

"No, I fell in love with you the moment I saw you through the window."

From where I'm standing here, we're nothing more than strangers.

But two seconds from now, I'm gonna make you mine forever.

"Love doesn't work that way, Jamie. You can't fall in love with someone you see through a window. You don't know anything about them."

"That's not true. I could see a great many things in you. I knew you were brave and strong because you came to my house, not knowing anyone there. And I knew you were kind because I watched you find something broken, that little pot, and try your best to make it whole again. I could see you had enough joy in your heart that you would leave a little piece of happiness behind for someone else to discover. And I knew you were waiting for someone—" he shrugged his shoulders— "I just hoped I could be the man you were waiting for."

"Jamie." I searched his face, wishing I could see the world as he did. I couldn't—probably never would—but loved that I could see it through him. Gratefully, I leaned my cheek into his chest and wrapped my arms around his waist. "No one has ever seen me the way you do."

"And yet, I've made you cry. Tell me how to make you happy again."

"I don't want to change you, Jamie. I just . . ." God, I looked at him in bewilderment as if he could supply the answer. "I just want you to be different."

A slow, earnest smile spread across his face in answer, though he didn't respond directly. Instead, he gave me the space to compose my thoughts, waiting patiently for me to put words to what I needed from him.

"I thought that being your muse would be like being Van Morrison's brown-eyed girl. I only considered the good things, the romantic things. I didn't realize I would feel so alone at times."

Jamie looked at me as though I'd just broken his heart. He knew something, too, about loneliness.

"I don't mind giving you space when you need it, Jamie—I just wish I had some warning. And I need to hear from you every day in some way, and I need to know that you're coming back to me. And I want to be a part of everything in your life—not just the easy stuff. Because how can I ask you to be there for me if you won't allow me to be there for you? I love you. And I want to be able to tell you that."

He wrapped his hand into my hair and looked at me with a depth of feeling that took my breath away. He was stunningly beautiful in the silhouette of the night sky, formidable and open, with a face that glowed with honesty and vigor.

"I love you, too, Melody, as if we share one heart. And I should have told you that every day because you are the glory and solace of my soul, every single day. If you'll let me love you still, I won't let another day go by without making sure you know it. Not one."

I didn't have to wonder whether he meant it; he always meant it. So I folded into him and let the boundary of my body disappear into his.

Somewhere during our earlier tangle, several buttons of his shirt had come open revealing the livid marks I'd made on his chest and neck. I ran my hand over them, caressing them soothingly in apology. He leaned into my touch as he always did, savoring it, gently cradling my face in his hands.

"I need you," he whispered. "Show me how to be everything you want, because I never want to be anything less."

"I need you too, Jamie." His eyes glistened, and he kissed me again, softly, his lips holding mine like he never wanted to let go. When he told me before he needed me, I hadn't been quite prepared to recognize the same feeling in myself. At that time, it had felt too dangerous—needing a man who came and went from my life without a moment's notice. This time, though, there was no hesitation in answering; the truth, like scratches on skin, is sometimes glaringly obvious. "Just promise me you won't disappear."

"I promise."

His assurance was enough because it was honest, and I knew that. I also knew that I needed his joyfulness and his sense of adventure in my life. And I needed to be the person he saw in me because it was the better version of myself.

He was the *daring* to my *measured*, the *possible* to my *expected*.

I could fight this feeling between us, or I could embrace it.

I decided to embrace.

So, under a blanket of stars and forgiveness, we promised, each in our own way, to make a new way forward together.

Chapter 27

Mel

Only on rare occasions did I wake up before Jamie. I came out of a dream I didn't fully remember just as my bedroom was emerging from the gray light of nighttime into the warm, yellow glow of morning. I was deliciously sore in any number of places, and Jamie was sound asleep in bed next to me.

I got to watch as the dawn touched each of his features in quiet succession. His long, lean, naked body lay on its side with one white pillow under his head and another clutched securely in his arms. There wasn't a single line in his face, except for a slight indentation where his mouth seemed to bend vaguely at the tips in a secret smile. His thick, cinnamon-brown lashes with their dark tips fanned out over his cheek and outlined the soft rise of his cheekbone. He looked as peaceful as a choirboy—well, a very naughty choirboy.

We'd been up half the night talking and touching—his chest, my breasts, his hips, my thighs—and paused several times to remind ourselves how enticingly well all these parts fit together. And finally, in the very early morning hours, we'd curled up in shared warmth to sleep with my back to his front, his hand cupping my breast, and our feet entangled among the rumpled sheets of my bed.

Now, as I watched him rest, with his hair in endearing disarray and his stubbled jaw just barely hanging slack, I had an urge to wake him again, to kiss the seam of his lips in both greeting and invitation, and sink again into the addictive pleasures of the flesh. But I understood myself well enough to know that the urge to have him wasn't just coming from my considerable lust for this man, but from a more basic desire to seek reassurance in the words we'd spoken, now in the full light of day.

I resisted though, barely, knowing how much he needed the rest and how rare it was for him to be sleeping so soundly. The thing I knew about Jamie above all else was that he always meant what he said. He had said he loved me, and I knew in my heart he did.

So instead of waking him, I snuck out of bed and off to the kitchen to see what I could pull together for breakfast.

Atticus, though, was not so considerate. He cared nothing for weekends or sleeping in and had no scruples whatsoever about waking Jamie for a little romping and snuggling in my absence. By the time I returned, Atticus was shamelessly on his back in bed, eyes closed in froglike bliss, as Jamie scratched him from throat to belly.

"Good morning," I said, leaning in to steal a kiss from Jamie's mouth as I disrobed and slipped back in bed with our plates.

"Good morning. God, you're grand. What have you managed, here?"

"Latkes. A glorified potato pancake."

"Mmm." He sliced off a large piece and engulfed it hungrily.

Breakfast was a relatively basic affair consisting of scrambled eggs, latkes and berries—and minus the dog, who grumbled on his way off the bed at my general lack of respect for his equality in the household.

When we finished eating, I gathered the plates and set them on the nightstand beside me. It was Sunday morning, and I could not think of a single thing I wanted to do more than to curl up beside

Jamie and spend the whole day in bed. He echoed my thoughts exactly, wrapping his arm around me and pulling my head down to rest on his inviting chest. His fingers ran again and again through my hair as I rested my cheek in the hollow of his sternum and stroked the many firm ridges of his abdomen.

"When did you start taking your cooking classes?"

Even without seeing his face, I could easily hear in his voice that this was not a simple question to ask. The answer illustrated just how far apart we had drifted.

"A couple of months ago. I didn't tell you at first because my original plan was to surprise you—to have you over for dinner and fix that stew I'd botched so badly the first time. But then . . . well, everything happened."

I could feel his chest rise and fall with each breath, but he didn't say anything for several beats. Then he picked up my hand and squeezed it softly.

"I'm sorry, love."

"It's okay." What else was there to say? The best laid plans . . .

"No, it isn't." With his accent, it sounded like *t'isn't*, and I thought of my crumpled little list. Maybe it could use a few more words.

"But I'm here now," he added with quiet conviction.

Those four words were even better. Almost as good as *I love you*.

"I know," I answered cheerfully. And I did know.

"So tell me your ritual." He said this in a tone that set aside for now all evidence of sorrow and regret. It was a total non sequitur and completely in keeping with his spiral-thinking brain.

"What do you mean?" I lifted my head to see his face.

"Your ritual. For cooking," he said, as if this should make perfect sense to me. It reminded me so much of a conversation we'd had months ago.

Tell me your passion.

And once again, I didn't think I had one. Did *other* people have rituals for cooking? His questions always seemed to throw me for such a loop. I kind of panicked for a minute, scrambling around in my brain for some sort of answer that didn't sound completely lame, and mentally retracing any routines I could possibly think of that even remotely related to cooking.

"Well, I guess I tend to grocery shop on Tuesdays because the sales usually start on Tuesdays, and *forget about* shopping on Saturdays . . . that's just—"

"Melody." He stopped me with a gentle touch. "That's not what I mean." His expression was pleasant and expectant, as if he knew I had an answer to this puzzle, but I was somehow the last one to realize it. "I'm curious to know what is your ritual when you cook?"

And that's when I realized with relief that I *did* have the answer. And true to the dynamic between Jamie and me, he knew it before I did. He had always observed the lawyer side of me with quiet fascination, but the creative side of me he understood perfectly—probably better than I did.

"I start by straightening up the kitchen," I answered with some surprise at the revelation. A full-dimpled smile grew on Jamie's face as if he had expected no less. "I want a fresh space to work with," I asserted now, with more certainty. "I like to have wide open countertops at my disposal because I'm a little messy; I use a lot of pots."

He laughed at that. "I can see it."

I nodded and sat up cross-legged to face him, catching my footing in the conversation and enjoying the intimacy of being able to relate to him on this level. He, too, must have a ritual in his creative process, but it never occurred to me to inquire what it was. "I also enjoy having a glass of wine when I'm cooking in the evening—red or white, doesn't matter—and I always cook with music."

"What kind of music do you choose?"

"I like a mix of happy and sad songs, and I put them on shuffle because I don't want to know what's coming next. Because that's kind of how life is, you know?"

"Indeed it is," he said with a grin. "And do you play it on the stereo or do you use headphones?"

It was funny to me that he would think to ask that question, but actually, I did have a strong preference in that department.

"I bought an iPod; I like listening through the headphones. I think I like to make the world very small during the time I'm cooking, and just focus on what's in my hands and in my head. I find it very cathartic."

"Isolating, do you mean?" he asked directly. "But in a good way."

And there it was, the destination of his spiral thinking that I did not foresee. More importantly, for the very first time I *truly* understood, on more than just an intellectual level, something elemental about Jamie.

"Yes, maybe you're right. Maybe it is a form of isolation."

As I stared at him, almost in wonder, another tiny piece of this complex man fell into place. I'm not saying that understanding his tendency to withdraw from the world made it suddenly okay for him to withdraw from me for long periods of time, but it helped me to feel for myself what it was that sometimes drove him into that place of seclusion.

He watched as the realization rolled through me, and he smiled gratefully in return.

"And what about you? Tell me about your creative process."

"Ah, well, you see," he began, and concurrently pulled me back down beside him where I could lay my head against him and smell the earthiness of his warm skin. "It's probably less of a process than a mindset, I think." And then, looking up at the ceiling in inward thought, he seemed to examine his own rituals. "I cannot say to myself, *I'm going to be creative between two o'clock and four o'clock on Sunday.* I need to be open to it all the time, whenever it comes. Because songwriting is a very mysterious process. It's not something I feel I can control.

"The most creative people I know walk around singing melodies to themselves like nutters. They write everywhere and anywhere, even in public when they're with other people."

"Really?"

"Yeah. I have a hard time getting to that level, myself, because there's always a part of me that says, no, you have to be a social individual. And I do—I can't be so self-absorbed. But if you're really open to your own creativity, it's almost a madness. John Lennon said it's like being possessed."

"Is that why you always carry that notebook?"

"Here, hand it to me. I want to show you something."

I reached over to the nightstand where Jamie's tattered blue notebook and pencil lay beneath the lamp. I was very familiar with that little book—the left back pocket of every pair of jeans he owned had a well-worn outline of it rubbed into the denim. It was his constant companion, though not one I'd ever had a glimpse into. It was almost like a diary for him, and it seemed too personal to intrude upon.

Still, with one arm wrapped around me and the other one free, he opened the book in front of us to a series of pages he'd apparently just written.

"I did this last night, while I watched you sleep."

"It's about me?"

"It's about us. About what we've been through."

On the pages were a series of musical notes and notations, along with a shorthand of words I couldn't make out.

"It was lovely and quiet watching you, and I could hear very clearly what was in my head. When I write, I need to be able to physically experience whatever emotion it is that's inspiring me because feelings are the very currency of songwriting. That's why, though it's often inconvenient, I have to do it when I'm having the intense emotion; I can never remember it in quite the same way."

I ran my fingers over the notes, as though in touching them I might be able to hear what he had written there. I wanted to, so badly. It felt like a secret code for all the thoughts and emotions he had about us—like if I could just crack that code, I'd finally know everything that went on in his brain.

"Will you sing it for me?"

"Not yet. But when it's finished I will."

Of course, I knew he would write songs about our relationship from time to time; that's one of the really weird things about dating a musician—particularly a songwriter, because everything in his life is fodder for his craft. So, ideally, you'll be the inspiration for that beautiful ballad, but you have to know that sometimes he'll sing really personal, hungry songs he wrote at some point about someone else, and sometimes he'll sing angry songs about you. And you have to just roll with it, knowing it's all part of that creativity he expresses through song. In this case, we'd had such a crazy last twelve hours that the notes on his page could be capturing any number of things— some more of a credit to my personality than others.

"Do you usually start with the lyrics or do you start with the melody?"

"It can happen either way, I suppose. I love brilliant lyrics, but for me the real magic is in the melody. The melody dictates the lyrics and ultimately is what captures the feeling I want to express. So usually I'll start there. When I feel like I have it right, I'll take my best shot at the lyrics and then Greg—"

Jamie caught himself midsentence and stopped. After a cautious pause, he cleared his throat and continued, "—Greg will complete the arrangement, and we'll beat up on the words a good bit more before we're done."

I tried my hardest to see his eyes, but he stubbornly wouldn't return the look, choosing instead to focus on the notepad in his hand. His face was very carefully blank, which in itself was his ultimate tell. Jamie was the most transparent person I knew, except when he was very determined not to be.

"Have you talked to Greg?" I asked the question with enough insistence that he would have to acknowledge it.

"No," he said quietly, his lips compressing to a firm line. "I've talked to Nash a few times and sent over some material to look at."

I nodded, my chin on his chest. "What do you think is going to happen?"

He lifted his shoulders and let them drop, kneading the curves of my ass as absently as he might knead handfuls of sand at the beach. "I think we both need time to sort our heads. If we're going to come back, we have to come back with clear hearts."

If was a very big word. It left significant room for any number of outcomes. And I knew this weighed heavily on Jamie's mind because the band was such an integral part of who he was. They were a family, and whether or not he would say it, he was not ready to acknowledge the fact that *if* was not an equal substitute for *when*.

I could see the shadows of doubt cross his face and searched for anything suitable to say. As I did, I happened to notice something I hadn't seen before.

"Jesus, did I do that?"

"What?"

I pushed his jaw to the side, turning his head so I could see him better. And sure enough, there was a red mark stretching from his hairline down his neck.

"This scratch behind your ear!"

He ran a hand carelessly over it. "Could be. I haven't seen it."

He was so nonchalant, but the evidence of my complete loss of control winded me. In the light of day, it was not a particularly proud moment.

"Jamie, I'm so sorry. I've never done *anything* like that. Does it hurt?"

He looked at me as if I'd said something very funny.

"No."

"God, you must think I'm a maniac."

I could not peel my eyes away from that scratch. And the fact that I'd done it in such a mad frenzy was unsettling. I was on the verge of leaping out of bed to find antibiotic cream and bandage him to the hilt. But he pulled his chin out of my grasp and looked at me. Jamie was no stranger to violence; I had always known that. And he had let me do my worst. He had wanted me to exorcize my pain so that we, too, could come back together with clear hearts.

It had worked, but I'd never allow it to happen again.

"Actually," he grinned, "I'm grateful."

"Why on *earth* would you be grateful?"

He laughed. "Well, remember, I've seen what you can do to a man's privates when you're mad, love, and not that I didn't probably deserve it, but I'm grateful you let me slide. All things considered."

"Oh, my god. I *have* done something like that before. I *am* a maniac."

Jamie rolled on top of me and grinned from ear to ear.

"You're only a tiny maniac," he said as he began nibbling at my earlobe and scraping my neck with his teeth. Goose bumps rose over my skin almost immediately. God, he was sexy.

I ran my hands down his back and over the muscular rounds of his ass. Riding a bicycle through San Francisco had given Jamie perhaps the most perfect ass known to man. Atlas, himself, would have been jealous.

"Oh, that's reassuring, thanks."

He pulled back, grinning widely. "I love you, though. Maniac or no."

All around us, sunshine was streaming in through the windows of my bedroom, lighting everything with clarity and hopefulness. And there was absolutely no hesitation in his face as he spoke the words I'd waited to hear.

If there were only two emotions, love and fear, then it had always been love between us.

I pulled his mouth down to mine and held him as close to my heart as I could manage. His body felt tautly alive, and I became aware of a hard, solid warmth growing between us. Jamie began to press himself to me in suggestion, but there was very little suggestion necessary; my own body was so ready to welcome him.

"I love you too," I said breathlessly, wrapping my legs around his waist and enjoying the way it exacerbated the situation between us. "But modifying *maniac* with *tiny* doesn't make it any better."

"But you have *breasts*," he said with total illogic. Then he proceeded to fasten his mouth on my nipple.

"What?"

I had about one shred of rational thought left in my brain and tried very hard to focus it on his line of thinking. But he just shrugged and made a face, now completely uninterested in pursuing any course of discussion involving maniacs. He had moved on to breasts, and he clearly found that subject far more engaging.

Chapter 28

Mel

Shortly before noon, the demands of Jamie's stomach had outrun certain other of his appetites. He climbed out of bed, pulled on his slacks, and left me to stretch out blissfully as he rummaged the kitchen for our lunch.

I could hear him in the refrigerator, opening various things and rejecting them, or in some cases opening things and consuming them on the spot as he prepared the rest of our meal. And he seemed to be giving Atticus a running commentary of his progress, though Atticus was likely much more focused on any slip-up that could result in something landing within his sphere of reach. Atticus followed Jamie around like a shadow, finding him endlessly curious and entertaining.

As for me, I was happy—just simply happy in a way I couldn't have imagined twenty-four hours earlier. I rolled over on my side between the soft white sheets of my bed and stared out at nothing in my room. My pillows smelled like him again; my body smelled like him again. Last night, I'd fallen asleep with his solid weight leaning against me as though reminding me, *but I'm here now.* He was, and that felt right to me. I didn't want to question it or second-guess myself. I was tired of thinking everything through. I was tired of

206

being sad. Instead, I just accepted his return to my life as a gift and coveted it greedily.

Jamie was still banging around in the kitchen when his cell phone began to vibrate on the nightstand next to me. At first, I just tried to ignore it. That wasn't particularly successful. Curiosity quickly got the better of me and I picked it up, noticing the 650 area code on the display. That could be anyone, I assured myself correctly, and put it back down where I found it. It was not right to invade his privacy, though I'll admit there was a little part of me that was *dying* to. Well, *little* may have been an understatement. A month and a half apart will do that.

But I'm here now.

Jamie appeared in the doorway with our lunch, rescuing me from any counterproductive thoughts.

"Your phone rang," I said with as much nonchalance as I could conjure on short notice. "I didn't answer it. I mean . . . of course I wouldn't . . . answer it. Or look. Well, I did look . . . but . . . yeah. Like that."

It was verbal diarrhea. And it just kept coming out. I wanted to stuff a sock in my own mouth, for Pete's sake. Not having one handy, I did my level best to avoid his gaze, busying myself instead by straightening the comforter and hoping he'd be more interested in settling down with his meal than in pursuing the hot mess I was serving up.

He was not.

His mouth twitched at the corners, and his eyes instantly lit with humor as he walked into the room. He didn't say a word, but he was clearly enjoying my discomfiture. Still, his long, teasing look overflowed with love and amusement, and rather than pressing any advantage he may have had in that moment, he simply leaned in and planted a firm and loving kiss on my lips.

Then he picked up the phone from the nightstand and dialed into his voicemail with the mirth in his expression still lingering on his face.

But slowly his face changed, and I watched the humor drain from it like water from a tub. He stilled, and his eyes focused inward on the voice at his ear. The change in his carriage was equally startling.

"What is it?"

"I have to go." He immediately began looking around the room for his shirt.

"Jamie?" I sat up in bed abruptly and reached for his wrist. I could not bear to have him leave me so suddenly and without explanation, not after everything we'd been through, and he knew it.

"It was about my mum." There was no time for more, but the worried look in his eyes was explanation enough.

I nodded quickly, jumping out of bed. "We'll take my car."

§

We shot across the city and down the peninsula in record time. Jamie was preoccupied and silent nearly the entire trip, except for one brief call placed to Killian. The only thing he'd told me was that the message had come from a family neighbor. His parents had had an argument, and it was escalating again. Killian was meeting us at the Callahan's house.

As Jamie drove, I could see a dozen scenarios playing out behind his eyes. Every muscle in his body was tense.

I didn't know a lot about Jamie's family or their relocation to the U.S., only that his uncle had had a plumbing company here in the Bay Area, and that his father had moved the family from Ireland when his uncle became terminally ill. Jamie's father had taken over the business and the small family home in which they lived. The business had at one time been lucrative, and would have continued on reasonably well, but alcoholism and depression sabotaged much of his father's success here in the States, as it had back in Ireland. They got by, but it was never a peaceful existence.

Over time, the family had scattered, leaving Jamie and Cara largely to fend for themselves.

As for Jamie's mother, I knew even less about her. He loved her, that was obvious, but it was a conflicted relationship and he rarely spoke of it.

We exited the 101 Freeway and weaved our way through a very middle-class neighborhood. Most of the houses were non-descript boxes of mid-century construction. They weren't large or fancy, but they all appeared carefully maintained. All except one.

As we approached the house by car, I knew almost instantly that it belonged to the Callahans. If its ill repair wasn't clue enough, the small gathering of neighbors rubbernecking from their lawns was all the confirmation necessary. I also noticed a plumbing van in the driveway, and something about it struck me as odd, but I didn't have time to consider it.

Jamie threw the car in park on the street outside the single-story home and bound up the walkway towards the front door. As I leaped out myself, I could instantly hear the sounds of shouting coming from the open kitchen window.

Jamie wouldn't have had time to notice the looks on the neighbors' faces, and I was glad for that small mercy. A few seemed to have at least *some* compassion for the situation, but most looked towards the house with blatant disdain, as though its occupants had long been the bane of the neighborhood. Jamie had spent many years in this house, among these people, and I wondered how he must have felt as he grew old enough to become aware of their opinions.

Still, my immediate concern was the unfolding drama inside. I ran up the walkway and just through the open door in time to hear a soft, but unquestionably threatening Irish burr.

"Let it go, or you can take it up with me."

A chill crept up my spine at the sound of Jamie's voice, pitched low and tight with anger. I stopped short in the doorway a few feet behind him and could see that his muscular back and shoulders were straight, and clearly stretching to their full height and breadth. His fists were clenched at his sides, and if he heard me come in, he didn't acknowledge it. His focus was laser trained on the man standing in front of him.

That man was Ronan Callahan. The stories Jamie had told me of him had left an impression in my head that was somewhat Stalinesque. To see him in person was sort of a shock. He was so badly weathered that it was impossible to tell his age with any degree of specificity. He'd clearly once been tall and solid like Jamie, though now the muscles had atrophied and his clothes were ill-fitting and shabby. His facial features were sunken behind a bone structure I plainly recognized, and his skin had taken on that unhealthy gray hue of alcoholism.

But the most striking thing about him was his eyes. They were Jamie's eyes exactly, that beautiful, light hazel shade, fringed in long auburn lashes—except where Jamie's eyes were vibrant and warm, these were flat and lifeless. And if he had any affection for his youngest son, there was nothing evident in his countenance to suggest it. It was an odd and disquieting thing to see these two men together, so similar in make and build, and yet they looked like different species entirely.

Ronan's eyes narrowed, and I saw his jaw set tightly, but he didn't move.

"You think you can come into *my* house and tell me somethin' about *my* wife? Get the fuck out before I throw ye out myself."

The cadence of his speech and the clear effort it took to expel the words made it obvious that Jamie's father was intoxicated, and very likely more volatile in that state. Even from my vantage point, I could almost feel the rage radiating from Jamie's body, but he seemed to be consciously aware of the necessity of keeping it under control.

"I'll gladly leave, but I'm takin' her with me."

I watched Ronan's face transform into a malicious toothy expression that could not, by any stretch, be considered a smile, and he glanced briefly to his left.

"She's not going anywhere."

That was the first time I became aware that Jamie's mother was also in the room. I'd been so intent on the tense scene before me, I hadn't noticed her. And it was an effort to peel my gaze from the two men, like the way you feel almost compelled to watch a grenade whose explosion is imminent. But there, sitting straight and stiff at the kitchen table was Fiona Callahan.

My first impression of her was that she was small. She wore a conservative green dress that was aging, but attractive on her. Like Jamie, she had the most gorgeous dark auburn hair, thick and long, I thought, judging by the stylish French twist she was able to achieve with it. What woman wouldn't give anything for hair like that? She wore almost no make-up to bring out her pretty blue eyes. And when she turned, she seemed to be holding a tiny gold cross on a chain around her neck.

"She'll come with me and you'll have nothin' to say about it." Jamie's voice was remarkably calm, but his accent was growing noticeably more pronounced, which I knew to be a sign of his growing vehemence. "Mum?" he said, now addressing his mother firmly, though his gaze remained trained on his father. "Let's go."

Jamie stepped forward and held out a hand, and I thought for a moment Fiona would take it. But before she had a chance to, Ronan startled us all by yanking Fiona out of her chair by her wrist and holding her possessively to him. It was a jarring movement that broke the chain she clutched and caused the twist in her hair to come loose.

"Let her go!" Jamie shouted, as all evidence of calm evaporated in a flash.

His voice was so forceful I flinched at the suddenness of it. A shock of fear gripped every muscle in my body. His fists were clenched tight at his sides and his chest cavity heaved with fury.

As I watched the situation unfold, I had a very strong notion that I shouldn't be here, should not be witnessing something so appalling and so personal to this family. This was a dark part of Jamie's life, one he would never readily acknowledge to outsiders. Still, I would not leave him to face this alone. I thought of the stories he'd told me; there weren't many he'd shared, but they were awful, and just the tip of the iceberg, I was sure. And they would certainly explain how a lonely child could easily grow into an angry young man. To Jamie's overwhelming credit, he had not given in to those feelings, and instead, had turned to music.

Music gave me a voice when I didn't have one. It was my emancipation.

I could see now what music had meant to him. It wasn't a hobby or a fascination; it was a lifeboat. Without it, he might have become any number of things. Suddenly, I understood with absolute clarity why he'd felt the need to turn down the record contract—to preserve his right to say what he wanted to say, or needed to say. Music was his way out of the darkness, and he could not let it be contaminated by the greed of others or the temptation of fame for fame's sake alone.

"Jamie, please, I'm fine. You should go." Fiona would not look Jamie in the eye, nor could she keep the tremor from her voice.

It was then I realized, seeing her on her feet between the two men, that she wasn't small. In fact she was taller than I, with long limbs and a shapely figure. She had the aura of someone small, though, the way she seemed to fold into herself and speak softly.

"You're not fine, Mum! None of this is fine. And you don't have to stay with him. I can take care of you. Please come. *Please.*"

Ronan's hand on her wrist relaxed and a self-satisfied grin crawled onto his face, as she sank back down into the chair. It made me absolutely sick to my stomach. He had Jamie's dimples too, but on him they looked cruel. He didn't speak a word; he didn't have to. Ronan knew Fiona would never go with Jamie.

Jamie knew it also, before she ever shook her head in negation. And I thought, in that moment, that his heart had been broken beyond all repair.

"This is my place," she answered quietly.

"God, Mum."

"Get out of my house." Ronan's voice was sharp and sinister, underscored by his cold, unfeeling eyes.

"What's wrong with you, Da? Have you *no* shame? Do ye feel like more of a man because you can bully a woman? Because you can beat her down to nothin'? Is that what gives ye back your pride? The whole neighborhood is out there talkin' about ye, about what a louse and drunk ye are."

Ronan made a humorless sound that impersonated a laugh, but most certainly wasn't one. "Do ye think I care? About any of 'em?" No, from his tone, it was a matter of complete indifference. "Or about you and your judgment? You who paints up your arm and parades around on stage for money? Singing all your songs about how mistreated ye were as a boy. How your mean ol' da didn't love ye. Have *you* no shame? What kind of a way is that to make a living?"

"An honest one," Jamie answered through clenched teeth. He didn't change expression; the only clue to his emotion was the slow creep of flush that rose on his neck. "But you wouldn't know about that, would you?"

"Ah, there he is, mister high and mighty. Mister so much better than the rest of us. You think you can shame me, boy? You're just like me, Séamus," he said, using the Irish Gaelic form of Jamie's name like an insult. "Not wanting to be tied down, always feelin' restless, lettin' your cock lead ye around like a dog. You think your life will be any different from mine? I tell you what; I'll do ye the favor of tellin' you how it will go. One day, you're happy, screwin' around, making a little coin, thinkin' who the fuck ye are. Next day, ye wake up with seven more mouths to feed and nothin' in your life but responsibility. More than ye can bear. And every day it's more of the same."

Behind the combative demeanor, there was a shadow of disillusionment. And, incredibly, he looked at Jamie almost as though he was seeking understanding.

Then his gaze drifted to Fiona and the flicker of baldness was gone.

"Now, despite everything I done for her, I got a wife that goes about doin' herself up like a common whore," he said, speaking directly to Fiona. "Who is it you're tryin' to impress?"

"I wasn't trying to impress anyone." Fiona dropped her face to her hands, sobbing.

"Then why the whore's hair?" He grabbed her mane sharply in one hand.

"I'll take it out!" she cried, and reached up to begin removing the pins of her twist. But he wouldn't let it go.

"You're right, ye will," he said, tugging her head back brusquely.

Jamie lunged forward, but not fast enough to prevent Ronan's barbaric intent. Ronan pulled a knife from his pocket—popping it open in a blink of metal—and sheared the twist clean off Fiona's head.

For one stunning moment, everything stopped.

It felt as though even time had stopped. Ronan opened his hand, and the gleaming strands of auburn hair, a perfect match for Jamie's own, wafted to the floor. Certain pieces appeared to float, catching the sunlight coming in from the kitchen window in a rainbow of copper and gold. Three jaws hung open; three hearts arrested in shock. And none of us could take our eyes off that twist of hair that now lay lifeless and ruined at Ronan's feet.

Fiona's hands shot to the back of her head in horrified disbelief. Mine covered my mouth in absolute incomprehension. I could not detach my eyes from the jagged, hideous cut of her hair. I shrank back in a sudden wave of nausea.

"There! Next time you think about—"

Jamie's fist hit Ronan's face in a neat, crushing blow, putting an end to his speech. He stumbled back, tripping and crashing into a small side table, and falling hard against the wall behind him. The force of the impact knocked a picture of the Virgin Mary askew on its nail.

Ronan looked stunned for a moment and then wiped a gush of blood from his nose with the back of his sleeve, leaving a dark red streak down his forearm. He seemed to be gathering himself, eyeing the man standing in front of him with cool dispassion.

I could see Jamie in profile, his chest heaving with apparent adrenaline, and his fists clenched at his sides. But his face was stony, the wariness in his eyes frozen into a look as cold as ice.

"Get up," he ordered, with a chilling threat in his voice I hadn't heard before.

Ronan didn't respond but heaved himself up slowly on all fours with the knife still clutched in his left hand. His nose flared with angry breath like a baited bull.

"Please, stop!" Fiona cried, her sobs ragged with terror and dismay.

But there could be no stopping; this was a conflict more than a decade in the making, and I knew in my heart it would be settled here and now.

Jamie took two large strides forward, picked Ronan up by the collar of his shirt, and slammed him into wall with a thud, evacuating the breath from Ronan's lungs. The older man made a thin wheezy noise, attempting to say something that was indiscernible, but clear in its contemptible intent.

"You are a vile man," Jamie breathed, barely an inch from his face. Cold hazel eyes held Jamie's, unblinking and unmoved. And in that space of a breath, Ronan recovered his wind and drove his fist viciously into Jamie's kidney.

Jamie let out a tortured grunt and was forced to let go. He drew back, steadying himself. But he had no more than a second before Ronan found his opening. Shifting on his feet like a boxer, Ronan brandished the knife in his hand.

"Get out of my house."

"Drop the knife."

"Why don't you take it from me?" Ronan goaded.

Jamie had youth and agility on his side—I was eternally grateful for that—but I knew he was hindered by the internal restraint of his conscience. By contrast, Ronan approached the conflict with the same callousness of an anonymous bar fight—as if no blood were shared, no history existed between them, no love at all. I was terrified for Jamie. Not just for the physical outcome, but also for the emotional toll that such a confrontation would have.

Jamie lunged for the knife with startling speed, grabbing Ronan's wrist, and pulling him off balance. Ronan tumbled forward, only regaining his footing as Jamie shoved him back against the couch where he had no leverage.

Jamie knew how to fight.

He squeezed Ronan's wrist so hard I thought it might break, and angled his body in close, so there was no way for Ronan to get enough momentum for a punch. Instead, the two locked together in a struggle of brute force—both grunting, one with effort, the other with pain. And all around us, the room was cast with the smell of sweat and fury.

There was tight strain in both their faces, matching crimson shades highlighted by the shine of perspiration. It went on for several minutes, but the conclusion became more and more obvious. Ronan was no match for Jamie's strength and endurance, his failing body worn away by years of abuse. All at once, he let the knife fall to the floor, clattering across the wooden planks.

"Give up," Jamie growled, finally relaxing his vise grip and letting go of the wrist, but keeping his formidable frame pressed against Ronan's weaker one.

Ronan rubbed the abused limb with his other hand and, for a moment, seemed to acquiesce. But seeing an opening in Jamie's stance, Ronan lunged forward in what appeared to be a final attempt to avenge his pride. He may have realized he would have to accept defeat at the hands of his son, but he would not do it graciously.

For his part, Jamie seemed to have grown tired of the fight. He was the stronger of the two by far and must have known it would be up to him to end this before any real damage was done. He reacted quickly and efficiently, as though he had no stomach for the confrontation. With a decisive blow to the jaw, he knocked Ronan against the wall with a force of impact that dislodged the Virgin Mary from her nail and sent the picture crashing to the floor. Ronan's eyes rolled back in his head, and he slumped to the ground in a loss of consciousness, piled like a heap of dirty laundry on the floor.

The room fell suddenly silent. The only sound was Jamie's labored breath. The reality of what he'd done seemed to hit him squarely, and he hung his head in exhaustion and regret. There were no winners here, no joy in prevailing, and the look on Jamie's face was neither satisfaction nor relief. He'd done what he had to, but he was not proud of it.

Solemnly, he bent to pick the knife up off the floor, folded it closed, and tucked it into his pocket.

It was then I realized I could breathe again. My heart was pounding furiously in my chest, and I ran a shaking hand through my hair as shock and sickness began to drain away. Distantly, I registered the sound of Fiona's high-pitched sobs.

Jamie suddenly noticed it too, and crossed the room in a few long strides to gather her in his arms.

"Ah God, Mum." His large, gentle hand stroked her butchered hair. She collapsed into him, weeping uncontrollably. He held her to him, carrying all her weight, while clumps of auburn hair began to scatter on the floor.

"Shhh. Don't cry. I'll take you somewhere right now, if you like, and we can get this fixed. You're so beautiful, Mum. It doesn't matter."

Tears ran into the corners of my mouth, though I didn't remember starting to cry. I could see the pain expressed in every feature of Jamie's face, and my heart broke for both of them.

Then, he pulled back and looked Fiona directly in the eye.

"But it's time for you to leave this house. I want you to come with me."

Fiona took in a deep ragged breath and wiped her eyes with both hands. Slowly, she turned her head towards Ronan, still crumpled on the floor and unconscious, breathing in ragged, uneven snores. The expression on her stoic face was complicated, the lines of weariness cut deep, and silently she shook her head.

Jamie looked like he'd been punched. "You can't be serious! What does he need to do to ye before you'll leave him?"

"Don't judge me."

"I'm not judging you, Mum. I'm trying to protect you!"

She shook her head and touched the jagged strands that fell

unevenly over her ears and neck. "Like you said, this can be fixed. And he'll be sorry for it when he sobers up." She was clenching her jaw to hold back tears and she would not meet Jamie's gaze. "He will be."

Jamie was stunned and frustrated beyond all measure. "What has he ever done for you?"

"He gave me you," she answered softly, but with resolve. "All of you."

"That's not enough!"

"It is for me." She met Jamie's eyes directly. For a very long moment, they just stood staring, willing the other to understand.

Jamie had no words.

"Whether or not he says it, he needs me. I'm his wife."

"I need you! I need you, Mum."

"Don't make me choose between ye," Fiona said, shaking her head. "You've always been a very independent lad."

Jamie made a sound of exasperation and outrage. "I wasn't *independent*. I was *alone*. With you and Da wrapped up in his madness, and five older brothers who didn't give a *shite* about what happened to me. I had Danny and Cara, was all. I couldn't have anyone else."

"What is that supposed to mean?" Fiona snapped, now directing her anger at Jamie.

"Because of this!" Jamie said, slamming his fist on the table. "This insanity! This is what I bloody grew up with every day of my life. I couldn't very well have friends and bring them into this."

"Well, you seemed to have done just fine, for all that." Fiona looked away, crossing her arms over her body in a gesture of pure defiance.

Jamie's eyes were laser trained on her and his breath was coming fast. "So, that's it? You're staying?"

Ronan began to stir, not quite waking, but showing signs of growing consciousness.

"I think you should go before he comes to. There's been enough trouble for one day."

"Mum, he's no good. Look what he's done to you—not just your hair."

"You don't know him like I do. He loses his head sometimes, I know. But he's never hurt me. He never would. He's just had a hard life and you need to have some respect."

"*Respect?*" Jamie practically choked on the word. "How could *you,* of all people, say such a thing to me? That bastard moved us half way across the world to avoid being arrested for theft."

"He moved us here to help with your uncle's business."

Jamie shook his head in disbelief. "That's a lie. If that was the reason we left, why did we have to change the spelling of our name?"

That's when it clicked about the van in the driveway. 'Callaghan' had been spelled with a g. In the traditional Irish spelling—not the way Jamie spelled his name today.

"He thought it would be more American."

"Another lie you tell yourself. He's been drunk my entire life, and when he's sober enough to stand, he's a brute and a bully. Tell me, now—what is there to respect?"

"You'll not speak that way, Jamie Callahan. He's your father, your flesh and blood."

"*God* help me, I know it."

Just then, Killian burst through the doorway carrying a large blue binder. All eyes swung in his direction, and that's when Fiona seemed to notice me for the first time too. She put her hand on her hair self-consciously and walked away into the kitchen. Killian didn't ask; he could see the carnage on the floor and the look on Jamie's face, full of hopelessness. He crossed the room and handed Jamie the binder, placing a supportive hand on his shoulder.

"Thank you," Jamie whispered, and a glance passed between the two men with a message I didn't understand. I looked from one face to the other, both closed and full of secrets.

Just then, Ronan came to. He opened his eyes and fixed them coolly on Jamie's face. Jamie walked over and knelt in front of him, the mass of his body looming over Ronan like an ominous thundercloud.

"Do you see this, Da?" he said, flipping through pages of the binder in front of Ronan's face. "While I worked for you, I kept my own records of your business—hiring undocumented workers, under reporting your income, substituting inferior parts for the ones you quoted, not pulling permits for certain jobs. It's all here." Ronan's eyes widened, but his expression was otherwise hard as stone. "I don't need to tell you that if you lay one finger on Mum again, I will ruin you. And then I will hurt you." Jamie spoke softly, a cold, hard threat beneath the subtle Irish lilt. "Are we clear?"

The air in the room around us was still. I didn't know how lucid Ronan was at that moment. But he eyed Jamie steadily, and then without uttering a word, nodded once. Finally, Jamie rose to stand dangerously over him, underscoring his point with the sheer size of his frame.

I knew how conflicted Jamie must have felt in that moment. Given all that had happened, I'm sure he wanted some sort of justice. As a woman and a witness to this hideous scene, I certainly did. But as a lawyer, I knew the likelihood of any real jail time from the infractions Jamie mentioned was doubtful, and at the end of it, Ronan and Fiona would be back together, but without their business as a means of an income—a hard life made even harder by their meager circumstance.

And Jamie might have had Ronan arrested for assault, but that wasn't what Fiona wanted, and he didn't want to hurt Fiona beyond what she'd already suffered. If she would not help herself, not get out of the situation or press charges against her husband, then neither Jamie, nor the law could do much for her without her cooperation.

Maybe she loved Ronan, maybe she thought she needed him, or maybe she felt a duty to her marriage. Emotional abuse can be insidious and elusive in that way. And though Jamie was offering a way out—money, a home, support—he couldn't make her take it.

I had to hope Jamie's threat would keep Ronan in check. After all, there was no question in anyone's mind that Jamie meant it. He always meant it.

He looked upon Ronan with contempt, one last time, and then turned on his heel to go.

"Séamus," Ronan said, softly, in a different way than before. Jamie heard the difference too, and stopped, but kept his back turned. "You never went to bed hungry. And ye always had a clean set of clothes to put on."

Jamie's jawline tightened, but his face showed little else. Only his eyes betrayed the deep emotion that threatened just below the surface.

"Was that where you set the bar for yourself, Da?" he answered in the same quiet tone.

Ronan raised his shoulders, and then dropped them in a painfully familiar way. He closed his eyes and leaned his head back against the wall.

"It was more than my da did for me," he said, with an exhaustion that seemed life-long.

Jamie said nothing further and did not turn back. He walked out the front door and was gone.

He knew, and I knew it too, that something in his life had changed irrevocably, and there was no going back.

§

Jamie strode silently back down the walkway towards the cars. The neighbors were all gone by then. It was only mid-afternoon, but it felt like it had been the longest day I could remember. When Killian and I reached the cars, he gave me a quick hug and whispered, "Take care of him," in my ear. I wanted to—god knows I did—but, in truth, I didn't know exactly how.

Jamie was already seated in the driver's seat when I got in. He didn't look at me as I buckled, and he wasn't saying a word. His hands were gripping the steering wheel tightly, causing the muscles and veins in his forearms to stand out even more prominently than usual. His chest was rising and falling rapidly, though his breath was inaudible.

I was at a total loss.

He eased the car into the street and made a turn at the first corner. The look in his eyes was distant and entirely closed off. He was, in that moment, impenetrable. It was as if I didn't exist.

"Jamie?" I said quietly.

But there was no response, no acknowledgement, whatsoever. He just continued to drive. Another turn down another street, more houses.

His breath was still coming rapidly, and now I could faintly hear it. His hands were locked on the wheel, and his eyes were trained on the road in front of him. Another turn.

I looked out the window to people I didn't know, and thought how odd it is that we go through our days, often totally oblivious to the pain being experienced by someone just an arm's length away. Lawns are mowed, groceries are unloaded, children play. And just out of reach, someone's life is coming completely apart.

I felt the car begin to slow, and Jamie eased it over to the side of the road. We weren't anywhere I recognized, just some random house on the verge of a business district. He brought the car to a careful stop, and he put it in park.

For a very long moment, he just sat there like a stone, his eyes focused on his hands in front of him. Then, he let go of the wheel. His breath was now coming in loud pants, and without warning he smashed his fists into the burled wood with a grunt. I jumped at the intensity of it.

A deep red flush developed on his face and he pounded the wheel again, triggering the horn. And then again, and again until his knuckles became bloody and raw. An explosion of sound came from his lungs with each blow, and his expression burned with agony and rage.

I couldn't breathe as I watched the manifestation of his pain, couldn't stop myself from crying, or adequately cover the quiver of my ragged breath. But he didn't seem aware of it.

At last, he stopped and gripped the wheel again with iron fists. He slumped forward in the seat, his forehead bracing against tenderized knuckles, and his whole body began to shake violently. I could hear his inhalations, heavy, like a man struggling against intense emotions.

"Jamie?" I whispered again. "I'm here." I reached my hand out to stroke his head and neck. Tears began pouring down my face, and I just let them come.

Jamie inhaled sharply, and I could see the glitter of moisture under his own closed lids. I could not bear to watch him suffer.

"Jamie." I tugged a little on his neck. I would have done anything to comfort him, anything at all. But he was rigid and unyielding in his seat.

I thought of the band, and how its breakup had driven him into the seclusion of his head. He was physically here now, though it felt like he'd left again—sitting close but, in fact, miles and miles away. I didn't want to lose him, and I didn't want to see him go through this alone.

"Jamie," I said one last time, trying desperately to reach him. I tugged a little harder.

And, suddenly, he gave way.

His large body shifted, and he turned his head blindly towards me and laid it heavily on my shoulder. His arms came around my waist, shaking with the tremors that racked his body. I'd never seen him like this. I immediately pulled him closer and rocked him gently in the warmth and protection of my love.

"I need you, Mel," he whispered roughly, struggling, in a voice I did not recognize. "Don't let me disappear."

His words were so broken I could barely make them out.

But it was then, with stunning clarity, that I finally realized what it was I could give him. All those months ago, I had stood outside a music venue wondering what I had to offer in exchange for the gifts he'd given me: the joy and adventure he'd brought into my life, his perspective on the world that changed the way I saw everything, including myself, for the better. I could give him my love, of course, but I had always believed that, perhaps, there was something more. And just then, I understood exactly what that was.

I could be his shelter; I could be that safe place from where he could make his stand in the world, a place to which he could feel grounded.

After all, everyone needs to know there's somewhere they belong; and, even more, that there's someone they belong *to. That* is the very essence of security, without which, we are adrift.

Jamie experienced things vividly and documented them painstakingly, but it was quite possible he had never really felt a *part* of anything. Maybe until the band. And now, even that was in question for him.

But I could give him a *home.*

Whereas I had always had one, strong and stable, Jamie had lived his life with near constant disruption and chaos. I could see that now, as clear as day. And I could see the toll it had taken on him—how absolutely tired he was. He was a wall of a man, but god, he could break like the rest of us.

I held him close, wrapping myself around him and squeezing his shivering body tightly to mine. I pressed my cheek to his head and willed the strength of my own solid foundation to be enough for the both of us. It would have to be. I would not give him anything less.

I think he knew it. I think he could see it in the way he saw everything else between us.

So there in my arms, in a car on a random street in a suburb of San Francisco, Jamie Callahan went utterly and completely to pieces.

Chapter 29

Mel

"Come sit and let me look at your hands," I said, as we walked back into my apartment.

"They're fine. It's just a scratch."

Jamie shrugged off my concern with a small wave of dismissal and pulled off his shirt as he started down the hallway towards my bathroom. He was bone tired, and in no mood for a fuss. What he wanted was a shower and a hot meal. Still . . .

"Your hands are bleeding. Sit down here and let me clean them."

The raw vehemence in my voice was as much of a surprise to him as it was to me. He stopped and turned back to face me. The truth of the matter was that the whole incident had left me feeling very shaken. In the moment, I was so overwhelmed by the horror of the events as they were unfolding that I was numb. But as time passed, the shock was wearing off and the reality was setting in that Jamie had been on the wrong side of a knife. I could do nothing for him then. Now, I just needed to. I needed to care for him. I needed to feel the warmth of his skin and the life coursing beneath it.

I needed for him to just sit the hell down.

And somehow understanding this in the way he understood so

many things about me, he gave up arguing.

"If you like." He nodded softly, and his face relaxed into a half-rueful smile.

By the time I returned to the living room with medical supplies, he was ready to submit himself to my care. He sat obligingly on the arm of the couch with his legs spread wide and his hands resting on his thighs.

And god, he was stunning, with his vibrant hazel eyes and that rugged, handsome face, and a body that looked like it was carved from stone, with definition around every muscle. Even after months together, I could still be mesmerized by the twist of his powerful torso, and the formidable swell of his biceps and shoulders when he moved. He was beautifully built—every inch of him—and none of it sculpted in a gym. Like everything else he had, his body had been forged from the rigors and the hardship of his everyday life.

Strong as he was, though, he was not impenetrable, and he had the cuts and bruises to prove it. A dozen images of my own fear and helplessness came rushing back to topple my reserves as I caught sight of his injuries. I felt myself begin to break.

He rose to his feet as I collided into his embrace. I let go of everything in my hands so I could just hold him.

I needed this. I needed him.

I pressed my cheek to the smooth skin of his sternum and squeezed my eyes closed to block out everything but the feel and smell of him. He was so vivid to me: warm and alive and earthy. I didn't ever want to let go.

"Shhh, love, don't cry," he whispered as he rocked gently on his feet. "I wasn't in any danger." One hand was around my back tightly, and the other clutched my head firmly to his chest, where his heartbeat was steady and strong.

"I was so scared, Jamie."

"I know. I'm sorry to have put you through it."

I shook my head against his body. "No. I wanted to be there for you. I love you," I whispered, and pressed my lips to him again.

He made a sound of deep contentment and squeezed me a little tighter. "Lord, I know it," he said in a voice uneven with emotion. "I asked the universe for a pony, and by some miracle, it saw fit to send me a unicorn."

§

Jamie was right; the cuts on his hands were superficial. The emotional damage from them, I knew, was not. He sat patiently and still as I wiped them clean with hydrogen peroxide and applied an antibiotic ointment. All the while, his soft eyes never left my face. He seemed to be drinking in every movement, every detail, and every gentle touch between us.

"Does anything else hurt?" I ran my fingertips lightly across the dark bruise that was developing over his kidney.

He shook his head, silently. The day was finally beginning to fade, giving way to a soft pink light that drenched the room in warmth and peacefulness. It was quiet too; there was almost no street noise outside. I picked up one large hand from his thigh and checked the bones again to make sure nothing was broken. He closed it around mine and then intertwined our fingers together. His hand was rough but gentle, engulfing mine completely.

"I'm glad you were there with me today," he said softly.

I could feel his gaze on my face and looked up, into the pale greens and golden browns that made up those amazing eyes. There was just a hint of a dimple on one cheek.

But I'm here now.

"Jamie, why didn't you show your dad the notebook before today?"

And just like that, in the blink of an eye, his face changed entirely.

"I should have," he said with regret, "for my mum's sake."

"No. I didn't mean . . . I wasn't suggesting—"

God, none of this was his fault. I was instantly sorry to have asked the question. It's just that the notebook had clearly made an impression on Ronan, as Jamie must have known it would, and I wondered if revealing it sooner would have eased some of his worry regarding Fiona.

Jamie lifted his other hand to touch my face. "I know you weren't." He took in a deep breath of resignation, and let his shoulders drop again.

"I have five brothers, as you know." I nodded, though I knew very little about them. "Two of them are back in Ireland, and one lives just outside London. I think—I've heard, that is—that one of my brothers is living somewhere on the East Coast, but none of us have talked to him in years. And my other brother, Allen, is in the military. None of us are close, nor are they close to my mum and da. Our family . . . well, you know."

Jamie stroked the side of my thumb with the pad of his own. "We're not much of a family. We never were."

"Jamie," I squeezed his hand in mine.

"Nah, it's just . . . Mad as it sounds—and I *know*, genuine idiocy—" he said directly— "some small part of me always thought that as my da got older, maybe he'd finally want a son."

Jamie shrugged matter-of-factly, though his words were anything but. He paused, gathering his thoughts, and I fought very hard to keep myself from expressing the sympathy that I deeply felt. He wouldn't have wanted it.

"I ended my relationship with him today," he said. "Not that we had much, but . . ." He shook his head in inward reflection. "Our fight—that's just men. But the notebook is a betrayal. He'll hate me for the weakness it gives him." He took a long deep breath and let it go. "That's why I didn't show it to him sooner."

Family is a noble passion, he had said, and not from experience. *Beautiful and noble.*

Over the months, I'd peppered him with silly stories of my family's raucous Christmas Eve dinners and family vacations. He had listened with rapt attention as I told him how, until my brother and I were eighteen, my mom would sneak into our bedrooms as we slept and decorate garishly for our birthdays. I complained about how my mom and dad were strict about curfews and homework and Sunday dinners. All of that must have seemed as foreign to Jamie's experience as today had been to mine.

"I wish I could make things easier for you," I said, meaning it more than he could know.

But he did know, and he smiled sweetly as if I had just said the perfect thing. Dimples graced his cheeks sincerely.

"You *do*, every day."

Then he took my other hand in his and studied it for a long moment. "I never wish my life were easier—" he said finally. "Only that I was better made for it."

That sentiment, I thought, conveyed Jamie to a tee. He didn't spare a thought for blame or negativity or self-pity; he only focused on action. And in doing so, he'd made his life as interesting and as rewarding as possible. That quality in him had called to me so powerfully from the very beginning and I loved it more with each passing day.

"I've always hoped," he continued, "that when the time came, I could be big enough to make allowances for human frailty. I want so much to believe that somewhere deep inside, my parents—both of them—had started out with good intentions; had hearts that were filled with love, but just couldn't quite put down the bottle, or got trapped in this continuous cycle of destructive behavior. Because I can forgive them for that. And, Mel, I want to."

His eyes lifted to mine. I could see he was working hard to bury the darkness inside him once and for all, with a certain degree of gentle compassion for his past—and no interest in going back.

As though speaking the words made them so, he seemed to relax and be at peace. The exhaustion left his face and the muscles of his neck and shoulders released their burdens. A light that had gone out of him for a time, now burned again with remarkable brightness. Jamie was the most resilient person I knew. And I just had this feeling—it wasn't a sage, or anything like that—but looking at him sitting there on the arm of the couch, with a spark in his eyes that made my heart skip a beat, I just knew that everything—everything!—was about to get so much better.

Chapter 30

Jamie

"Oh, Holy God," I said out loud. I'd been flashed many times on stage, but that was distant and impersonal, a blur of faces in the blinding lights. Experiencing it from the proximity of Mel's laptop felt weirdly scandalous. "Someone has just sent us a picture of her—" Well, the word that came to mind wasn't an actual word, but eight-year-old me always felt it should have been.

This whole MySpace thing had the potential to be a bit unwieldy, in my opinion. But I was fascinated by it, nonetheless. Not by its capability for sending mounds of flesh to an unsuspecting Irishman, but by the sheer fact that it bypassed so many roadblocks that artists faced today—being heard, developing a following, just getting your name out there. And the comments—the direct dialog with fans was intriguing. It was such a personal connection, and one that was very different from what we experienced on stage; this was one-to-one. And for that very reason, I had the sense that "social media," as it was being called, could soon become something very powerful.

I sat at Mel's kitchen table in my sweats, fresh from a shower after work while she and Hope circled around me, recreating another recipe from their class. I enjoyed these nights, actually. Loved the hum of activity and laughter, the aroma that filled the apartment, and the sheer domesticity of it all. More than anything, I loved the feeling of being tethered to something I didn't want to leave in the first place.

Hope set down the spoon from a pot of marinara she was stirring, and leaned over my shoulder, squinting at the screen. The tips of her white-blonde hair tickled my forearm. "Is that a banana between her boobs?"

I looked at her lightly freckled face in horror, and then back at the screen. I think she may have been right. *Holy God.*

"Huh." Mel came over to stand on the other side of my chair, a dishtowel slung over her shoulder, and put her soft hand on my neck. I relaxed into the sudden warmth of it and couldn't help staring at her flawless features and supple skin. She was so unbearably lovely.

She tilted her head to one side, all the while stroking me with her thumb. "You kind of have to admire the composition, though. Do you think she took that herself?" Mel looked down at her own endowments. "I don't think I could get the banana to stay."

Hope was in agreement. "Well, Irish, that is one hell of a proposition." She patted my shoulder and turned to head back to the stove.

"I'll *pass*," I said to the screen, and promptly hit delete. Personally, I didn't think the composition was particularly inspired, either.

Mel stepped away to address the pile of pots they had used, leaving me to miss her hands almost immediately. So much so that I pushed back from my chair and went to stand directly behind her, pulling her hips to mine. She was tiny, but she had the most astonishing curves.

I could feel her smile, even without seeing it, and leaned forward to press my lips to her elegant neck.

"I'm more than happy to let you practice with my banana," I whispered against her skin. "I might even moan a little to encourage you."

"How very selfless of you, frontman," she laughed, and turned in my hands to face me. Her shapely breasts crushed against my chest and I reached down to cup her arse, which fit nearly perfectly in my palms. She was grinning widely, matching my expression exactly. I took a moment to just stare at her lips, ample and slightly moist. Red.

Quite suddenly, I was taken back in memory to another evening in this very kitchen. Right here in this exact spot, I realized. And for a moment, I saw her again on her knees, her small hand wrapped around my base where she worked me with that succulent mouth. I could picture my fist tangled in her hair as I braced myself against the counter and let go for all it was worth, shouting my release.

Just looking at her lips tonight, I felt that same shiver rack my body as it did when she slid me spent from her mouth.

My cock was immediately engaged in the memory, aching to be back there, skimming over her velvet tongue. Every muscle in my lower stomach contracted tightly, and the smile slipped away as my breath accelerated with my heart rate.

She was my undoing.

When I met her eyes again, I found her watching me, serious now. And her cheeks were flushed, too, as if she was thinking of the very same thing.

I swallowed hard, flicking a glance at Hope, who still had her back turned and was adding salt to the marinara. Mel looked over as well, and then pressed her palm firmly against my erection. I closed my eyes and exhaled a jagged breath.

Admittedly, it didn't take a lot for her to rouse me, but when she reached up, pulling my mouth to hers, and I felt her wet tongue against mine, I nearly lost it all. I squeezed her arse and ground myself into her hand. The relief was—

Hope cleared her throat conspicuously. "Uh, single girl here—wondering when it's going to be safe to turn around."

Oh sweet Mary, mother of God; the relief was not nearly enough, and the timing was complete shite. To make matters worse, I looked like I was smuggling a telephone pole in my pants. I laughed against Mel's lips.

"The Irish aren't ones to rush, Hope." I rubbed the back of my neck in physical frustration. "We're passionate about everything: ale, music, women, life—pretty much anything that involves having fun, having an orgasm, or having no recollection of the previous twenty-four hours." I glanced in her direction. "Had you not heard that?"

"It's so true!" Mel agreed lightheartedly. She gave my resentful cock one last squeeze before releasing me to sit back down at the table where I could conceal its tender state. "It makes us passion-less people feel a little lacking."

She went to the fridge, grabbed three beers, and kicked the door closed with her foot.

"What is that supposed to mean?" Hope was facing us now, spoon in hand, and her question came out in precisely the incredulous tone I was hearing in my own head. It seemed to take Mel by surprise.

"No, I'm not being self-deprecating," she tried to clarify. "I just mean that I've never really had a *thing* like Jamie does. He has like a *million* passions."

She looked to me as if for help in explaining this.

"I disagree," I said, not offering any help, whatsoever. "I think you *do* have a passion."

Mel shot me a level glance. "If you're about to say I have a passion for musicians, I will end you." Then pointing at Hope, she added, "You, too."

Hope laughed, but actually, Mel wasn't far off, in my mind.

"Not musicians, precisely, but music." I crossed my arms over my chest and leaned back in my chair, feeling the blood return to my head where it could be of more use for this conversation. "I think you have a passion for music. I think you always have. That's where the fascination with musicians comes from."

"Well, sure, I love music, but I have no talent for it."

"For creating it, perhaps," I responded directly. "But you have a passion for listening, for understanding the artistry behind it, for the instruments, for the culture. By your own admission, you're a great admirer of music and musicians."

"That may be true but—"

"I think you'd make a smashing band manager."

My interruption derailed her objection and she paused, examining me. If she was expecting to see any hint of a jest in my face, she found none. I was absolutely serious.

"You can't just become a band manager, Jamie. That's a huge job. It requires a lot of expertise."

"True. Managing a band is very much about making connections, which you don't yet have. But it's mostly about steering artists through the process of negotiating recording and publishing contracts, supporting them through record development process, and helping them to make smart career decisions. I think you'd be fantastic."

She shifted a little in her stance, serious, and still holding the beer. I saw her glance at Hope, who wasn't laughing either.

"But you'd need to start with something like a road manager first," I continued, when I felt she was listening to me again. "Learn the ropes, make contacts."

"Still, aren't most road managers also sound engineers?"

"The fact that you know that is exactly what I'm talking about."

"I dated some musicians, as we well know," Mel said with her perfect blend of sarcasm and irony.

"And you paid attention because it interests you. There's no job training for road managers; most of them get their start from just being in a band. And yes, some road managers also have technical skills, but they don't have to. You have legal and business expertise that's every bit as valuable. And mostly, a road manager's job is to know the venues, take care of logistics, make sure the contractual riders are met, and that the artists and crew are paid on time. You did all that for us when we went up to Washington State. You were *brilliant* at it. And you loved it."

She blinked at me, absorbing the case I had laid out for her. She did love it, and I could see in her face that she was looking for a reason to disagree but couldn't come up with one.

"Well, who *wouldn't?*" she asked earnestly.

"I wouldn't," Hope answered. And she was right. Touring was not for everyone. It's a nomadic existence, with long hours, and far removed from the normal rhythms of life. But if you have a passion for music, it's a front row seat; and it's different and exciting every day.

"Jamie's right," Hope continued. "You wouldn't shut up about it. I think you'd be *smashing* also." Hope turned to me with a sassy grin on the word "smashing." Why did Americans think that word was so funny? It's a lovely word.

"My parents would *shit* if I gave up a career in law."

"You wouldn't be giving it up," I pointed out, "just using it in a different way."

"Besides," Hope said. "This is your *life*, Mel. You don't live it for someone else. If you think for a minute it's going to get easier as you get older to change course and do something you love, you're wrong."

I could see the chaos in my lovely Mel's eyes, as she processed the challenge that Hope and I laid down before her. She'd long carried the career expectations of well-meaning friends and family, but what of her own expectations? What did *she* want? That was the question.

Hope removed two of the bottles from Mel's hand and opened

them, offering one to me. Mel looked at the remaining bottle without really seeing it and picked up the opener.

"Well, it doesn't matter. No one would hire me. I don't have any experience."

"I would," I said, holding her gaze unblinking. "I would hire you."

In an instant, the room fell completely silent, even the city seemed to pause and listen. Mel's eyes locked on mine.

And then, from somewhere out in the universe came the sound of a click, as the best of what we were together dropped definitively into place.

No one could've blamed Mel for making light of my offer. No one needed to remind her of my circumstance. But those thoughts were not at all what I saw in her exquisite face. The opposite, actually. She had absolute faith in me that I would one day be in a position to follow through on that promise, even though I had no means to do it today. And I had absolute faith in her that she could apply an extraordinary skillset to a career path she was truly suited for, even though making such a drastic change would require a tremendous amount of courage.

That's what passed between us as the world fell away, leaving only the sound of two hearts sharing a measure of time. And then, slowly, I could see her imagining a different life for herself; one she hadn't even considered, but one I knew she would be madly passionate about.

A life in music.

A life with me.

Chapter 31

Mel

Sometimes the greatest milestones are met with the smallest amount of fanfare, but their effects are often the most enduring. In the weeks that followed the incident at Jamie's parents' house, I held him as close to me as I could. I wanted to show him that he could have the time he needed in his head to write music, and think, and process everything. But he didn't have to isolate himself completely, as he'd always done in the past.

He had asked me not to let him disappear, and I answered.

For Jamie, giving himself over to another's care was an enormous act of faith. And though we didn't make a big deal of it, every night that he showed up at my doorstep after work—ready to talk or listen or just hang out—the trust left me almost speechless.

It was a joy for me, too, spending so much unstructured time together. Jamie put his passions at the heart of everything he did—not under the heading of *someday* or *if only*. He well understood the necessity of working jobs you didn't enjoy, but he couldn't fathom the idea of making a career out of anything you didn't love. He was my inspiration.

Sometimes, he would let me help him with song lyrics, though I had nowhere near his ability to conjure a complex image with just a few words. Still, every once in a while, I'd stumble upon just the thing he was looking for and I was ridiculously proud of my contribution. When he wrote about me, though, it was different. He wouldn't let me help. He told me that those words came from his soul, and he needed to say them in exactly the way they felt to him.

I melted for that. *Melted.*

I also noticed he spent a lot of time on MySpace and realized one day that he had begun posting acoustic versions of things he was writing on Cadence's page. Their following was becoming enormous, despite the break in touring. And it was driven primarily by Jamie's active cultivation of Cadence's online presence. This was fueling an enthusiastic and ongoing dialog between fans, rave reviews for their music, and many, many questions about their next performance. Jamie said the feedback helped him to shape certain parts of a song and let him know if he was onto something worthwhile.

But I didn't think that was the whole story.

I knew Greg had begun posting things on their page too. And I thought that maybe Jamie was holding out an olive branch. Or perhaps leaving a trail of breadcrumbs, so that one day soon . . .

Chapter 32

Mel

"Show me what you were working on," I asked him one Sunday after finishing some notes on a brief. I shut the lid on my laptop and set it on the coffee table.

Jamie hesitated for just a second, then picked up the Gibson that was sitting on the floor next to his chair. He positioned it across his lap and began to work out a bright, complex melody. Each time he played it he changed it in some way, though the essential chords remained the same. Sometimes, he changed the key, sometimes he added embellishments, but he played it over and over and over until the progression sounded exactly right to him.

Occasionally, he'd pull a pencil from behind his ear and make a note or two, but mostly, the work was occurring from memory and from some mysterious creative reserve. It was amazing to me how fast he became fully absorbed in the process. In fact, I wondered for a moment if he'd forgotten I was there, so focused was he inward. His brows pulled together slightly and his eyes were listening, rather than seeing. It was fascinating.

I watched his fingers move nimbly, finding exactly the chords and strings he wanted without any thought to their placement, as if the work—the fretting, the muting of strings and so forth—just got out of the way to make room for his creativity. With his guitar, he was able to achieve a sound that was so precise, with such a beautiful vibrato, that it really sounded like a human voice; like a very distinct, signature voice.

I was thinking about all this when my buzzer rang.

Jamie glanced up in question, his attention suddenly back in the room with me. We weren't expecting anyone that I could think of.

I got up from the couch and pushed the button on the intercom. What came back through the speaker was a rapid-fire set of words, spoken with scarcely a fraction of a second between them.

"Melit'sgregiwaslookingforjamie."

Jamie snapped to attention, instantaneously decoding their meaning like a complicated foreign language. For me, it took a few seconds longer to register that Greg Van de Meer was at my door.

Jamie was already on his feet by the time I made the connection, and he nodded quickly for me to answer. I have to admit, I was nervous, myself, for this reunion, and more so at the sight of Jamie. He looked so earnest, with mixed feelings of hope and apprehension written all over his handsome face. I don't think I had any inkling until this very moment of just how much he'd missed Greg—missed his band—in the many weeks they'd spent apart. But he was the most openly expressive person I knew, and as he stood listening to Greg's footsteps climbing the stairwell, I could see he was overjoyed.

A smile burst across his face as soon as Greg stepped through the doorway.

They paused for just a moment, finding each other in sight. And then Jamie took two large paces forward and surrounded Greg in a tight embrace. There was a lot of hearty back thumping and manly sounds of pleasure. Finally, the two broke apart.

Greg quickly wiped a tear from his face, and Jamie tactfully looked away as though he hadn't seen it. That was the tacit agreement men had with each other.

"I'm . . . ah . . . sorry to barge in," Greg started to say, clearing his throat.

"Not at all," both Jamie and I answered in chorus, though Jamie's voice was thicker and less composed.

Greg didn't seem to notice. Or maybe he did. Men.

He ran a hand through his unruly hair, and then placed them both carefully on his hips. I thought I saw them tremble. Then his blue eyes came to rest on Jamie's hazel ones, and he appeared to find his center.

"I've been working on that new song you wrote, 'Yours,'" he blurted, like it was a race to get the words out. "And I like it, it's really good, but I think it needs something."

I didn't know if he was waiting for Jamie to acknowledge this, but for his part, Jamie seemed to have gone completely mute, so Greg barreled on.

"Well, see, I thought maybe we could rewrite it for the piano. You know, make it feel a little more personal, and add kind of a build up at the front. What do you think?"

The look he gave Jamie was nothing short of hopeful. Jamie was stunned, nodding and blinking like a bobble head, but at last managed to push out an answer. "I could see that," he said, roughly. "Definitely."

Greg face lit up with pleasure. "And I was also thinking it could use a coda before the last verse, to give it a little variation. I've been working on a couple of ideas."

"Yeah?" Jamie was now glowing in his own right. "That's brilliant."

"Okay. I just wanted to check."

I just wanted to make sure we were still a band, I thought he was actually saying. Greg had never been very predictable for me. He was the most introverted and the hardest to read. But the one thing I knew for sure about him was that he was extremely loyal. He loved Jamie more than anything in the world and you had to love him for it.

Greg looked down at his hands self-consciously, as though, having concluded his stated business, he wasn't sure what to do next. He didn't seem to have a plan beyond this point in the conversation.

"How have you been?" Jamie asked gently, understanding instinctively what was needed.

"Good." That seemed like an overstatement, if he was even half as invested in the band as Jamie, and I knew he was.

But with every passing minute, he appeared to relax a little more, to grow a little more comfortable in the circumstance. Finally, he took a deep breath and exhaled, pushing his hands into the pockets of his jeans. "Been working a lot. I've missed you guys," he added with surprising candor. "You know, playing together and . . . hanging out and shit."

That seemed to strike Jamie hard. But before he could answer, Greg cut in.

"Derek White called me yesterday."

"Oh, yeah?"

"He said they're doing a show at The Fillmore next weekend and one of the bands in the line-up had to drop out. The lead singer's got nodules on his vocal cords or some shit like that." He looked at Jamie questioningly and with such acute vulnerability. "He wanted to know if we might want to step in."

"Fuck, yeah!" Jamie affirmed without hesitation, and shoved his own hands deep into his pockets, exposing a tempting line of taught skin just below the hem of his T-shirt.

"Yeah?" Greg's eyebrows shot up comically on his forehead, and a medley of emotion careened across his face. "Okay. I'll let him know. I told him I would talk to you."

Though both men seemed determined to contain their joy under the thin veil of male bravado, it radiated from them, nonetheless.

"We'regonnaneedtorehearse," Greg said in one long, happy syllable. "Weprobablysoundlikeshit."

"I'm sure we do." Jamie nodded eagerly, as though he hadn't just agreed that they probably sounded like shit. "And I want to hear what you came up with for 'Yours.' I've been feeling like it could be better, but I didn't know how to fix it."

"Yeah, okay. I'm free tonight, even," Greg shrugged, feigning nonchalance. "I just have to photograph an apartment in North Beach first."

"Want to meet at Nash's flat at seven?"

"Yeah." Greg smiled, turquoise eyes shining brightly. "Good plan."

And then neither of them said anything. I watched them just stare at each other awkwardly, as if they both had to fart and neither wanted to be the first to let it out.

"You know, I hear Nash wants your arse off his couch," Jamie told him.

Greg laughed wryly, rubbing his dark goatee in what I had come to know was an unconscious habit. "I'm sure you're right."

"Maybe it's time you came back to our place."

There was a long pause, so full of unspoken sentiment. I had nothing to do with this conversation, yet even *my* heart was practically ramming itself into my throat.

"Maybe so," Greg answered softly, setting the butterflies in my stomach free at last. He looked at Jamie with so much love it spilled from him, genuine and unrestrained. "Good to see you, brother." Then he smiled shyly and turned to leave.

Jamie halted him by placing a hand on his shoulder and squeezing gently. He returned the affection in Greg's eyes in equal measure. "Good to see you too, my brother."

Chapter 33

Mel

Magic. It was high on my list of favorite words that Jamie says, and it was the very best way to describe Cadence's return to the stage. And what better stage to make that return than The Fillmore? It was a magical place, after all—a cornerstone of the San Francisco music scene, richly steeped in music history. Many, many great bands had played here; many incredible performances had taken place here.

The standing room-only venue was filled to its capacity of about thirteen hundred people, and though the band had only signed on to do the show a week in advance, the number of Cadence fans in attendance was astounding. Everywhere I looked, people were holding up signs for the band and wearing those cheesy Cadence T-shirts.

One such person happened to be an insanely good-looking megafan with strawberry-blond hair and intense green eyes.

"Danny! I didn't know you were coming," I shouted over the backstage changeover as Danny snuck up on me from behind. "Does he know you're here?"

"Yeah." Danny beamed with his broad smile. "I just surprised him. I couldn't miss this."

To look at Danny, it would be easy to get distracted by his outward attributes and not see the substantive person beneath. I had the sense that, in some ways, he counted on that. Almost like camouflage. He wasn't shy, but he was harder to get to know on a real level. He and Jamie shared a bond I didn't think either of them shared with many others. I knew for a fact that Jamie kept a pretty tight circle of friendships. Still, the ones he had were extraordinary.

§

Right from the start, the stage lit up with a sound that was so distinctly Cadence, and the crowd erupted in a roar, unlike any I'd heard. It was both fearsome and exhilarating. In a monumental crush, the entire audience seemed to press forward, pushing against the barriers, closing every inch of available space between them. I'd never seen anything like it. The front row was reaching as far onto the stage as they could, shouting pleas for drumsticks or guitar picks. Male and female alike, they were frothy with excitement.

Weeks' worth of tensions dissolved in an instant, and nothing in the band's recent past could dull the glory of being onstage for the better part of that hour. They seemed to rejoice in their reunion, knowing exactly what it was they had missed.

Beach balls began popping up from the crowd, painted with the band's name in glow-in-the-dark letters. They were tossed about in a sea of outstretched arms, a joyful, mirror image of the emotion flowing on stage.

It felt as though the whole room was suspended in a reverie of music and light, and together the band became something even greater than the collection of extraordinary artists they were. It was very much the way a group of carbon atoms under the right circumstance becomes a diamond.

That was Cadence, live at The Fillmore.

And I realized, for the very first time since I met Jamie, when I watched him on stage, *all* I felt was pride. Wild, ferocious, crazy pride. Gone was the fear, gone was the envy, and gone was any insecurity about being able to hold him.

Because, although I loved this part of him fiercely, I could readily share it knowing that I alone was privileged to see the other side. And I alone was trusted to keep it safe.

He had taught me so much about myself, given me gifts of faith and confidence I could never repay. He'd shown me the world through a different lens and helped me to celebrate every aspect of who I was.

I smiled to myself . . . or maybe not so much to myself because Danny elbowed me. "What?" he mouthed.

"I'm just happy," I yelled back into his ear.

He grinned, put his arm around my shoulder, and kissed the top of the head. Yes, he would be a great friend to have.

§

It was almost eerie the way Jamie echoed my thoughts.

The band was nearing the end of its set, when they finished the song they were playing and Jamie began, once again, to chat with the crowd. The band waited patiently, keeping up a steady, quiet beat.

"So, I have a question for you," he mugged as he strode across the stage, prompting wild cheering from all sides. "I wondered if you'd mind if we played a new song tonight?" he asked, as if he needed to. "It's *kind* of a love song." The crowd roared enthusiastically, and he laughed into the mic.

"Now," he paused dramatically to the soft sound of Nash's cymbals, "how many of you would say you're in love *right now*? Show of hands." Jamie put up his own hand expectantly, and then more shot up from all over the venue. He seemed to be counting them.

"I love you, Jamie!" shouted someone from the audience.

"Ah, you make me blush," he mugged to the roaring crowd, shamelessly employing his dimples. "But now you've gone and banjaxed my count."

Killian snarled on the guitar. More cheering followed, and various calls, inexplicably, for Jamie to remove his shirt or to play "Free Bird."

"No matter. We'll go ahead and play the new song, anyway. And if you like it, maybe you could clap a little at the end. Make us feel good. All right?" he asked, still smiling. "It's settled."

Then, to my surprise, he turned to the balcony, and spoke to me as though the room was suddenly empty, save for the two of us. "This one's for you, Mel."

The audience was still cheering as Jamie sat down at the piano. He adjusted the mic to his preference as the music from the band came to a close, and then began to play.

Jamie had often said that the magic of a song was in its melody. This one was simply gorgeous. It was passionate and aching, and I wished I could have seen his hands as he played. From my vantage point, I could only see the way he leaned into the instrument and the movement of his shoulders as he reached for the keys.

It started out slowly, and as I listened, my mind flashed to the scribbles in his notebook. Was this the tune he'd heard in his head while he watched me sleep? Were these the notations I could touch with my fingertips, but not yet understand? Suddenly, the room seemed very small to me, like we were back in his apartment, sitting shoulder to shoulder as he delivered a piece from memory.

As with every song he sung, the emotion flowed through him like a river. He glided effortlessly from that soft baritone that called to me, to his beautiful, clear falsetto. He was positioned to face me, with the expanse of the instrument between us. And as he played, he looked up in the balcony and sang the words he'd said came directly from his soul.

§

Stolen is the kiss, angel, you've lifted from my lips
Stolen is the fight I loathed, wiped clean from my fists
Gone may be the lock you shattered when you pried it from my door
Makes no difference, we both know I'm captive as never before

Because you alone know something the rest would never see
You alone had faith that there was so much more to me
More than just the lonely fading of footsteps on the floor
More than just the hollow echo in darkness, closing a door

I'd listened far too long to the man who bears my face
Listened to every doubt I'd had that I could make a place
But you wouldn't let me turn away from what I'm meant to be
I point to you; you're my proof I'm what you've seen in me

Now the sound effects of my leaving you are receding into memory
In the aftereffects of your loving me, you've torn away my boundaries
And still I'm more than all these things, my love. So much more
The best of what I am, my love, is yours. I'm yours
Can't think of anything I'd rather be than yours

Chapter 34

Mel

Cadence's job was done. They finished the set with a rousing rendition of "False," as they often did, and walked off the stage to the crowd's deafening approval.

Greg and Nash planned to take the van and drop the equipment at Nash's place, and then meet the rest of us at an all-night breakfast place nearby. Killian and Jamie were signing a few T-shirts and CDs by the side of the stage.

"Jamie looks the happiest I've seen him in a long time," Danny said to me as we waited for them to finish.

"Being back together with the band has been really good for him."

"That's part of it," he agreed. But he paused, still looking at me, and there seemed to be something more on his mind. "Did he ever tell you how we met?"

"Only that you were nine."

"That's right," Danny nodded. "I was at school on a Saturday, shooting hoops on the playground, when I heard this kid shouting the worst obscenities I'd ever heard in my life. I didn't even know what half of them meant. Later I realized he'd made up a lot of the words, but I'm telling you, he was convincing."

I laughed. "Why was he yelling?"

He shrugged. "Some kids had taken his guitar and they were fucking around with it. He was so pissed. But there were three of them, and it wasn't exactly an even fight."

"So you stepped in?"

"We were *nine*," Danny said, brushing off any overstatement. "But yes, I was always big for my age, and my uncle had taught me a few things. Truthfully, though, I think Jamie would've fought to his last breath for that guitar. It was this beat-up old piece of junk, but you could tell it was really important to him."

"From what I know, it was probably everything to him."

"Yeah," he said, holding my gaze for several counts. "Anyway, I'll spare you the details but needless to say, we went home with the guitar, and we've had each other's backs ever since." His angular jaw set firmly, and for a moment he fell quiet. "Mel, it killed me not to be here for him when all this was going down. The only thing that made it easier was that I knew you were here."

"I love him, Danny."

"I know. So does he." Danny nodded his chin in Jamie's direction. "Just look at him."

Jamie stood about twenty feet away, arms crossed over his chest, and he was laughing with Killian and Derek White. He was nearly impossible to overlook in a room on a normal day, but Danny was right, tonight his glowing, vigorous presence felt disproportionately large. He was happy—and the emotion fell from his body like glitter in the air. It was an effort just to tear my eyes away.

"So, what's next for you after graduation?" I asked him.

"I just put in my application for the master's program at Stanford. It looks pretty promising."

"Wow! Danny, that's great. You could be back on the West Coast this fall."

"Yeah. Keep your fingers crossed. I'm pretty excited."

"God, your parents must be so proud of you."

Juvenile as the words sounded, they were a revelation. Clearly, they illustrated my point of reference, having grown up in an environment of unconditional support. And as I considered the possibility of my own major life change, I realized that external obligations weren't holding me back.

I was holding me back.

Yes, my parents had invested in my education, but they had done so for the same reason most parents do: because education enables choices, provides opportunity, creates empowerment. Their intention was never that I be limited to a career I didn't love.

No, any restrictions I felt were of my own creation, born of fear, and I had to either break them, or own them.

But just as I was coming to understand this about *my* circumstance, Danny laughed in a way that made me question his.

He shrugged circumspectly. "That's another story for another time."

He didn't elaborate. Instead, he quickly glanced away, his hooded green eyes seeking distance and privacy. And in honor of the friendship that was beginning to grow between us, I did him the courtesy of letting it go.

§

Jamie finished packing up the Cadence merchandise and strode in our direction. When he was within earshot, Danny turned to me with a wry smile.

"So, apart from the whole sensitive songwriter thing, one of these days you'll have to tell me why in the hell you chose *this guy* over me?"

"It's quite simple, mate," Jamie answered easily as we started for the exit. "She gave me a little rub down at the barbecue and found I was packing more than a banana slug."

At the first chance I got, I was going to kill Jamie.

I had no idea what a banana slug had to do with anything, but Danny's gaze snapped to mine, and he assessed my face with his trademark intensity.

It was a supreme effort to meet that look with a poker face worthy of his scrutiny. Then, he smiled widely with perfect, supermodel teeth.

"Yeah, sure she did."

Jamie, too, was grinning like the idiot he was, as he held the door open that led onto Geary Street.

"I'll tell you this much, mate—I wasn't talking to her about *leeks*."

Danny shook his head, laughing. "Noted."

The corner of Geary and Fillmore was a busy place at nearly any time of the day, and the noise of the nighttime traffic assailed us the minute we stepped outside. Buses passed in a near constant flow, and the activity around the Kabuki Theater in Japantown, which was just across the street, gave one the feeling that this part of the city never slept.

"Jamie?"

A young girl was waiting for us by the entrance of The Fillmore. She could not have been more than fifteen years old—tall and lanky with curly brown hair and braces. She looked painfully nervous.

Jamie recognized it too, and smiled encouragingly, shifting the black duffel bag on his shoulder as he paused to return the greeting.

"Hi. I was . . . I was wondering—"

"What's your name?" he asked kindly.

"Eliza."

"Pleased to meet you, Eliza. Would you like me to sign something?"

It wasn't hard to see that she did. She was holding a Sharpie, a little notebook, two of Cadence's self-produced CDs, and two band T-shirts.

"Could you sign this?" She fumbled with the mass of items and finally handed him a pen and the notebook. He signed it with a flourish and handed it back.

"And these too?" Next came both CDs and T-shirts.

Jamie laughed. "I think you may be my biggest fan."

"My friend and I have been following you for a while on MySpace. That's actually how we found out about you."

"Really?" Jamie asked, and not in an idle way.

"Yeah." Her confidence was growing. "You guys have been posting a lot of music. And you and Greg always respond to my questions."

The expression that came over Jamie's face was one of pure fascination. MySpace was a curious thing for him. He'd been engaging in it much like a science experiment—unsure of the outcome, or even the merits of the process, but possessing enough conviction in his hypothesis to give it an earnest try.

"Well, I'm glad to know it's been useful for you. It's been quite useful for us, as well."

"I saw on your page you were playing tonight, so I came up here for the show."

"Up here?" Danny asked.

Danny towered over this girl. And whether it was the intimidation of his picture-perfect face or the fact that he wasn't a member of the band, Eliza ignored his question completely and quickly turned back to Jamie.

"From L.A. I convinced my dad to bring me."

The mention of Eliza's father seemed to conjure his presence. A tall, slight man in a button-down shirt and jeans pushed off the wall and stepped forward. I hadn't noticed him and had no idea how long he'd been there. Jamie seemed surprised too, and held out a hand to shake.

"I understand you were brought here under some duress," Jamie said good-naturedly.

The man laughed. "Pretty much. Eliza insisted we come."

"Well, then, I may owe you an apology," Jamie responded, winking at Eliza.

"Not at all, actually," he replied with the same humor. "When your teenage daughter tells you she wants to spend time with you, you jump at the chance, believe me. Even knowing you're just the wallet and the ride."

He smiled widely in Eliza's direction, a warm, genuine look that made me like him instantly. Eliza, on the other hand, was *mortified*. Although, in fairness, she probably could've had Bono for a dad and felt the same way.

"Besides," he continued. "It was one of the best shows I've seen in a long time."

"That's kind of you to say. I'm Jamie Callahan. And this is Melody Grayson and Dan Moore."

"Paul Westergard."

Jamie's expression changed in a way I didn't yet understand. It was just a slight shift, but knowing him as I did, I noticed it. Danny did too.

Jamie glanced peculiarly at Eliza, who was beaming, and then back at Paul. I looked to Danny in question, but he didn't seem to get it either.

"D'you mean—?" Jamie started to ask.

"EFI Records."

The words just hung between us for what felt like an eternity.

As they did, they voraciously consumed all breathable air.

Danny's eyes grew comically round, darting back and forth between Jamie and Paul, as the pieces fell into place. I found that my ability to speak was severely limited by the fact that my stomach had promptly relocated to my throat and showed no inclination of returning to its proper location.

Jamie, too, appeared embattled in a momentary struggle for his composure. I watched the muscles of his neck contract with a forceful swallow. Thoughts moved rapidly behind his eyes as he took measurement of every conceivable implication. Then his chest cavity expanded with a restorative breath, and his expression relaxed.

"It's a pleasure."

He spoke with a clear, steady voice, but I could feel the reserve in his countenance. Months ago, a chance meeting with a record executive—following one of the best shows Cadence had ever played, no less—would have left him brimming with excitement. And there were plenty of reasons to feel that way. But I understood his trepidation. The wounds from Cadence's break-up were still very fresh in his mind, as was the responsibility he thought he bore for it.

No, Jamie understood better than most that every opportunity carried real risk. He had been seasoned in a way that was necessary, if not a little disheartening. And suddenly, I could see that the man standing before me, while still hopeful and open, was also shrewder and more cautious than he had been, and probably better equipped now to navigate the perilous waters of the recording industry.

"I think you may actually have half dozen of our demo tapes circling your trash bin," he said with both charm and calculated wit.

"Really?" Paul answered with a wince. "I'll feel like a *real* jack ass if that's true."

"Dad!" Eliza chided.

His attention flickered to her before shifting back to Jamie in explanation. "My team receives a lot of unsolicited material. We simply can't get through it all. We try—" he said, shrugging.

"Of course."

"Did I hear correctly that you signed with Spire?" Paul asked, as an ambulance rushed past.

"We talked to them. But in the end, it wasn't a good fit."

By the way Paul nodded knowingly, I would have bet my life he understood there was a lot more to that statement than was said, but there was little more that was needed.

"Are you guys looking for a label?" He reached around to pull a wallet from his back pocket.

"Under the right circumstances."

"Meaning?" Paul removed a business card from the center fold and handed it to Jamie. Sure enough, on it was the logo for EFI Records, a subsidiary of one of the largest media conglomerates in the world. Paul Westergard was Executive Vice President of A&R.

Danny saw it too, and his wide eyes met mine excitedly.

"Meaning that any contract we'd sign would have to be on par with the market, of course, and also allow us a reasonable amount of artistic control. We want to know that the label would respect our choices."

Paul looked at him evenly as he absorbed the stipulations. Christ Almighty, this felt like the beginning of a negotiation.

"I hear you," he finally said. "The industry's getting nervous, though. With everything going digital, there's so much disruption to our business model, and we're all struggling to get ahead of it. By and large, most labels are taking fewer risks these days."

"With fewer rewards," Jamie said pointedly.

"Yeah," Paul agreed thoughtfully. "That's true. We all know we have to get much leaner. But beyond that, there are a lot of conflicting opinions on how we survive this long-term. Many of my peers are going the route of producing more generic music, hoping they can make up in volume what they're losing in individual record sales."

"But you don't agree?"

"No, I don't," he said in a way that felt honest. "We need to recognize that big-selling albums like "Thriller" are going to be fewer and farther between. We can't rely on that to drive profits anymore.

I think we need to offer more diversity of music, and get people excited about hearing it live. And we need to give our artists the tools to build more direct relationships with their fans. Like you're doing with MySpace. That's smart."

"In a few years, bands may be able to make a go of it on their own—without a label. Your daughter discovered us on social media."

"Yes, she did," he said, looking at Eliza in a proud parental way before returning his focus to Jamie. "It's definitely not just about radio play anymore. But I'll tell you this, there's still nothing like having a label go all in on your record. There's a lot of marketing power behind that."

I could almost see Jamie's brain at work as he studied Paul for a long moment. Then, very subtly, he shifted his gaze to me. And I knew in my heart what he was asking. *What do you think?*

He didn't really need my opinion—he was savvy enough to make the right call—but I understood his motivation for wanting it. Jamie knew I would give him a considered answer he could trust.

And my instincts about Paul told me *yes*. I didn't need to say it, though. Jamie could read it, just like he read everything else between us.

"We'd definitely be interested in talking."

"Good," Paul said. "Because I think we can come to an agreement on terms. I like what you're doing. And I especially like that you don't sound like anyone else."

"I like that you feel that way," Jamie said wryly, and I knew he was thinking of Spire.

"On the back of that card is the number for my assistant, Sharon. Give her a call on Monday, if you would, and find a time that's convenient for the four of you to come down to L.A. We'll meet at my office. And we can cover your travel."

"Thank you. Will do."

"Let's try to make it next week."

"All right. That should be fine," Jamie agreed.

Paul extended his arm in a firm handshake. It wasn't a *good to meet you* kind of handshake; it was one full of promise and expectation. Then he nodded to Danny and me and smiled.

An elephant-sized chill ran up my spine.

The Fillmore was, indeed, a magical place. Many great bands had played there, and many careers were launched there. People loved music and musicians at The Fillmore. And I couldn't think of a more fitting place for Cadence to have that moment that would change everything.

Paul tucked his daughter protectively under his arm and started to go. But then suddenly he stopped and turned back.

"I have a good feeling about this," he said.

Jamie laughed. "Oh, yeah?"

"You guys have a lot of talent," he said. And then he broke into a broad grin. "And I'm *very* good at being the wallet and the ride."

Chapter 35

Jamie

MySpace Blog Entry, January 6, 2005

I can't remember who said it or where I heard it so, among other things, you'll forgive me for paraphrasing badly. But it's said that if you never push yourself to do something you find a challenge, you'll never be anything more than you are today.

Creative pursuits are often that way. They're joyful and interesting and lovely. But just as often, they are very, very hard. You have a stellar idea, but you can't quite do it justice; your work faces rejection by someone you respect, or worse, by someone you don't; you compare yourself to others and suffer for the comparisons. That's when you wonder if what you're doing is *too* hard—if it's even worth doing. Or maybe you're just wasting your energy. I've felt like that at times in recent months, felt deflated and not quite motivated to pick up where I left off. In this business, it's easy to get discouraged, even for the most assured. It's easy to get distracted or weighed down by all the things that make artistry difficult: life and self-doubt, chief among them.

But that's where you have come in. To all of you who have shown up, sung out, carried signs, posted reviews and sent your generous words of encouragement, I thank you more than I can say. Your positive thoughts seemed to come when I most needed the reinforcement that I had something of value to offer. You helped me to push through the hard bits and continue to add my voice to the chorus.

I tell you this because today we signed a record deal with EFI. I have no idea where adventure may take us from here, but I do know this: when it's all said and done, there will be a list of words used to describe me. And this list will encompass who I was, and who I became. Whatever those words may ultimately be, you have added one that I'm quite proud of—storyteller. You see, one can compose music for his own edification and catharsis, and there is some value in that. But add an audience, and the tale he tells himself becomes a story that grows in meaning with each person who relates to it. There is incredible power and beauty in that, and for no one more than the composer himself.

It's magic, really.

There are a lot of things I may be without you, but I can say with certainty that you continue to make me far more than I could've ever been on my own. And I am forever grateful.

Until we meet again,
Jamie

Chapter 36

Mel

As it turns out, record companies are no different than other companies. A few like EFI are visionary; most are just average. Some act like bullies, others like babies.

And let's be very clear here, the relationship forged between Cadence and EFI, sealed definitively with a recording contract, was not a relationship rooted in love. Despite Paul's considerable influence, EFI attorneys had no compunction about dragging Gavin around the block several times before finally agreeing to the terms for which Cadence was asking.

No, this was definitely a relationship rooted in business. The difference was, it was *good* business.

At the end of the negotiations, the label was thrilled with their newest acquisition, and Cadence had the freedom to make their own brand of music in a trusting and artist-friendly environment. It was a relationship that would go on to prove very profitable for all involved, despite the growing challenges that both artists and labels would face in the years that followed.

Under Paul's watchful eye, EFI did its job promoting the band, and then some. In fact, at one point Rolling Stone would write about the phenomenon of Cadence "exploding onto the music scene." Jamie laughed about that, saying that for the band, it felt more like collapsing across the threshold. But there's a certain attraction to the idea of overnight success. The reality of paying your dues on the club circuit for years and working menial jobs to make ends meet is a far less romantic notion. Still, it gave the band professionalism and perspective, two things that are essential in any long-term career in music.

As for me, things changed pretty quickly. When the debut album was finished, Cadence hit the road for a lengthy promotional tour, employing a wet-behind-the-ears tour manager who made up in passion what she lacked in experience. And Jamie was right; I would not be the one to assist in testing the sound equipment, but god help anyone who divided tour manager by woman and thought they could short-change the band or crew on any contract stipulations.

Music was in my blood, and I felt like I, too, had found my calling.

On one of our breaks, we came home for a few of days to rest and recharge. I needed a haircut and wanted a pedicure so badly it was all I could think about. When I finally got back to my apartment, groomed and no longer feeling like I had the toes of a sloth, I threw my keys on the table by the front door and called to Jamie. No answer, but Atticus came running in from the yard with enthusiasm. He was covered in dirt.

I walked out to find Jamie, dressed neatly in a button-down shirt and slacks, and standing beside a large wood-framed vegetable garden that had mysteriously come into existence in the hours I was gone.

When Jamie saw me, he grinned proudly and gestured like a magician revealing his trick.

I was stunned, just stunned. I truly think my eyes may have popped out of my head.

The garden was beautifully crafted from reclaimed redwood and positioned in the sunniest part of my yard. It was still mostly dirt, but Jamie had planted a number of herbs, and labeled stakes marking what was there. I noticed he'd installed irrigation on timers and had a system of netting to keep out pests.

And right in the middle of the planter was a decorative metal sign. *Sow what you love*, it said in large block letters.

"Do you like the sign?" Jamie asked, eyes wide with anticipation. "I designed it myself."

It was a gorgeous aged-copper piece with scrolling detail around its border. At the top was a small copper bird whose body resembled a treble clef—just like Jamie's tattoo. Jamie had designed it to be decorative, but as was his calling, the words were chosen with precision and economy. *Sow what you love*. True for gardens, I thought, and also true for lives.

"I *love* it," I gasped in shock. A remarkable array of emotions clawed at my chest to get out.

Jamie knew I had grown to love cooking, and that I was rarely able to cook while we were on the road. In fact, I looked forward to our breaks when I had access to a real kitchen and a generous number of pots at my disposal. This garden was an acknowledgement of that—truly the most thoughtful gift anyone could give me.

"You did this all yourself?" I could hardly believe he'd had time to make plans for this while on tour, let alone execute them in the hours I was gone.

But he pointed at his chest with a dimpled smile. "Manure spreader, hole digger, and rock hauler, remember?"

"Not anymore, frontman," I grinned. "Now, you're a recording artist."

Jamie's eyes sparkled with pleasure, and the warm sunlight that flooded my yard lit his beautiful auburn hair like a flame. He was stunning standing there, so strong and peaceful and happy. We were home, but for both of us, home wasn't a place anymore; it was a person, and stepping into his waiting arms was like crossing a threshold.

"From your lips to God's ears, angel," he murmured in his low Irish burr.

His voice had always been the most powerful aphrodisiac, the way it melted over me, warm and tempting. It oozed into the cracks in my composure and broke apart any resistance.

"Thank you for this." I folded into his embrace, and let the earthy, masculine scent of his skin wash over me. Where the collar of his shirt was open, I pressed my lips to his neck, tasting his lively flesh with the tip of my tongue. A hoarse, guttural exhale rumbled through his chest, and I couldn't help myself; I reached up and pulled his mouth down to mine.

Soft lips crushed against my own. Lips that wanted, just as I wanted. I could not get close enough to his body, warm through the folds of his shirt, which I clutched tightly in my fists. He always kissed me like I was *everything*.

But all too soon, he pulled back slightly, and then pressed his nose to mine. His breath was still coming in short bursts and his hands were threaded into my hair, but his eyes were open and never blinked. He looked like a Cyclops.

"Do you trust me?" the Cyclops whispered.

"With my life," I answered without hesitation.

He smiled sweetly, letting go of my hair and reaching forward with his lips to brush mine tenderly.

"What about with your heart?"

"That's a given, of course."

I could feel his smile grow broad, pulling his cheeks to their breaking point and producing deep dimples on both sides of his face.

"So then, we have a bit of unfinished business—a challenge, if you'll recall."

"Okay," I said with suspicion.

Jamie released me from his hold and took a half step back. He put one hand on his hip and nervously rubbed his jaw with the other. Then he steadied his thoughts and . . .

"So, this bloke walks into a bar and sees the most beautiful woman he's ever seen in his life. No . . . wait," he said, looking a little lost. "I forgot. He's a *musician*. This musician walks into a bar and sees a woman. Well, she's a *lawyer*," he told me emphatically. "And she's really lovely."

I raised an eyebrow.

"*Fuck*," he said explosively to himself. "I'm fucking this up, aren't I?"

I just shrugged. But if this was his lawyer joke, it was terrible. Honestly, just so terrible.

Jamie dragged both hands across his head, causing his hair to shoot off in every conceivable direction, like a porcupine. I wanted to giggle. It was the most discomposed I'd ever seen him—a man who was a born performer, but clearly not a born joke teller. Some of his stories were a little iffy, as well.

"I'm going to be honest," I told him with a straight face. "It's not going well so far."

The resigned look on his face acknowledged this, but Jamie was resilient, as always. He took a deep breath and forged on.

"Right. So. This *musician*, you see, he meets this *lawyer*. In a bar."

"Yeah, I got that."

He wrinkled his brow. "Actually, I'm not sure it's a bar."

I laughed. "You're the *worst* joke teller. I have no idea if you'll ever get to the punch line, but I swear just watching you try to tell it is the funniest part."

He knew it too. He closed his eyes and shook his head, while tiny dimples formed on his cheeks. Then suddenly, he dropped to one knee, and the stupid grin was wiped right off my face.

"So he says to the lawyer," Jamie continued in a voice so calm it was stunning. "'Will you be my wife?'"

Hazel eyes rested on mine with a look of vulnerability and hope. He was the most expressive person I knew, absolutely incapable of artifice. For a moment I just studied that gorgeous face that I loved so much—those beautiful soft eyes and chiseled jaw, the nose that had been broken once before, the little crooked tooth that gave his smile its character. He was crazy handsome—and sexy beyond words—but he was so very much more.

I just stared at him, unable to form a coherent response. I didn't even notice when he took my hand in his. I was trembling as something tight finally worked its way past my throat.

"Is this a joke?"

"*Yes*," he answered, eyes wide with certainty. And then he realized my meaning. "I mean . . . no! Fuck! No! I mean, yes, it *was* a joke, but now it's *not* a joke. Oh Christ, I am fucking this up."

He popped to his feet, now taking both my hands in his substantial grasp. He looked comically ruffled, but I'm sure I looked comically stunned.

"My beautiful Melody," he said, regaining command of himself. "I love you." He heaved a great sigh of relief for getting at least that far. "You are my home. The only one I've ever had. You are the heart of everything I do, and everything I am as a man. You came into my life and made me whole. And I need you and want you with me forever. Please marry me . . . This is not a joke," he added hastily.

It seemed as if the world was suddenly made up of just the two of us. Like the only thing that carried any significance on earth was happening right here in my yard. My chest tightened, feeling far too small for everything I held for him inside it.

"Well, it happens to be the best lawyer joke I've ever heard in my life," I said, now streaming tears down my face. "You win."

L.J. GREENE

Finally, it was his turn to laugh.

"We're quite a pair, you and I." He took me in his arms again and held me tight.

"Yes, we are," I agreed, sniffling. "But it's like I told you before, if you get into badness, I'm your girl."

"Is that a *yes*?" he said, pulling back to see my eyes.

"It's a yes."

Relief coated his expression, and he cupped my face in his strong, rough hands, kissing me again with the promise of a lifetime.

"Love you," he whispered, like the words held his soul.

In my mind's eye, I reached back in our time together and retrieved the crumpled, worn out, but carefully preserved list of my favorite words that Jamie says.

And *love you* was still at the very top, just exactly where it should be, framed in that long O of an Irish burr that I would never grow tired of listening to.

It was the joy of my life, and one of many that now defined me.

I had traded in the clack clack clack of my stilettos for the echo of kick-ass boots on a stage floor. In doing so, I had welcomed an entirely different set of sounds: that of airplanes and buses and travel cases snapping shut. Of laughter and the roar of the crowd and, of course, great, great music. But underneath it all was the sound of two hearts beating—not in time, but each in its own distinct way. One was slow and steady, a methodical, constant sound. The other was a bit faster, a bit more excitable and keeping pace with a life lived in endless awe. But that's what harmony is, after all—two notes made better, a chord made possible, by the presence of the other.

§§§

Acknowledgements and Epilogues

Whew! They say even the tallest mountains can be climbed one small step at a time. That's the way this book felt for me—a lot of tiny steps leading somewhere I wasn't sure I could reach. With a few additional complexities than my first book, *Sound Effects* challenged me to do just a little more than I thought I could—to get things exactly right for the characters I had grown to love so very much, and to create a story that would be worthy of your time and investment in reading it. I hope you love it as much as I do.

And this brings me to the first group of people I really need to thank for its completion. The funny/eerie/awesome thing about life is that over the course of writing *Sound Effects*, my first adventure, *Ripple Effects*, was finding its audience. And periodically readers would post kind reviews to Goodreads or Amazon, or send me messages via Twitter. And those posts always seemed to come when I most needed a little boost of confidence to push through a tough spot in the process. They were a big part of the reason I never lost steam. So to that small but mighty group of you—and it's a pretty defined universe so you know exactly who you are!—I want to express my profound gratitude for your kindness and encouragement. Chapter 35 was inspired by you, and is dedicated to you.

To Sarah at Books She Reads, you are certainly included in this first group, but I wanted to mention you specifically because I appreciate so much that you took a chance on a brand new author, posting the first chapter of *Ripple Effects* on your blog and writing a review. Thank you so much for your generosity, and for lending support to authors like me, who might otherwise be lost in the shuffle.

As always, I want to extend a huge thanks to Joshua Jaden for his unbelievable cover art. His talent leaves me speechless every time. Although I write the books, he manages to bring them to life in way that exceeds all expectations. Josh, you're a master!

To Ashley at TCB Editing, I worked with you blindly for my first book, and sought you out specifically for the second. Your honesty and your thoughtful suggestions always make me better.

To Polgarus Studio, I wouldn't even attempt to do what you do so professionally and beautifully. I love that I never have to think twice about how to turn my stories into books.

Finally, I want to express my gratitude to my amazing husband who would probably rather pull out his own teeth than read a romance novel, but who does so anyway, with surprising insight. (Although, that thing you keep telling me I should include? No. Just, no.) Thank you for respecting every facet of me, even the ones you never saw coming. I promise never to take up singing or interpretive dance.

And now to the subject of epilogues . . . one of the best (and admittedly most challenging) things about writing *Sound Effects* was that Jamie and Mel are significant characters in *Ripple Effects*, which takes place in the present. As such, I had to go back eleven years to write their beginning, which also meant that I had to weave in the threads of their backstory and set them along the path to where they will eventually land.

For that reason, *Ripple Effects* is a perfect epilogue to *Sound Effects*.

While I aimed to leave Jamie and Mel in a very good place at the conclusion of this novel, for those of you interested in knowing how it all turns out, you can revisit these characters (and see a slightly older Danny in his post-cologne phase, finally ready to meet *his* better half!) in what I hope you'll agree is a satisfying postscript to *Sound Effects*.

So I guess that's it! As always, thank you for welcoming these characters into your hearts and homes, and thank you for taking this incredible journey with me.

You're *magic*!

Come find me on Twitter: @authorljgreene, and online at www.ljgreenebooks.com.

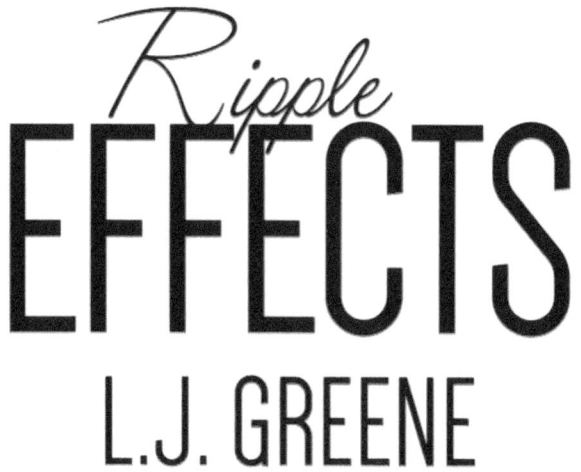

Ripple EFFECTS

L.J. GREENE

Science teachers are supposed to be nerdy, combed-over and, quite frankly, a little dull. They're not supposed to be like *him*. And while he may be the ideal person to help 22-year-old Sarah Kyle nail her fellowship essay for Stanford's master's program, he may also be far more life changing than she bargained for.

Daniel Moore is certain he would never date a former student. No question. Still, he's not quite prepared for the schooling he's about to receive from that four-chambered muscle in his chest that is suddenly adapting to an entirely new mandate. Yep, evolution is a bitch!

Because life is only one part science; the rest is art. And life can turn on a dime; they both know that, all too well. In their own ways, they both live with the enduring effects—the ripple effects—of sudden loss. This powerful connection draws them together in the unspoken understanding of things that are just hard to explain. But will it ultimately prove to be the bond that unites them or the force that tears them apart?

RIPPLE EFFECTS is a standalone dual POV adult contemporary romance that contains no twenty-something-year-old billionaires, no private jets and no bedroom accouterment. It does contain the first reference to dinoflagellates in romance (full disclosure: this may not be true), an ardent love affair sparked by the misuse of a hyphen (that is true), and a heartfelt and generously humorous journey of self-discovery, forgiveness, and the restorative quality of love.

Chapter 1

June 2015
Sarah

Like ground zero for nerd chic, Charlie's Bar & Grill on University Avenue stood as a mecca—a funky kind of place, equally favored by the hoodie-clad Silicon Valley professionals as by their similarly dressed student counterparts. It was Friday night happy hour on the last day of Stanford's spring semester finals and the place was packed.

"Here, take this." Selene tossed back her long, dark hair, and handed me a very pink, very sweet cosmopolitan. "For the next three months, we have nothing to do but relax. And we're going to start that *tonight*." She raised her drink in a toast, took a large sip, and melted into cranberry bliss.

In truth, neither of us was without responsibility for the next three months, but I understood what she meant. Selene Georgiou and I had been roommates for the past four years, and were heading into our final semesters of undergraduate study in the fall. After that, we'd be going our separate ways—she likely moving to San Francisco for a graphic design job and, me, hopefully continuing on at Stanford for my master's degree in education. This was our last summer together and neither of us was ready to face up to that reality just yet.

So despite the onset of a ham-like state of post-finals exhaustion, I agreed to come out for a drink, and even let her dress me up in an outfit she insisted was very flattering to my figure.

Selene was tall, like me, but lithe to my curvy athleticism, which explained why her floral print blouse felt a little sexier than I had intended. I pulled at the front of it for the millionth time.

"Wow, that is strong." I winced, swallowing another sip of the lethal concoction she'd handed me. Even the sugared rim couldn't disguise the heavy alcohol content. "Who'd you flash to get this?"

Selene rolled her eyes—not exactly a denial. "I'm going to the restroom. I'll be right back."

I took another small sip of my drink and glanced around the bar. I grew up in the Silicon Valley, but in truth, I was still in awe of it. Nowhere else in the world was quite like it. With its frenetic pace of life and vibrant cultural diversity, you couldn't help but feel like people here were always inventing, always trying to solve problems in an out-of-the-box, disruptive kind of way. And it's true that many of the companies founded here had literally changed the world—Fairchild Semiconductor, Cisco Systems, Genentech, Google, Facebook. As a result, the collective wealth in the Bay Area was absolutely staggering.

Of course, that made me a bit of an outlier. Though my childhood home was only miles from the Stanford campus, it was a great distance in terms of economics. But growing up, I was never discouraged by that. The Silicon Valley was rich with lore of seemingly crazy ideas that took shape in a garage and went on to become Apple or Hewlett Packard. It had always given me the feeling that if you worked hard enough, you could do anything—even get into Stanford on a full academic scholarship.

I still counted my blessings for that one, and often looked around myself with a deep sense of gratitude. Tonight was one of those nights. Apparently I was in good company; everyone here seemed to celebrating something.

Charlie's was known for its big open spaces that never felt claustrophobic, no matter how crowded it was. Plus, the used brick interior and cement flooring gave it a chic warehouse vibe that perfectly suited Charlie's passion for showcasing the eclectic artwork of local artists—everything from paintings to sculptures to scrap metal creations.

Today's artist was a photographer, and the restaurant's pin lighting accentuated many sweeping landscapes of the Bay Area, as well as interesting close-ups of local flora and fauna. They were incredibly beautiful, and it was a full minute before I realized I actually recognized a few of the photographs—one in particular. It was an image of the Golden Gate Bridge, with the bridge sitting almost eerily behind a ghostlike band of fog, and the rich, brown sand and rolling waves of Baker Beach in the foreground. The original focal point, whatever it was, appeared to have been cropped out, giving the image a soft, dreamy quality.

It was so distinctive I was nearly certain it was the one I remembered from many years ago, and glancing at the placard beside it, I discovered I was right. *Daniel Moore.*

Wow.

That name brought back more than a few memories—memories from a time in my life I would hardly call a high point. Most of the time I purposely avoided them. Every so often they found me anyway. Like now, when the small-world theory decided to prove itself once again. The photographer in question was standing just a foot away, scrolling through messages on his phone.

"Mr. Moore?"

Penetrating green eyes lifted to absorb me blankly. But I could see he was fighting to place me in his own memory. After a long, awkward beat, we both said my name at once. Though for him, it was definitely more of a question.

Daniel R. Moore was one of three biology teachers at McKinley High School. He couldn't have been more than a few of years into his career when I last knew him, and always strictly reserved with students. But he was definitely passionate about teaching. His lectures famously prompted some pretty memorable discussions on scientific advancements, and ethics, and conservation. When he was in full flow, he was absolutely captivating.

"Yes, of course, Sarah." He shook his head in apology and slid his phone into his pocket. "And, please, call me Dan."

His expression unexpectedly developed into a large, good-natured grin that was *far* from any recollection I had of him.

"I was just admiring your photographs."

"Ah. Charlie's a friend of mine. I blame him for all this." He looked around at the impressive display and his smile became more self-deprecating.

"No, they're really good.

"You're generous to say so."

We both stood silently for a moment as the pause turned awkward. What do you say to someone you haven't seen in more than five years and never really knew to begin with? Plus, I was now highly conscious of the fact that my blouse felt far too small, which was not ideal for a reunion of this kind. I found myself discreetly tugging at it *again*. To Moore's credit, his eyes remained on my face—a bit of professionalism that did ring true to what I remembered of him.

"Are you still teaching?"

"Yes, but not at McKinley. I'm at Taft now. Seventh grade life science."

"Oh. Nice."

For me, it was almost surreal to see him in this completely

different setting and to be talking with him as an adult; I'd been a student the last time we'd spoken. I wondered if he found it strange too. If he did, he didn't let on, but he was a hard one to read. I'd always thought so. Maybe it was a teacher thing.

After a beat, his eyes flickered down to my drink and it dawned on me what was very likely going through his head.

"Don't worry, I'm twenty-two," I reassured him, gesturing with the glass.

"Oh, I . . ."

He looked confused. Like maybe he didn't believe me? Did I look underage? I couldn't explain the ridiculous impulse behind it, but I pushed my hand into the pocket of my jeans and pulled out my driver's license and student ID, thrusting them in his direction.

Dan took the license and ID card from my hand and laughed uncomfortably, as though he wasn't quite sure what to do.

"Well, I . . . okay. I wasn't actually . . . Here, you can keep these," he said, handing the cards back. "So, you're graduating soon?"

I took another sip of the cosmo, definitely not looking like I needed the fortification. "Actually, I've still got one more year to go on my bachelor's. I'm doing an internship at Stanford Medical Center so I haven't been able to take a full load. Thus, the five-year plan."

"The medical center?"

"Working with kids with autism."

He narrowed his eyes as if digging even deeper in his memory. "Your brother."

"Yes. Well, Asperger's Syndrome in his case—but that's where the interest comes from."

"That's really great."

He was examining me even closer now, tilting his head slightly as if this was a revelation—like he was suddenly seeing me for the very first time. Evidently, I'd managed to progress in his mind from underage drinker to semirespectable societal contributor. I smiled, pleased with myself, and put the IDs back in my pocket.

But that's when I realized nothing else was *in* my pocket and the happy feeling quickly evaporated. I looked down to find that my neatly folded cash and house key were on the ground next to my foot, apparently dislodged when I took out the cards. And to my unmitigated horror, the tampon from my pocket was *also* on the ground, lying conspicuously close to his shoe.

Adrenaline shot through my veins. Oblivious to what was happening, Dan shifted casually in his stance and his foot came down on top of the tampon, crushing it.

His eyes went wide when he realized what it was, and worse *whose* it was. He looked back at me. "I'm sorry. Did I . . . ah . . . disable it?"

Disable it? Like a tampon bomb?

"No, no I'm sure it's fine," I insisted in high-pitched distress.

I sank to my knees, mortification gripping my body like a vise, and scrambled around at his feet to retrieve the items. Dan seemed to be of the opinion that keeping the conversation going while I did this was the best way for us to pretend he didn't just step on my tampon. But I couldn't focus at all on what he was saying. There was something about his completing a PhD in education at Stanford, which I wouldn't have thought was necessary for a middle school teaching position.

With one hand, I was able to stuff the tampon and the rest of my things back into my pocket. Unfortunately, I did it with enough gusto that the cosmo in my other hand sloshed over the edge of its delicate glass and all over his pristine leather loafer.

"Oh my god, I'm so sorry!" I was mortified. I tried brushing at it vigorously with my hand, but to little effect. The leather was soaked and the sticky sweet liquid was now running over the top of his foot and into his shoe.

"Sarah, stop. Please. It's not a big deal."

He gently grasped my arm and began tugging me back up before I had the chance to humiliate myself any further. But even that was not to be—another wave of liquid shot from the mouth of the glass as I rose, this time soaking the leg of his pants, just inches from his crotch. He let out a little grunt and released me.

We were both gaping at the wet spot now and it was clear there was no hope of a dignified recovery for either of us.

He spoke first: "Okay. . . well . . . uh . . ."

The only thing I had handy to help him dry himself was a tampon and believe me *no one* wanted to see that again. And no one wanted my hand anywhere near his crotch.

Suddenly I found myself on the verge of tears. Real tears. The big ugly kind that required a nose blow and usually ended up in hiccups. I looked up at his face, my eyes wide, fully expecting to see the return of the stern Mr. Moore I remembered from five years earlier—the one who seemed to compensate for his youth and stunning good looks with somber formality.

Instead, his expression was . . . well, it was shockingly patient. Maybe even a little amused. I hardly knew what to make of that.

"It's okay," he said kindly. "This won't be the first time I've left a bar wearing a cosmopolitan. Though it's been a while," he added.

Then he made a playful show of squishing the liquid in his shoe and I had to laugh, in spite of my absolute horror. I wondered if it was always this way for insanely attractive men—women doing bat-shit crazy things in their presence. He seemed to know just how to handle it.

I took in a deep breath and let it out, making the best effort I could to gather myself.

"I'm so embarrassed."

"Please don't be." He waved a hand dismissively. He was being much nicer than he needed to be, given that he was going to spend the rest of the evening looking like he'd urinated himself, courtesy of me.

"And I'm really sorry—I missed what you said. Did you tell me your PhD is on education reform?"

"I did, yes."

"That's so funny—I'm writing my grad school fellowship essay on the same topic."

"Really?" he said with interest.

"Yes," I said, lifting my glass in a toast. "And here's to hoping yours is going much better than mine."

Education reform was turning out to be an especially broad and complex topic and I was hopelessly stuck on how to deal with it properly. It was a major source of stress for me because my fellowship depended on getting it right.

But I didn't want to think about that now. The room was warm, and I was still radiating with the heat of humiliation from my scalp to my toes. Oddly the skin between my breasts felt cool. And something about that registered in my brain, distracting me from our conversation. I turned to see if there was a breeze coming in from an open door.

"I think mine's coming along pretty well, actually," he told me.

"Good, maybe I'll just copy it and save myself some trouble."

It's fair to say that *thoughtless* was an adequate description for how I was keeping up my side of the exchange. Glancing around the space, I couldn't see any open door, or any reason there should be a breeze where we were standing. Tiny alarm bells began to go off in my head, which was probably why it was a second or two before I realized what I'd just done: I'd proposed plagiarism to a teacher. My former teacher. And then it dawned.

My attention snapped back to the tall, athletic man standing in front of me and he had the strangest expression on his face. He seemed to be searching politely for some appropriate thing to say— which, god knows what in the world that might be.

"No, I didn't mean I would *actually* want to plagiarize your PhD. I never do that sort of thing. *Ever.*"

He laughed again, but there was something definitely uncomfortable beneath it. "No, I didn't think . . ."

Rubbing the back of his neck, he looked away briefly. Then, he turned again in my direction. But he wasn't really looking at *me*; he was looking pointedly at my forehead. Something wasn't right here. His eyes darted around the room again, as if searching the place for any kind of help he could find. At last, he refocused his attention precisely on my face.

Clearing his throat, he continued in a businesslike manner: "What I was going to say was, it's definitely an ambitious topic for a short essay. You'll have to narrow your focus considerably or your work will come off as superficial." The intensity returned to those devastating green eyes. "If you want, I'd be glad to review your outline and give you a few ideas."

I was flooded with relief that we seemed to have returned to more stable ground. Okay, see, *this* was how a normal conversation was conducted. He was just a regular person, after all—no more or less than I.

"You forget I've had a pretty intimidating experience with your infamous red pen," I teased, then watched his reaction.

Mr. Moore was not known for his sense of humor, and in light of his surprisingly personable manner tonight, I was suddenly curious to know how he'd respond to mine.

Before my eyes, his gaze turned from intense to almost sparkling. He was still oddly rigid, but he cocked his head to the side and adjusted his stance.

"What are you implying?" That disorienting smile was back, and something about his demeanor eased my concern.

"I'm not *implying* anything," I said, relieved to feel like myself again for the first time since he uttered my name. "Our papers always looked like they'd been victims of a violent crime."

He blinked for a moment, and then threw his head back and laughed. Actually laughed. It was a hearty, masculine sound with a bit of a rasp around the edges, and it washed over me with unexpected warmth.

"Some of them definitely were a crime. A crime against science— and against my intelligence, for that matter."

I'd never heard him laugh.

Years ago, I wouldn't have thought he was capable of it. This whole exchange showed a side of him I could not have imagined back then. He had an actual sense of humor.

And an incredibly sexy laugh.

It was an altogether pleasurable discovery. Unfortunately, it was followed by a rather cataclysmic one: The three middle buttons on my blouse had popped clean off. And now my shirt was hanging open—*wide* open. And it had likely been this way for many minutes!

My eyes leaped to Dan's face. I frantically groped at my blouse with my one free hand, hoping he hadn't noticed the malfunction. But *of course* he had; his ears were now the same shade of pink as my cosmopolitan. He quickly looked away, avoiding my conspicuous attempts to somehow pull the two sides of my shirt back together. But there was no mistaking the fact that I was failing miserably. Finally, he reached back across his shoulder and tugged the light gray sweatshirt over his head. His thick, wavy strawberry-blond hair was sent into wild abandon, which he mostly righted with a quick shake of his head.

"Here—in case you're . . . cold."

He handed me the sweatshirt with one hand, and took the sticky drink from my shaking fist with the other. Then he stepped away to set it down on the bar.

"Run!" my brain shouted, helpfully. *"Or cry!"* That was much less helpful. Dan must've already thought I was a barely legal flasher—crying would just make him think I was an *unstable* barely legal flasher.

This night was a complete disaster!

I gratefully pulled the sweatshirt on, still warm from his body and roomy enough to accommodate his size. With truly heroic effort, I forced myself back to rightness. Or the best version of it I could fake under the circumstances.

"I'll send this back to you," I offered when he returned. He waved that off and scribbled something on a napkin.

"Here's my email. Send me your outline. I'd like to help." He looked at me earnestly, as though rightly sensing some hesitation on my part.

Honestly, I wanted to cry. My whole composure was in disarray. I nodded, looking down at the napkin, and fought to hold myself together.

"I mean it, Sarah," he added gently.

"Okay. Thank you." Finally, I lifted my gaze to his.

He was being so incredibly nice that I scolded myself for every bad thing I'd ever thought about him, and in doing so tried to reconcile my memories of that humorless teacher with the man standing before me. I simply couldn't.

Selene walked up to my left, smiled pleasantly at Dan, and then turned to me. "Are you ready to go?"

"Yes." *God yes!* I could not have been more ready to go. "It was really good to see you again . . . Dan. And thank you for—" I gestured to the sweatshirt.

"It was good to see you too. Glad to hear you're doing well."

The sincerity in his face was oddly comforting. It was impossible to think I'd conveyed anything remotely resembling my best self, but his genuine kindness made the calamity of the last half hour feel, maybe, slightly less calamitous. If only for a moment . . .

§

Leaving Charlie's, Selene and I walked along University Avenue. Neither of us said a word for long minutes.

"He was my high school biology teacher," I finally whispered as the indignity seeped back into my consciousness.

"*That* guy is a science teacher?" She was definitely taken aback by this little nugget of information, and gave herself a moment to process. "He's not like any science teacher I've ever had."

That was probably true for most people, but it didn't help my humiliation in the least to dwell on it.

"That was *horrifying*."

"Yeah, it pretty much was." Selene never pulled punches. It was actually one of the things I liked best about her. Although every once in a while, I wouldn't have minded being lied to, just a little bit. "Someone needed to step in there before you reprised the Celtic dance you did at Sheryl's twenty-first birthday. You were definitely heading in that direction."

"Was it that bad?"

"So to recap: You dropped your tampon at his feet; bent to pick it up, thus, spilling your drink on his shoes and pants; and carried on a full conversation while exposing your breasts. Did I leave anything out?"

"I told him I wanted to plagiarize his PhD."

"Oh, nicely done!" She said this as if it were an achievement. "Well, look at it this way—you probably won't ever have to see him again."

I took a deep breath. *That's true*, I told myself in a consoling manner. Although . . .

"He offered to help me with my fellowship essay."

Selene turned to me, eyebrows raised. "Was that before or after you popped your blouse open?"

"Oh my god." A fresh wave of nausea rippled through my stomach.

"You should definitely take him up on it, though."

"There is no *way* I could do that now. I just gave him a peep show!"

"So what. They're just boobs. He's a biology teacher, after all."

Right.

"What was up with you, anyway? He's ridiculously hot, but that was . . ." She shook her head as if she was at a loss to commit an innocent adjective to that particular scene.

"I really don't know what that was. I think I'm just tired."

Truthfully, it was probably more than that. It's a funny thing to see someone after many years, and to find him so different from what you remember. Maybe he seemed different to me because *I* was different, but I would never have described him as friendly or warm.

Although to be fair, I couldn't imagine I'd weather much better in his memory. I could only guess how I would've come across at that tumultuous time in my life: introverted, sullen, obsessively focused on my college resume. I stopped short before allowing myself to consider how I might have come across tonight.

When we finally reached our apartment, I went quickly to my room and collapsed on the bed. For a long time I just stared up at the sparkling popcorn ceiling. It was astonishing how running into someone you knew years ago threw you back immediately to who you were when you knew him. I felt the need to mentally shake off that person I once was. But it was also a good reminder of what had changed in the time between—how far I'd come in many ways, and what was still in front of me to do.

On an impulse, I dialed my friend Marcus.

"I need to ask you a favor . . ."

About the Author

LJ Greene is a self-professed obsessive multi-tasker who writes boring stuff by day and lets her inner romantic fly by night. This California native is married to the most amazing man and has two incredible children who feed her soul every day. She's an avid reader of all genres with an embarrassingly large ebook collection, and a weird penchant for reading the acknowledgements at the end of a novel. She's also a music lover with no apparent musical talent, a travel enthusiast, and a cheese connoisseur.

Website: www.ljgreenebooks.com
Twitter: @authorljgreene

www.ingramcontent.com/pod-product-compliance
Lightning Source LLC
Chambersburg PA
CBHW020240180626
46810CB00006B/2284